FIRE, WATER, AND ROCK

Visit us at www.boldstrokesbooks.com

FIRE, WATER, AND ROCK

by
Alaina Erdell

2022

FIRE, WATER, AND ROCK
© 2022 By Alaina Erdell. All Rights Reserved.

ISBN 13: 978-1-63679-274-3

This Trade Paperback Original Is Published By
Bold Strokes Books, Inc.
P.O. Box 249
Valley Falls, NY 12185

First Edition: December 2022

CREDITS
Editors: Victoria Villaseñor and Cindy Cresap
Production Design: Susan Ramundo
Cover Design By Jeanine Henning

Acknowledgments

Bold Strokes Books gave me this wonderful opportunity to see my story in print, and I'm so thankful. Rad, I'm so appreciative you took a chance on me and then took another chance when I'd not yet proven myself. I wasn't expecting such an in-depth, personalized response when I submitted my original manuscript. It was my first glimpse into how much Bold Strokes cares about its authors and makes a concerted effort to give authors the tools they need to become better at their craft. I'm eternally grateful.

It seems unfair I get to put my name on the cover of the book when it takes so much energy, effort, knowledge, and cooperation from a team of people to get a book to market.

Sandy Lowe has a keen knack for assessing a manuscript or proposal and asking, "This is great, but what if you did this, too?" It's always an excellent suggestion. Her ability to multitask and keep the gears of the Bold Stokes Books machine moving forward astounds me. Despite all her irons in the fire, she remains approachable and generous with her knowledge. I'm so grateful for her gentle guidance and foresight.

My editor, Victoria Villaseñor, took a manuscript with significant issues and helped me craft it into something stronger by leaps and bounds. Working with Vic was revelatory. I'll use what I've learned from her in every future book I write. She strikes a perfect balance between suggesting necessary edits without damaging the fragile psyches of her authors. Her experience shines when she'd anticipate an emotional reaction from me during the editing process, but she'd always show me the light at the end of the tunnel before I could ever get too worried. She knew what I needed when I needed it, and that meant everything. Thank you.

Thank you to Cindy Cresap for catching all those annoying little things I do and explaining why I shouldn't be doing them. I promise I'll do better next time. I look forward to working more with you.

Thank you to everyone behind the scenes at Bold Strokes Books who do the oft-unsung work needed to get a book into the hands of readers. To Toni, Ruth, the typesetters, the proofreaders, and all whose names I don't know or unintentionally omitted, thank you.

Jeanine Henning did a tremendous job of listening to what I wanted in terms of a cover and branding. I'm proud to have her design work on the cover of this book and my next few books.

I'd like to give special thanks to Jeannie Levig. Jeannie took me under her wing, and I'm forever grateful for the time she took to guide me through my debut novel's infancy. She must have answered no fewer than a hundred questions about the publishing process and writing in general without making me feel like a single one was inane. If I ever manage to write a book half as good as one of hers, I'll consider myself successful.

To my ever-supportive friends Anne-Sophie, Beth, Robin, and Win: the years of friendship, advice, motivation, encouragement, and time spent lending your ears have meant so much to me. Each of you has enriched my life in different, wonderful ways. Win, your eye for inconsistencies is unparalleled. Thank you for all your help.

A special group of readers exists who have encouraged me over the years to try to get my stories published. They might not believe me, but it wouldn't have felt possible without their unwavering support. I'm so appreciative of each one of you who cheered me on and inspired me.

My family has always made me feel I could do anything, and I've never doubted their love and support. I just wish some of them wouldn't have waited until I moved three time zones away to have the cutest babies.

My brother was kind enough to share his hard-earned knowledge of wildfires and wildland firefighting. Thank you for making me sound like I know what I'm talking about and for keeping so many lives and properties safe over your career.

Years ago, my girlfriend and I went hiking in Pfeiffer Big Sur State Park. I casually mentioned how I had this idea for a sapphic romance that took place in a state park. What we discussed that day became the genesis for *Fire, Water, and Rock.* She encouraged me to write the story as soon as possible, and she's never stopped encouraging me. She's quick with motivation, helpful suggestions, and praise. I'm extremely lucky to have her in my life. It doesn't hurt that she's an amazing writer and makes an excellent sounding board. All my love and thanks.

Lastly, I'm eternally thankful to my youngest brother, who taught me the joy in which life should be lived. I'm sorry you never found your goggles in Park Lake that summer, but you certainly had fun looking. I loved watching you.

Dedication

For A with love

Chapter One

Jessica Sterling waited for an older Winnebago the color of a coffee stain to chug uphill in the opposite direction before she pulled across the oncoming lane into the overlook's parking lot. She took the first available spot, only a few spaces from the Dry Falls visitor center. She got out, leaving the Outback's air-conditioned interior. It wasn't necessary to lock her car which held a summer's worth of belongings. A low rock wall a few feet away marked the edge of the canyon's rim.

She gazed across the expanse, hands on her hips, duly impressed. The photos she'd seen while doing research didn't do it justice. What stood before her in this rural, out-of-the-way, and relatively unknown area of Washington state was one of Earth's finest marvels: the largest known waterfall to have ever graced the planet. However, the 400-foot-high falls that once rushed with a flow ten times that of all the rivers of the world combined now stood dry. The falls had once been five times as wide as Niagara Falls, and twice its height. Jess let her gaze roam across the plateau-like top and down nearly vertical walls to the slanted talus slopes. Deep blue plunge pools dotted the valley floor below, the spring-filled lakes reminiscent of what once cascaded over the edges at freeway speeds.

Far below, toward the southern part of the canyon, a verdant expanse caught her attention. She made out the long green fairways of a nine-hole golf course and her destination, the campground dotted with lush and vibrant non-native deciduous shade trees, obviously irrigated. The rest of the drab canyon consisted of parched ground dotted by low-lying, shrub-steppe vegetation.

The sun seared her back through her shirt. She walked toward plaques that explained the area's history. Most of the information etched on the weather-worn plaques mirrored what she already knew, but she still had trouble imagining water flowing three hundred feet above her head, as one plaque described. She already stood on the rim of the canyon. That meant the floodwaters had been eight hundred feet deep. Jess couldn't wrap her mind around the massive events that had created the area.

She walked to the next plaque, newer than the previous plaques, and read with interest. It described how the state park had dedicated the overlook to a ranger and firefighter who had lost her life in a blaze a few years back. Jess read her birth date and realized the ranger had only been two years older than she was now. She'd been so young.

"Tragic." The deep voice came from behind her.

She turned to find a uniformed park ranger leaning against a handicapped parking sign watching her. He straightened and stepped over the curb, his six-foot-plus frame dwarfing her. He was good-looking, dark-haired and hazel-eyed, and everything about his body language told her he knew it. He invaded her space enough that she could smell his musky cologne and read his name badge: *B. Rolland.*

"That was quite the fire. It's too bad. She was a good ranger." He rested his hands on his service belt and jutted his chest out. He seemed to be trying to be suave and charming, but he came off as smarmy and overconfident. She wasn't fond of random conversations with strangers, especially when she felt like they wanted something, and she classified the beginning of this conversation into that category and took a step back.

After expressing her condolences, she managed to weather another four or five minutes of small talk involving the fire, the brave woman who had died fighting it, and his unabashed surprise that Jess planned to camp alone the entire summer. Upon hearing that tidbit of information, he introduced himself as Brett and suggested she join him and some friends at a party up near Steamboat Rock on Monday. He explained it was casual, a Memorial Day barbecue and some drinks with his friends, but he was "certain a pretty girl like her would enjoy herself."

With forced politeness, she declined twice and retreated to the safety and serenity of her Outback. Cranking the air conditioning to high, she watched him ignore all the other visitors sprinkled along the scenic vista's edge as he ambled along to the visitor center. The cool air did nothing to dispel the unpleasant feeling he gave her. How many young female campers fell for the good-looking man in uniform's act throughout a summer? She wasn't going to be one of them, that was certain.

❖

As Clare snapped her firearm into its holster on her right hip, she mused about how long she'd been doing the same thing. A bit of quick math told her that the upcoming Memorial Day would mark her ninth anniversary of working as a commissioned law-enforcement officer and ranger at Sun Lakes-Dry Falls State Park. She broke the nine years into parts: three of those years had been educational, four of those years full of happiness, and two of those years…well, she forced herself not to think about those years.

How many times had she buttoned herself into a tan polyester shirt? How many times had she slid into the drab, olive-green tactical pants? How many months had she lugged around her nine-pound belt until its weight no longer felt like it hung on her, but rather became a part of her? She had to admit she enjoyed attaching her gold-plated name badge to her uniform each day. It gave her a sense of pride and accomplishment, even after all this time. Her passion for her job might be waning, but her sense of duty wasn't.

Clare perched her sunglasses on her head and tucked stray hairs behind her ears. She wouldn't need the sunglasses for a few more hours, but she'd forget them if they weren't there. The sky outside the living room window showed hints of pinks and reds as she walked to the kitchen. She could reach anything in the tiny kitchen by standing between the two counters. She couldn't complain though. The park provided her housing, and not paying a mortgage or rent allowed her to put most of her paycheck into savings.

She doctored the coffee she'd poured into her travel mug, dropped the spoon in the sink, unplugged the coffee maker, and glanced around as she took her first hit of sweet, liquid caffeine. The small living room and two bedrooms felt like home after all these years, but she expected the administration to assign her a roommate or offer her single quarters soon. While they'd been kind and understanding up until this point, she didn't expect it would last much longer. Not after two years. She only used the second bedroom for storage anyway. It contained two bicycles, boxes of clothing that were more suitable for colder climates, and two suitcases despite the fact she couldn't recall the last time she'd traveled. Living alone in the house felt comfortable, and the thought of living somewhere else or with someone else unsettled her. On the other hand, memories made in the house also upset her. Fate, or rather the administration, would have to play its hand, and she'd have to live with it.

The activity would pick up in the park starting today. Memorial Day weekend marked the beginning of summer and was always one of their busiest times. She'd get little sleep over the next few days. Duties during her long shifts included safety issues like patrolling roads and waterways, dealing with legal and underage drinkers, trying to maintain the park's quiet hours when the party atmosphere got a bit rowdy, and worst of all, dealing with registration.

Registration was one of her least favorite parts of the job. The ranger station's booth was small and the fan that was supposed to keep the rangers cool was even smaller. With over 150 campsites, the lines could get long at times, both at the walk-up window and at the drive-up window. Campers got anxious and agitated having to wait in the heat, and she didn't blame them.

She knew it would be a long and tedious day, and she already dreaded it, but she grabbed her phone, her coffee, and her keys, and took a glance in the mirror by the door. Lifeless eyes stared back. Would there again come a time when she could look in the mirror and recognize the woman she saw? She slammed the front door behind her and got in her white truck with its light bar on top for the short drive to the ranger station.

CHAPTER TWO

Jess slowed her speed as she reached the campground at Sun Lakes State Park. A covered walkway leading up to the registration window ran the length of the small ranger station located at the entrance. Across the main road stretched the park's biggest lake, Park Lake, with its uninspired nomenclature. Children and adults of all sizes dotted both the sandy beach and the shallows. Between skinny, one-lane ingress and egress roads stood the small, yellow ranger station, the Checkpoint Charlie to the campground portion of the park. No campers waited in line at the walk-up window. A red stop sign attached to the side of the building urged incoming vehicles to stop at the side window to register.

Jess pulled the Outback's nose up to the stop sign and rolled down her window. She fumbled in her backpack for the reservation confirmation she'd printed before leaving Seattle. The sound of the ranger station's window sliding open made her turn.

"Do you have a reservation?" A female ranger leaned out the window.

Jess found her intense blue eyes captivating. The uniform was one she'd already seen, a pressed tan shirt with olive pants, but it was the woman wearing it who captured her attention. Jess was already starting to feel beads of sweat gather on the back of her neck from the five seconds the window had been down. In contrast, the woman looked perfectly and elegantly cool down to her crisp uniform. She'd pinned her blond hair back in a simple roll except where a few baby curls escaped near the nape of her neck.

"Uh…yes. I have the printout here somewhere." She dug in her backpack and chided herself for appearing so disorganized.

"What's your name? I don't mind looking it up." She flashed Jess a kind smile.

"Jessica Sterling." She couldn't tear her eyes away. The gold-plated name badge pinned over her right breast read *C. DeVere.*

"You're with us for a while!" She looked over Jess's reservation. "Is that correct?"

"Yes, through Labor Day." In a few days, it would be Memorial Day. The State Park Department had given special approval for her months-long stay until Labor Day. It came with a few stipulations, but it was worth it. Her sojourn here would give her what she needed to finish her thesis.

Her mind returned to the ranger like a rubber ball tethered by a taut elastic string to a wooden paddle. Christine? Catherine? Courtney? Crystal? No, she didn't look like a Crystal. Caroline?

"Would you like to pay the full amount or by the month?" The woman's long fingers hovered over her keyboard.

"Full please." Jess even found her profile beguiling, from her perfect nose to her high cheekbones, to the elegant expanse of her neck where it peeked out above her collar. Jess handed over her credit card, hoping the trembling in her hands went unnoticed. Why was she so nervous? A bit late, it occurred to her that she should have offered to pay by the month. She wouldn't mind having an excuse to see her again.

Jess tried to focus on something else since ogling an attractive woman wasn't why she was here. Closing her eyes, she thought of the cost of the trip. The sum of her stay pleased her. Staying in a hotel or even a motel would have made this trip impossible. The inexpensive nightly fee for a campsite, however, *was* in her budget, and it meant she could be right where she needed to be. Coin showers and flush toilets a short walk away might be inconvenient, but she could think of worse places to spend three months, although currently she was melting and hadn't yet gotten out of her car.

"Here you go."

The low, soothing voice made Jess open her eyes. She caught the glimmer of a smile as she accepted her credit card, the receipt, a brochure about the state park, a map, and a half-sheet of campground dos and don'ts. Jess looked at the black, sporty watch the woman wore on her thin wrist, the watch's face large and masculine in contrast to her feminine features. More importantly, she wasn't wearing a wedding ring. Jess reached for the controls on her dash and surreptitiously turned the AC up a few notches. The sudden sound of blasting air gave her away.

"Fire danger is high this weekend, so campfires aren't allowed. Propane stoves are fine though. Here's how you get to your campsite. We're here. Follow this road straight ahead." She drew a line for Jess with her pen. "Your campsite will be off to the left, here. Number 145." She circled it for her. "Be sure and set your tent up on the dirt and not on the grass."

Jess would have done almost anything she'd asked her to do.

"Welcome to Sun Lakes, Jessica. I'm sure I'll see you around." She smiled, her perfect teeth bookended between the slightest parenthetical creases around her mouth. Laugh lines deepened around her eyes, paradoxically making her even more beautiful.

Jess thanked her and reluctantly pulled away, map in hand.

During her drive across the state, she'd been worried about setting up a tent she'd never used before without anyone to help her. Her father had always done that for her on camping trips. Earlier, she'd been concerned about whether she'd be able to find enough foods to suit her tastes at the general store without having to eat junk food all summer. Whether she could gather enough data to complete her thesis had kept her up many nights.

Since registering at the campground, only one question occupied her thoughts. Who was C. DeVere? A pleasurable warmth spread through her that had nothing to do with the weather.

"You'll want to stake that down."

Jess turned from setting up her propane stove on one end of her picnic table. C. DeVere stood at the edge of her campsite, the ranger she'd met earlier.

She pointed to Jess's tent. "It can get windy at night."

Her tent was already a greenhouse in the ninety-degree heat. Jess watched as C. DeVere shifted her weight to one leg. She held a clipboard in the crook of her arm. She was taller than Jess expected, her legs long and her body trim. Jess glanced toward her tent, halting her brazen appraisal. A little wind would be welcome to cut through some of the heat.

"Okay, thanks." Jess had tossed the stakes into the nylon tent bag and thrown them in the back of her car. She knew she wouldn't need them with the weight of her queen-size air mattress and a summer's worth of supplies stored in her tent. Plus, she hadn't thought to bring a mallet.

"Make sure all your food is locked up at night, otherwise you'll have raccoon problems."

Jess suppressed a smile. The cool and composed ranger took her job seriously, even when it came to warning campers about furry critters. She tucked a lock of hair behind her ear as she talked, a habit Jess found she enjoyed watching. Jess also liked how it held the curled imprint when the same piece of hair fell again moments later.

"Same with your garbage. Make sure you put it in the locked containers on site. The raccoons will get into everything."

"Got it." Jess pressed her lips together, amused.

"Remember, stake that tent down." She smiled and turned to go to the next campsite.

Jess stood glued to the spot, eavesdropping on her neighbors as the ranger spoke to them. The ranger asked them to move one of their tents because they hadn't followed instructions and had pitched it on the grass strip that separated the rows of campsites. Jess listened with interest as C. DeVere managed to be both commanding and respectful. Her voice had a melodic lilt, low and soft. As she moved to the next site, one of the guys began pulling up the stakes on the offending tent.

"I told you we weren't supposed to set it up on the grass." The shorter of the two chastised the other as he watched him drag his tent off the grass.

"The grass is softer. I don't know why we have to put the tent on the dirt and gravel."

"It kills the grass. Why do you care? You have a sleeping pad. It's not like you're sleeping on the ground."

"This is the spot that's going to have the most shade in the morning. You could at least get me a beer instead of watching me work."

The way they interacted made her think they must be related. Brothers probably.

His companion swung his legs from the picnic table and opened a red and white cooler. As he made eye contact with her, he held up a beer. "You want one, too?"

Caught observing, she stuttered her response. "Um. Yeah, I guess so. Sure." She walked around her picnic table and crossed through some low brush into their campsite. "Thanks." She cracked it open and took a long swig of the lager. She nearly moaned when the cool, refreshing beverage hit her throat.

"Tim Reardon." The shorter guy extended his hand, still wet and icy cold. "Sorry about that." He wiped it on his cargo shorts. "That's my brother, Ian."

He greeted her with a raise of his rubber mallet.

"I'm Jess. Is this your first time camping here?" She watched Ian try to find the perfect spot for his tent.

"Yeah. It's been on our list of places to camp for a while though. Have you been here before?"

"No, it's my first time." With feigned indifference, Jess watched C. DeVere make her circuit, checking in with each campsite.

"Are you camping alone or meeting friends?" Tim ran his fingers through his hair.

"It's just me. I'm working on my thesis this summer. I'm writing about Dry Falls, so I thought there was no better place to do that than here."

Ranger DeVere laughed at something the next row over.

"That's awesome." Tim seemed sincere when he said it. "We're here for two weeks. We have some hikes we want to do, some bike trails to check out, and we want to swim and chill in the sun with some beers. We've heard it's a fun place during the summer. You're always welcome to join us. I see you brought your bike, too."

She glanced to where her beloved Trek sat atop her car. "I'd like that. Based on what I've seen so far, I can probably park my car and use my bike to get everywhere this summer."

"Yeah, it's not that big here in the canyon. I looked at the map. If you want to go into town or up to Steamboat Rock, then driving is best." He finished his beer and crushed the can under his foot before tossing it into a garbage bag. "I wanted to drive past it on our way here, but we came from the opposite direction."

"Where are you from?"

"Portland. We own a barbershop there. Someone has to trim the hipsters' beards for them."

She grinned at his quip. He seemed like a nice guy even if his jokes were terrible.

"How about you?"

"I'm from Seattle."

"Are you studying at U Dub then?" He used the Pacific Northwest's slang for the University of Washington.

"Yeah, I'm working on my master of science. I'm a geology nerd." She shrugged and grinned.

"That's cool." He seemed a little too earnest. They watched Ian pound his stakes into the ground.

She didn't know if Tim was flirting with her. Jess had rarely been able to tell in similar situations, although her encounter earlier with Brett had been obvious.

The nerd part was half-joke, half-truth. She was self-admittedly socially awkward and had difficulty reading others. As a server, patrons often hit on her, or at least that's what her coworkers told her. She never was able to delineate when someone was being nice and when someone was coming on to her. Now hyper-sensitive to the possibility he was flirting with her, she turned to go back to her campsite.

"I better finish unpacking before sunset. It was nice meeting you both. Thanks for the beer." She delicately stepped over rocks and brush into her campsite.

"No problem." Tim raised his voice to reach her. "Come by anytime if you want to join us for a bike ride."

Thankful he'd said, *us* and not *me,* she dispelled the notion that he'd been flirting. She was embarrassed for even thinking it. She loved her chosen profession, even if it made her less attractive to some people. Most people didn't consider a love of rocks sexy. She knew this from experience.

Had anyone asked, she would have said she considered herself average looking, but she rarely thought about those things. Her pale skin required copious amounts of sunscreen, and her straight dark hair was, well…just straight and dark. She had nice eyes though.

She finished arranging her belongings in her tent and went outside to relax in what would be her home for the next three months. From her camp chair, she watched the long rays of the setting sun stretch over the campground. The campground that had been nearly empty when she set up her tent now buzzed with cars, bikes, and pedestrians as campers tried to find their homes away from home. She missed the quiet. The din of the campground rose as those who had spent the day on hikes or at the lakes gathered for dinner.

Campers all around her bent over propane grills or trudged toward the showers carrying towels and wearing wet bathing suits. Children who had probably expended far more energy than normal showed signs of being tired and cranky. Smells of grilled burgers and hot dogs wafted toward her campsite, and her stomach growled. She pulled out an unappetizing, pre-made ham and cheese sandwich and a Gatorade from her cooler.

Tuning out the activity around her, she made a list of items she needed on the back of a gas station receipt. She'd passed the small general store as she drove into the valley. It likely had a limited selection of overpriced items, but she'd check it out tomorrow. If they didn't carry what she needed, she could drive into Coulee City or even Ephrata.

Noticing her eyes begin to strain, she glanced upward. The sky had darkened, night fast on its way. Her sweaty shirt still clung to her skin. She hoped the night would provide some relief from the heat and found herself wondering what kind of hours the rangers worked.

Jess flicked on the lamp above her, leaving it swaying on the metal arm she'd attached to her picnic table. The lantern illuminated one end of the table, but not much more. The swinging fixture made the shadow of her pen dance. She scrawled *bug repellent* as winged creatures frequented the attractive light. She wouldn't have to suffer the bugs for long. It had been a long drive, and she intended to turn in early. She had much to do in the morning.

As 10:00 p.m. rolled around, a state park truck with its flashing bar of lights crept down the rows of campsites. Her heartbeat quickened. As promised, the rangers strictly enforced the campground's quiet hours, and the truck stopped to speak to parties playing loud games or blasting music. As the truck crawled past her, the silhouette of a man turned toward her. The magnitude of her disappointment surprised her.

Chapter Three

I thought about you last night."

Clare had been watching Jessica drive her tent stakes into the ground with a large rock. Jessica rose from her crouched position. She already wore a bright smile, her dimples on full display. She wiped her brow with the back of her hand and looked genuinely happy at the intrusion.

"I'm Clare."

"Jessica, as you might recall, but most people call me Jess."

Jess held her hand a bit longer than appropriate. Her skin felt soft but slightly gritty from the rock she'd been using.

"Did you have a wild night?" Clare couldn't refrain from teasing her and giving her a small smirk. A blush crept up Jess's neck and culminated in a sheepish smile. Clare had noticed her advice had gone unheeded on her final patrol the day before, and Jess's tent had remained without tether. When the wind had kicked up, she'd briefly considered going to check on her but had decided against it. Some lessons had to be learned.

"Well, it started quite nicely. I could see the stars through the mesh top of my tent. Occasionally, I heard other people, but mostly the only sounds were insects. It was quite peaceful—at first." Her soft features turned into a scowl.

"Then the wind started." Clare laughed.

Jess nodded. "I woke to a horrifying noise. I didn't know what was happening. The tent pitched to the side, throwing me off my air mattress. I struggled to right myself, but the mattress and sleeping bag were on top of me. My face smashed into the side of the tent." Her eyes looked like saucers.

Clare grinned at the image, trying not to laugh.

"Oh, that's not all." Jess took a deep breath. "It sounded like a freight train. I almost ducked my head so it could barrel over me. I heard the wind tossing items around the campground. People were shrieking and a baby was crying. I managed to get back on top of the air mattress and used my duffel bags to weigh two corners of the tent. That didn't last thirty seconds. The wind gusted again, and they landed squarely on my chest. Everything inside them spilled out. The wind sounded like it was howling. If I didn't know better, I'd think it was angry." Breathless, she paused.

"Did it settle down after that so you could sleep?" Clare enjoyed teasing her a bit, but she didn't want to seem uncompassionate. The first time she'd experienced the wind years ago, it had terrified her.

"Sleep? I had to lie on my stomach like the Vitruvian Man, my arms and legs stretched out toward the four corners of the tent, all my clothing and belongings beneath me. It was sheer will that kept it attached to the earth. I envisioned my tent with me inside it flying through the air like the house in *The Wizard of Oz*." She motioned dramatically through the air.

Clare chortled and felt her entire service belt shake as the laugh came from low in her belly. It felt good to laugh. "Did you consider sleeping in your car?"

Jess looked pleased to have elicited such a reaction from her. "I did, but I thought the tent would have little chance of staying put without the weight of me inside it. I also didn't want to have to canvass the county for it in the morning. Plus, fleeing to the safety of my Outback on the first night would have been downright embarrassing." She grinned and shrugged a shoulder. "So, I held down the fort, literally."

Clare's cheeks had started to hurt from smiling. "The physical architecture of the canyon coalesces the wind and sends it rocketing along the coulee toward the campground. That's why I suggested you stake down your tent."

"I feel like that's a subtle way of saying, 'I told you so.'" Her lips twitched like she was holding back a grin.

Clare shrugged. "I've been doing this a while. I give good advice." She liked how Jess teased her back. How old *was* she? Jess might have been in high school when Clare started working at the park. She winced.

Jess bit one side of her lower lip and grinned. "Do you have any more advice for me?"

Did she have more advice, or did she simply want an excuse to continue flirting with her? Clare couldn't remember the last time she'd enjoyed a conversation so much. "As I said before, be careful of the raccoons. They'll stop at nothing."

"Is that so?" Jess lifted an eyebrow. She appeared amused.

"They'll get into any food you leave out. You should wedge your cooler under the picnic table or, better yet, put it in your car." Clare pointed at the cooler on the picnic table bench. "You got lucky last night because of the hurricane-strength winds, but when the raccoons come out, they'll easily find their way into any food."

Jess nodded, more serious. "Okay, I'll keep all my food in my car."

"Good." Clare tucked her hair behind her ear. "You'll take my advice this time? Not like the stakes?"

"Yes, not like the stakes." Jess grinned.

She should get back to work, but she didn't want to go. They stood looking at each other for a moment.

"Well, if you think of any more advice for me, feel free to stop by anytime. I'll be here all summer." Jess held out her arms.

Surprised by the invitation, Clare nodded and smiled. She had the feeling Jess wouldn't turn her away even if she arrived without any words of wisdom. She turned to leave, taking the fluttering in her chest and much to think about with her.

As she walked back to the ranger station, she thought about what she'd said. It hadn't been a lie. While futilely trying to sleep, Clare had thought about Jess far too much. Even when Jess had surely been fighting in the battle between the wind and her tent, deep down, Clare knew that she'd be fine. She seemed to be quite independent. After all, she intended to spend the summer camping alone. Plus, she earned bonus points for not finishing the night sleeping in her car. Furthermore, the first thing Jess had done at sunrise was to remedy the situation, with a rock no less. Clare liked what she saw.

However, Clare wasn't in the practice of looking at women and hadn't for years. Having a sudden interest in someone felt strange and terrifying, and she wanted to step back from the dangerous precipice even though she was metaphorically still in the parking lot. In her vehicle. Belted in.

Later that night after her shift, she lay in bed, her two-way radio on quietly. Nothing much of interest was going on. She'd grown accustomed to hearing the voices of her best friend, Lyn; and Helen, the other dispatcher, in her home. She usually left her radio on even when she wasn't on duty, and it frightened her what silence might sound like if she ever turned it off.

Helen was working since she and Lyn always requested the same shifts so they could spend time together on their off days. Helen was in her fifties and had worked at the park longer than any of the park's staff members.

There wasn't a strict rule against fraternization with campers, but the system frowned upon it. Over the years, Clare had worked with rangers who disregarded the vague policy. Certain culprits had a new liaison every weekend. She'd never been interested in stepping over that line.

Maybe talking to Helen would help her sort out her thoughts. Clare flopped over on her side, kicked the sheet to the foot of the bed, and called her.

"My work daughter!"

"Hey." Clare chuckled. Helen had taken her under her wing during her first few weeks of working in the park. "Do you have time to talk as long as there's no chatter?"

"For you, always, dear. How is the weekend treating you?" Even in her no-nonsense dispatcher's role, Helen managed to be sweet to everyone.

"It's been interesting so far." Tentatively, she continued. "I met a woman who will be camping alone all summer while she's working on her thesis. She had approval in the system, so she must've received permission."

"That concerns you?"

"No, no. Nothing like that. It's just that she's…well, it's the first time that someone has made me…" Strangely, Clare couldn't verbalize her feelings.

After a long pause, Helen spoke. "Oh, I see. You're interested in her."

Helen's knowing tone helped her relax.

"Yes, I suppose so. I hardly recall what that feels like. She's young, but something about her intrigues me."

Another voice came over the radio and then through her cell phone a split second later, creating an eerie echo.

"Hold, please." Helen took care of the request before she addressed her again. "Okay, I'm back. Say again?"

"I was just saying she intrigues me. While part of me would like to get to know her better, I don't know if I'm ready for that. I know it's been two years, but sometimes it feels like yesterday. Some mornings I wake up and the pain still feels so fresh. Maybe self-preservation is the way to go, no matter how nice Jess might seem."

"Jess? That's her name? That's pretty." Helen sighed. "Hon, I've known you for a long time. I can't recall the last time you asked me anything like this. Don't you think it's about time you deserve some happiness, something good, even if it's just friendship? Maybe you two can be friends for the summer. You could stand to have a few more friends."

Clare didn't answer at first, thinking it over. "No, I don't think I could be friends with her. It would have to be all or nothing. It feels… different with her." She hated how words were failing her, but it didn't matter. Helen seemed to understand.

"As in happy, breathless, giddy?"

"Yes." It was a perfect description of how she felt each time she'd been around Jess. It was how she felt now, just talking about her, like the mere thought of Jess made her shimmer. Granted, they'd known one another for all of a millisecond, but she couldn't deny the attraction. What would happen if she invested her heart for the summer? Would she survive having it ripped out come fall? The stakes seemed too high. Yet, she knew Helen was right, as usual. She deserved some happiness.

"My dear, you're thinking too much about this. You already have your answer."

Clare smiled, even though Helen couldn't see her. "I don't know why you put up with me. Thank you."

"I'm always here for you, dear. You haven't been over for dinner in a while." Her tone had a hint of motherly disapproval. "Hank misses you."

"I miss him, too. Let's pick a night you and I both have off. Give him my love."

"I will, darling."

As she tried to fall asleep again, a sense of calm washed over her. It gave her hope. She wasn't quite ready yet, but perhaps this meant she might be soon. The summer might turn out to be more interesting than she'd anticipated.

CHAPTER FOUR

Jess straddled the wooden bench of her picnic table. She added firewood and marshmallows to her growing shopping list.

"Hey, I noticed you haven't eaten or cooked much since you arrived, so I brought over some breakfast Ian made." Tim held a paper plate. "We had a couple of extra pancakes and some scrambled eggs and bacon, so I made you a sandwich." He handed her the plate.

She hadn't taken her eyes off the food. "Oh my God, that looks so good. I'm starving." She managed to pick up the assemblage in one piece and took a huge bite. It was still warm. She closed her eyes in enjoyment. After she swallowed, she shouted over to the next campsite. "Thank you, Ian!"

He saluted her with a spatula he was washing.

"The slice of cheese was my idea." Tim sat on the picnic table bench with his back to the tabletop. He splayed out his legs, a bright shade of Pacific Northwest white.

"Thank you. It's delicious. I didn't realize how hungry I was. I haven't shopped for groceries yet. I'm going to the general store before I head out in the field to do some work." She hoped he understood the words she mumbled around the food in her mouth.

"I can't believe you're working the whole time you're here. Are you planning on having *any* fun?" He scowled. "It's Memorial Day weekend, you know. You should relax a little and come with us to watch the laser light show tonight on Grand Coulee Dam."

"I don't know. I need to get stuff done while I'm here." She picked out a piece of bacon and folded it into her mouth.

"Hey." Ian walked over while drying his hands on a paper towel. He wadded it up and tossed it into her fire ring. "What are you doing tonight? We're going to see the laser show. You should come with us."

Tim was right. It was summer, and summertime was meant to be enjoyed. It wouldn't hurt her to have a little fun while she was here if she stayed on top of her work. She looked between them. They were relentless.

"How could I say no?" She smiled and popped another bite of bacon into her mouth.

"That's what we like to hear." Ian grinned.

Happy with her response, they retreated to their campsite.

As she took in her surroundings, her new home away from home, she became aware of the rare sense of joy that came from making new friends. She'd been so focused on her research that she'd neglected to include any plans for enjoying the summer. She'd become so used to being independent that she hadn't considered the opportunities for social interaction that might arise from being at the campground. Yet, Ian and Tim were already friendly enough with her to make plans. Then there was Clare.

What was Clare? Jess enjoyed talking to her but calling her an acquaintance made their interactions seem superficial and fleeting. That didn't feel quite right. The word friend didn't feel right either. All she knew was that thinking about seeing Clare again sent a little rush through her. She hoped she'd see her again soon.

Jess drove past the ranger station that looked closed. She exited the campground and enjoyed the air conditioning that had started to blow cool. She pulled into a space in front of the general store, a full three-minute drive from her campsite, if that. She could easily walk or bike for smaller shopping trips.

A middle-aged woman working the cash register greeted her as she stepped inside, the bells on the door tinkling behind her. A handful of people milled about. The air smelled of microwaved burritos and industrial cleaner.

The small space was well-organized and geared toward tourists, with souvenirs available all around the store. In addition to groceries, they carried many other sundries. The items were overpriced, but the store had most of the things she needed. She filled her cart with bottled water, beer, meats and veggies to grill, a lighter, sunscreen, bug repellent, firewood, and ice. An endcap loaded with everything needed to make s'mores caught her eye, and she stopped to choose between the various kinds of chocolate bars.

A masculine voice in the next aisle said a name that jerked her attention like a fishhook snagged in a trout's jaw.

"So, how's it going with Clare? Any luck with the Ice Queen?"

Jess could almost hear his sneer and recognized the voice as Brett's, the smarmy ranger who had spoken to her at the lookout. She remained out of sight at the end of the aisle.

A feminine voice, just above a whisper, snapped at him. "You're so rude. Just because she won't date you doesn't mean she's an ice queen."

"Well, it doesn't sound like you're having much luck in that department either, sweetheart." He growled the last word.

Was it true? If this woman was interested in Clare, did that mean Clare was interested in women? An unexpected shiver raced up her spine.

"She doesn't date. Everyone knows that. So, go to hell, Brett."

"Watch it, sister. You should be fired for talking to me like that."

"I don't work for you—thank God—so bite me."

Someone stomped off. The bells on the door dinged moments later.

Setting the bag of marshmallows and two Hershey's Cookies 'n' Creme bars in her cart, she waited, hoping he would go the opposite direction. She heard him at the register.

"Here. Keep the change, Maggie."

The bells on the door dinged again.

Jess finished her shopping, the conversation she'd overheard replaying in her mind. The cashier rang up her items and bagged her groceries while participating in a bit of small talk about the recent heat. Receipt in hand, she wheeled her cart out the door to see a white truck with the state park's insignia outside. Jess wanted to groan upon seeing he hadn't left yet. She dreaded dealing with him again. Her heart skipped a beat when Clare opened the truck's door.

She carefully exited the vehicle in the manner that law enforcement officers do while wearing a loaded service belt of equipment. She smiled when she saw Jess. Jess opened the rear hatch of her car.

"Hi, you. Want some help?" Without waiting for an answer, Clare picked up the heavy bag of ice and put it in the back of her car.

"Thanks." Jess unloaded the last bag of groceries. "I have a huge favor to ask."

Clare rested her hands on her belt. She'd pulled her hair back into a tiny ponytail. Jess couldn't see her eyes through her dark sunglasses.

"Sure. What?"

"Do you remember the guys at the campsite beside me? You asked one of them to move his tent off the grass." Jess squinted in the bright sunlight.

Clare chuckled. "Yes. If I recall, they staked down *their* tents." She pushed her sunglasses up on top of her head. Her eyes seemed to shine.

Jess rolled her eyes at the jab. "Well, they asked me to see the laser light show up at Grand Coulee Dam tonight. They seem like nice guys, but I'd feel better if someone knew where I was, and sort of…" Palms up, she fumbled for the right words.

"Made sure you returned?"

"Yeah, I mean, I'm sure it's not necess—"

"I need to grab an iced coffee, then I'm going on vehicular patrol. I'll swing by your campsite in a few minutes and make it known that I'm aware of where you'll be tonight." She gestured toward the campground.

"They seem like nice guys." She liked Tim and Ian, but she wasn't keen on getting in a car with two guys she'd just met without someone knowing where she was going. Jess felt relieved that Clare understood.

"Most do. You're right to be careful. We don't truly know anyone, do we?" Clare dipped her head and tucked her sunglasses into the collar of her shirt.

"I guess not." She wondered at the vague sense of hurt beneath the surface of Clare's words and wished she knew her better.

"Okay, I'll see you soon." Clare trailed her fingers down Jess's arm from elbow to wrist as she passed.

Goosebumps ascended her arm, and her visceral reaction to the touch startled her. To her surprise, she found the sensation both welcome and pleasant.

❖

Jess had just finished putting away her groceries when Clare's truck rolled through the campground. She watched her park and get out. Clare wore her hair down now, and it framed her face with gentle waves.

Jess had bought Tim and Ian ice cream sandwiches as a thank you for making her breakfast, and they ate them while manspreading on top of her picnic table, their feet resting on the bench.

"Good morning. Breakfast of champions." Clare motioned to their half-eaten ice cream bars.

They laughed.

"Are you three going to the laser show tonight?" She stood with her hand on her hip.

"Yeah. We're all going." Ian licked a drop of ice cream from his wrist.

"Well, I wanted to remind you that it will be quiet hours when you return, so please respect other campers and keep noise levels low."

"Sure." Tim crumpled the empty wrapper in his fist. "No problem."

"Gates lock at ten o'clock, but I'll be at the entrance letting you in, so make sure your driver is sober. I'll see you all tonight. Enjoy the show." With that, Clare turned her back to the guys and winked at her as she walked away.

The wink seemed to fly through the air and pierce Jess right in the sternum. She sucked in a breath. She'd asked Clare to look out for her, but the wink had been unexpected. Feelings bubbled up inside her, too many to sort out. Clare would be watching for her tonight. It made her feel safe but nervous, too. No one had looked out for her in some time.

Would Clare have looked for her later even without her asking? Jess wanted the answer to be yes. While she looked forward to spending the evening having fun with Ian and Tim, she looked forward to returning to the campground and seeing Clare even more, if only for a moment.

She recalled the conversation she'd overheard inside the general store. Clare didn't seem cold. She'd been warm and generous with her. They'd joked and laughed, and maybe even flirted a little. Jess was stumped and more than a little pleased. No, Clare didn't seem like an ice queen at all.

CHAPTER FIVE

Clare smiled as she left the ranger station and drove along Dry Falls Lake Road. She'd already seen Jess twice during her short morning shift. Could that have anything to do with the sudden lifting of her spirits?

It was still mid-morning, but waves of heat already rose from the asphalt, making the scenery in the distance waver and dance. Air conditioning blasted from the vents. Her stomach rumbled, and she counted the minutes until she could clock out and grab some lunch. After that, she'd try to get a few hours of sleep before her shift tonight.

She surveyed the park's morning activity. Not much was happening yet. Some hikers and kayakers were trying to beat the midday heat. In a few more hours, the park would be a happening place, especially around the lakes. She'd be on duty again for all the craziness tonight.

As she came around a curve, someone walked on her side of the road. Jess, wearing a Huskies baseball cap, turned her head when Clare pulled up beside her.

"You know there are trails around here, right?"

Jess smiled. "Yes, but I want to get to the eastern face of Umatilla Rock while the morning sun is still on it, so I thought the road would be the fastest option."

"You should walk against traffic then, so you can see the cars coming." She pointed to the other side of the road. "I don't want you getting hit by someone coming around a corner."

"Good point. I will." Jess folded her arms and leaned on the passenger side door, her head poking inside the truck's cab. "Do you ever sleep?" She scrunched up her nose.

"We have long shifts and extra shifts on holiday weekends. Normally, I work nights, which I prefer. I like hearing the park breathe at night. It makes me feel connected, part of something."

Jess scowled. "I've heard the park breathe at night. It sounds like a fire-breathing dragon."

"It can be peaceful, too. You'll see." She grinned, then hesitated a moment. "I'm heading that way. Do you want a ride?"

"Can I? I mean, is that allowed?" Jess looked surprised.

"Unless you plan on suing me, it's fine."

Jess grinned, opened the door, and swung her backpack into the truck.

Clare continued her slow crawl along Dry Falls Lake Road, grateful for the reduced speed limit that would extend the time she was in Jess's company. "Are you a photographer?" She motioned to the camera that hung around her neck.

"No, I take photographs, but they're for research. I'm working on my thesis."

"What kind of research?" Clare turned to look at her. Jess had lovely green eyes. They reminded her of the antique glass bottles her father collected and displayed on his study's windowsill. She always admired their bright translucence.

"I'm a geologist."

"You are?"

"Yeah, I know it's nerdy, but I love it." Jess rubbed her palms together.

Clare could sense she did because she seemed to glow as she started talking about her passion.

"My interest mainly involves stratigraphy, studying the composition of the rock layers and the order of the layers themselves. I love researching the different layers. There's so much to learn, so much more than meets the eye. Did you know there are two kinds of stratigraphy? Lithostratigraphy and biostratigraphy. But I'm probably boring you." She ended her passionate exposition, and her shoulders dropped a little.

"Not at all. So, which of the two are you interested in, or is it both?" They were almost to Umatilla Rock, and Clare wished she could slow down. Their conversation would soon be over, and then Jess would be gone, taking her stunning eyes and excitement with her.

"Well, by default, I'm interested in both, but I love biostratigraphy. That deals with using the fossils found within the rock layers to determine the relative age of the rock."

Clare pulled to the side of the road and stopped. "Fossils, huh?" Umatilla Rock rose before them. Jess didn't move to get out. On impulse, Clare said, "Tell me something about Umatilla Rock." She turned her attention to the massive formation that knifed its way through the valley floor.

Jess took a moment, either because she'd been put on the spot or because she wasn't expecting her interest.

"Well, it's a monadnock."

"*MON-ad-nock?*" Clare echoed her pronunciation.

"Yes, that means it's like an island. It's an isolated ridge that rises abruptly from a level area. Sometimes they're called inselbergs. It's composed of more erosion-resistant rock than all the rock around it that washed away over time. I'm going to go climb it." Her eyes sparkled.

"You're quite interesting. Do you know that?"

Clearly at a loss for words, Jess opened her mouth a few times like a fish out of water.

"I can imagine you as a little girl all excited about your rock collection." Clare rested her wrist over the top of the steering wheel.

Jess grinned and her glorious dimples appeared. "I *still* have a rock collection. I brought it with me."

Clare matched her contagious smile.

"Come by my campsite sometime. I'll show it to you." Jess got out of the truck. She grabbed her backpack and stood by the open door. "I have beer, too, if you need more incentive than rocks and fossils."

Before she could answer, Jess called out her thanks for the ride and closed the door. Clare watched her start up the path toward Umatilla Rock.

No, she didn't need more incentive than that. She didn't even need the rocks.

Jess had been itching to get in the field for months. Bursting with excitement, she'd stuffed her backpack with her notebook, pens, binoculars, sunscreen, sunglasses, granola bar, water bottle, and phone.

She wasn't sure she'd have cell service in the park, but she took her phone anyway. She'd been on her own long enough to know that being independent meant being prepared. Now sweaty and standing at the top of Umatilla Rock after taking a quick assessment and some photos of the strata on its eastern face, she was pleased to find that she did indeed have service. Not as pleased as she'd been with the company during her ride to the rock, but pleased, nonetheless.

She glanced at her phone, but she still didn't have any text messages since the *ok* she'd received from her boyfriend, Jackson, after letting him know that the drive had been nice and that she'd arrived safely. It irritated her that he couldn't bother to text more than two letters. He also hadn't answered when she called. Either he was acting like he didn't care that she was going away for the summer, or he really didn't care. The worst part was that she hoped it was the latter, even if she sometimes dwelled on how she had no one who cared about her well-being. It was a lingering feeling she couldn't shake. Still, she'd rather deal with that than deal with him.

Jess stood in a crevice atop the formation where she could cross from one side of the rock blade to the other. She surveyed the valley from her central position. It was a glorious day, and she was thrilled to be here. The sun heated her bare shoulders. She was glad she'd chosen to wear a baseball cap, even if the cap had once belonged to *him*.

She'd met him at UW during her last year as an undergrad. His father owned an upscale Italian restaurant and bar on Capitol Hill, and she waited tables there. Tips were great, and she'd been able to afford her classes and her small apartment, and still be able to put some money away for this trip.

She took out her water bottle and sat on a flat rock facing the visitor center that stood on the western edge of the canyon. A few kids used the stationary binoculars mounted near the bright white building. Were they looking at her? If so, what would they see? She scoffed. If they looked close enough, they would see a coward, someone too afraid to be on her own.

Over the years, she'd learned how to fend for herself out of necessity. It'd been the only option, and she'd had no choice in the matter. Independence had meant survival, but it was a lonely type of existence. She'd been so lonely that she'd filled the void with Jackson.

She picked up a shard of rock that had fallen from the stone façade and turned it over in her hand. Part of her wished she'd bitten the bullet and ended the relationship before she left Seattle. She knew she wanted more than he could ever offer. When they met, all her close friends were dating great guys, and she'd succumbed to the pressure to be part of a couple. He was attractive, nice enough, and got along well with her friends, but she'd never felt that special something with him. Despite his dullness and the utter lack of sexual chemistry between them, he gave her something to lean on. She'd decided she'd rather be with someone uninspiring than be alone. Having no one terrified her. Loneliness was a shadow she'd been trying to evade her entire life.

She needed to focus on what was important, and that wasn't a relationship that was going nowhere. With the on-site data she planned to gather this summer, she'd write her thesis and be close to being and doing everything she'd dreamed of since she was a little girl.

Jess decided to deal with him later. He'd be there when summer ended. Keeping him around until then reassured her that she'd have something to go home to in the fall, even if she planned to end the relationship upon her return. She could reassure herself that she wasn't alone in the world, at least for a little while longer. Even if it wasn't totally true…

She tossed the rock she'd been holding in her hand, and it skipped and fell somewhere below her. She stood and began her descent down Umatilla Rock. Loose rocks skidded beneath her hiking boots as she picked her way down the steep terrain. While not necessarily heavy, the weight of her backpack shifting with each step made it difficult to keep her balance. The canyon floor far below made her realize how high up she was and how far she'd tumble if she made a misstep. Laser-focused on reaching the top during her ascent, she hadn't noticed the steepness. She stepped on a flat rock the size of a brick, but a smaller rock beneath it made it teeter-totter. Her leg skidded out from beneath her. She reached out. Her hand contacted an outcrop of rock, and she held on with all her might. It was enough to slow her fall. Her other leg folded beneath her. Her ass hit the uneven, rocky slope, and the fall shoved her backpack up around her shoulders. Her head snapped back, but it slammed into the cushion of her pack and not the rock-hard trail.

Staring at the sky, she lay there for a moment to assess the damage. Her ass hurt, sharp rocks still poking into her. Her elbow felt scraped, but she found no major bleeding. Relief replaced terror, and her pulse began to slow a little. She sat up.

As she brushed herself off, she started to get excited again about what she was about to accomplish over the summer. Camping by herself had been *her* choice, a rare instance in which she didn't mind being solitary. Could she have asked Jackson or a friend to come along? Sure, but she didn't want that. She'd chosen to go alone, and that gave more significance to her accomplishment.

However, in the back of her mind, she knew independence was all fine and good until it wasn't. When it came to matters of safety— like falling off a steep trail—or needing someone for other reasons, independence morphed into something darker, something akin to isolation or loneliness. Jess banished those thoughts. She'd slipped, but she'd survived. She could do this alone. She was strong. She'd succeed this summer and prove it.

CHAPTER SIX

I s that decaf?"

"It's decaf." Lyn pushed an iced coffee toward her as Clare slid into the booth. "Difficult shift?"

"No, hardly." Clare wiped at the back of her neck with a napkin. The heat was intense. "I'm back on tonight though." Even though her shift had ended, she kept the radio clipped to her shoulder at a volume she could still hear, even if others couldn't. She reached for one of the bistro's sticky, laminated menus sandwiched between bottles of mustard and malt vinegar at the end of the table. Bistro was being generous. It was a glorified coffee shop attached to a gas station, but dining options near the park left them with few choices.

"I'm on duty tonight, too." Lyn stopped her as she opened the menu. "I took the liberty of ordering our usual. I'm starving."

She let out a grateful sigh. "Thanks. Me, too. All I've had today is coffee." She could feel Lyn's eyes on her. Her best friend was sharp and missed nothing. Lyn was a great dispatcher, but she would have made an excellent detective, too.

"You seem off. Or different. Is everything okay?" Lyn picked some lint from the sleeve of her shirt and attempted to inconspicuously drop it on the floor.

Clare flipped her hair from her eyes with a toss of her head. "No, nothing. I mean, I'm fine." She bent her flexible straw back and forth.

"You're such a terrible liar and have been since college." Lyn shook her head.

"I am not!"

She laughed. "Do you remember when you tried to convince the RA that the liquid in our—"

"Okay, enough. Yes, I remember. I was younger then. I've learned." Clare grinned. "We had fun that night though, didn't we?"

"You're so annoying when you try to evade my questions." Lyn scowled at her and only stopped because their food arrived. The server placed the salad in front of her and a panini in front of Lyn.

"That looks good." She eyed the melted cheese oozing from Lyn's sandwich as she drizzled the dressing on her salad.

"Well, you can't have any because you won't tell me what's going on." Lyn took a huge bite and stared at her expectantly as she chewed.

Clare pushed diced egg and chicken chunks around with her fork. "I don't know how to explain it." She usually told Lyn the most mundane details of her day, yet she was having trouble finding the right words to talk to her, the person who knew her better than anyone. "A geologist checked into the campground." She glanced up to see Lyn's reaction.

"Okay. So?" Lyn's stare was no longer harsh, but unreadable. She reached over and dipped one of her fries into Clare's ranch dressing.

"She's interesting." Clare hated how high-pitched her voice sounded. She stabbed a forkful of romaine.

Lyn swallowed and stopped eating. "Interesting how?"

They made eye contact. She didn't need to say more.

"Oh. And?"

"And what? There's nothing more to say. I met her and she's interesting." Clare took another bite. Maybe if she had food in her mouth, she wouldn't have to answer any more questions.

"That's it? She's interesting? Is she interested in you?"

"I don't know." It was the truth. She motioned to Lyn's abandoned food. "Eat. What's wrong with you?"

Lyn picked up a fry and gnawed at one end. "It's not like you to fraternize with campers."

"No, it's not." She held eye contact as she chose her words. "But she might be worth changing my ways."

"Wow, this is monumental." Lyn took a sip of coffee.

Clare couldn't ignore the growing unease between them and hoped to find a way to alleviate it. Lyn's friendship was important to her. She'd been in her life to help celebrate the good and had consoled her through the bad. She knew when Clare needed space and when she needed someone to pull her out of bed and drag her into town for a coffee and croissant.

Over the years, Clare began to realize that Lyn would like to have more than a platonic relationship, but she didn't share the same inclination. During times like this, the awkwardness loomed larger than the canyon at the bistro's doorstep. They'd spent so much time together since they were teenagers that Lyn felt like the sister she never had. Yet, as close as they seemed at times, because of Lyn's feelings for her, Clare had never been comfortable telling her everything.

"Nothing has happened, and maybe nothing will happen. But if something did happen, I think I might be…happy about it." She offered up a wry smile.

"Well, you'll have to point her out." Lyn seemed to remember her food and took another bite of her panini. She swallowed and continued. "I want to see this *interesting* woman. I can't remember the last time I heard you mention being happy."

Her radio crackled, and Lyn leaned across the table to hear. She turned up the volume to make Helen's voice more audible.

"Papa Romeo 687, this is Dispatch. Over."

Gordon responded. "Dispatch, this is Papa Romeo 687 at the boat ramp. Over."

"Report of smoke and a possible brush fire north of Charlie Delta. Over." Helen's perfunctory report had Clare standing and pulling money from her wallet.

Gordon's answer came through her walkie. "Copy. On my way. Over and out."

"I'm sorry." She threw some cash on the table.

"You're off duty." Lyn slowly shook her head.

She'd already keyed the mic on her shoulder. "Dispatch, this is Papa Romeo 645 at Banks Lake. Over."

Helen responded right away. "Papa Romeo 645, Dispatch. Over."

"Papa Romeo 645, responding to brush fire. Over." She squeezed Lyn's shoulder and dodged other patrons on her way out, ignoring their inquisitive stares and whispers. Time was of the essence. She knew how dangerous even the smallest fire could become. Minutes mattered. When dispatch informed them of a fire, it made her heart race and her stomach roil. The anxiety alone nearly crippled her, and she hated how she always rushed out expecting the worst. Yet all that paled in comparison to the fear of what might happen if she didn't respond.

❖

Clare stripped off her dirty uniform while the shower warmed. She kicked the pile of smoky clothing into a corner of the bathroom and ran her fingers through her hair. It stank of smoke. She and Gordon had contained the small fire with ease. They dug a fire line using a shovel and a Pulaski, trapping the flames between it and the roadway before the real firefighters arrived. The sense of relief she gained from stopping these little brush fires before they became something more helped mask her other, bigger feelings.

She looked in the mirror and hardly recognized the image looking back at her. She felt like she'd aged a decade during the last two years. Leaning closer, she inspected her hairline for grays. She found the three she already knew about, but no more. Still, she cursed the genetics or stress that had caused them. Mid-thirties were far too young for gray hair. She stepped into the lukewarm shower. A hot shower was the last thing she wanted in this weather.

The last couple of years had worn on her, much more than anyone knew. Her parents still worried about her. She continued to assure them she was fine, and she saw them for the usual holidays: Thanksgiving, Christmas, and Easter. She mostly stayed in touch with her mom via text, and occasionally her dad, although his willingness to text versus call continued to be a work in progress.

As she worked shampoo into her hair, her mind wandered to her upcoming shift. She wondered who else would be on duty and hoped it wasn't Brett. She was friendly with the park staff, although she wasn't especially close to any of them, aside from the two dispatchers.

Brett, the head ranger, also served as her boss. Still, he'd asked her out on more than one occasion. Keenly aware of state park policy against supervisors and employees dating, combined with the fact that she felt no attraction to him or other members of his gender whatsoever, she'd turned him down. As a ranger, he was strict, too strict for her taste. Sometimes, an illegally parked vehicle needed a warning, not a citation. It was a park, not a prison. She tended to focus her law enforcement attention on graver matters.

He'd sulked for a bit, but then made an obvious effort to be nicer to her over the last two years. Maybe he felt sorry for her. Or he was wearing her down to ask her out on a date again. Either way, his attentiveness bordered on clinginess, and so she quit saying yes to his invitations altogether, even if it was stopping at the concession stand during their shift for an ice cream cone.

Her fellow rangers were all people with whom she was friendly. She had no qualms about working with any of them. Gordon was an athletic-looking young man who'd served in Syria before he began working at the park. He spent most of his days off at Steamboat Rock, or wherever the young people's party de jour was happening. That said, he always showed up for work sober and took the job seriously.

Pedro, with a few months under his belt, was by far the best-looking of all the guys, something she believed Brett held against him. While others extolled the exploits of their off days, especially Gordon, who had a fondness for chasing after college-age women on vacation, Pedro never talked about what he did on his days off. She rarely saw his vehicle when he wasn't working. She and Lyn had mused he might have a proclivity for the same sex and couldn't find what he was looking for in the conservative small towns surrounding the park. Of course, Brett would never pick up on those clues, so he continued to see Pedro as a threat.

Nicole was a slightly flighty, confident, red-headed social butterfly in her early twenties. She loved working registration and getting the chance to chat with all the incoming campers. In contrast, Clare loved quiet nights walking the park alone, flipping her Maglite in time with her steps, making sure all the gates were locked, and all was well. She loved when Brett scheduled Nicole with her since they both could focus on the aspects of the job that they found gratifying.

For the past two years, all her coworkers had tiptoed around her to some extent, even Lyn. However, over time and with the help of the ever-changing seasons, things were starting to feel more normal, at least at work.

She rinsed the conditioner from her hair and turned off the water. A realization struck her. She felt different—better, lighter. As she dried off, she admitted this might be the best she'd felt in a long time. She was physically fit and had to be for her job. Mentally and emotionally though, the last two years had wrung everything from her until she felt as dry as the desiccated ground of the park.

However, the last couple of days had felt like someone had given her a life-saving sip of water. Could she be feeling excitement for the future instead of dread? The woman she used to be might still be in there somewhere, waiting for some water.

CHAPTER SEVEN

Jess grilled cheeseburgers for Ian and Tim for dinner. Ian provided a bag of barbeque potato chips, and they all sat at her picnic table, elbows spread wide and heads low as they devoured oozing burgers. Tim and Ian enjoyed a couple of IPAs, and they ate together in relative silence. She offered to drive up to the dam and back since she didn't plan on drinking. She wanted to get up around sunrise and do some work before the hottest part of the day.

"So, it's a laser show?" She abandoned her burger and crunched a chip.

"Mm-hmm." Ian worked on his second burger. He swallowed. "They project the laser show on the dam itself, from what I hear. It's supposed to be an entertaining thirty minutes if you come prepared." He winked at his brother.

She glanced at them through narrowed eyes.

Tim reached into his pocket and slid out a marijuana vape pen the size of a USB drive and showed her. He put it away. "A hit of that, and it should be an amazing show."

"You guys are perpetuating the Portland stereotype." They didn't seem to mind friendly teasing and gave back as good as they received.

Tim pretended to act appalled and searched for a comeback. "Well, you drive a Subaru."

"What's that mean?" She frowned.

Ian glanced at him in a way that suggested the two of them had discussed the topic before. He looked uncomfortable, especially since Ian seemed content to let him dig himself out of the hole.

"Well." He cleared his throat. "You know…"

"I know what?"

"Women…" He avoided eye contact with her and focused instead on picking at a weathered sliver of wood on the part of the table not covered by the tablecloth. "Women who drive Subarus…" He trailed off and glanced at Ian for assistance.

"Subarus. Lesbians. Lesbians drive Subarus." Ian waved his hand as if trying to hurry along the conversation.

She laughed. "Don't women who *aren't* lesbians also drive Subarus?"

They exchanged glances again. This time Tim found his courage and spoke up. "It's more than that though. It's the way you look at her. That's what made us think that, more than the Subaru stereotype."

Her cheeks felt like they were on fire. "Who?" Her voice sounded meek. She knew exactly who they were referring to.

They ignored her question.

"Remember when she asked me to move my tent off the grass?" Ian pushed his plate away. "If Tim hadn't offered you that beer, I think you might still be standing there." He smiled at her in a way that made her feel like he was an older brother giving her a tough time, but a brother who would have her back if necessary.

She laughed and threw her wadded-up napkin at him. What she had to say was less humorous, so she became serious. "You're right, and you're wrong. I do find her…attractive, but I have a boyfriend in Seattle."

They glanced at each other. The news seemed to surprise them.

"It's complicated." She studied the tablecloth.

"So, you're bi?" Ian's brow furrowed.

She thought about how she wanted to answer. Was she willing to acknowledge what she'd suspected for some time? She sighed. "No, I'm not sure that fits me. To make it simple, I'm in a relationship I shouldn't be in. I needed to end it long ago but haven't, for one reason or another." She smoothed the tablecloth. "I'm not proud of it." Still, opening the door the tiniest crack on her deepest feelings felt exhilarating and terrifying.

Tim playfully pushed her shoulder. "We've all been there. Breaking up with someone is hard. You might need a hit of this before we go." He slid the vape pen out of his pocket and offered it to her.

She laughed. "I'll take you up on that once we get there. I promise."

She would because she needed it. Maybe it would make her stomach feel less queasy. Why had she told them? To prove a point? And what point would that be? She didn't even know what message she'd been trying to convey. That she wasn't a Subaru-driving lesbian? Or was she? How did she feel so at ease with them that she already felt safe sharing details about her personal life?

Now that they knew, and even though her relationship with Jackson was going nowhere, embarrassment hit her. They'd noticed her flirting with Clare, and her actions filled her with guilt. This wasn't her. This wasn't like her at all. What had come over her? On the other hand, she didn't regret how she'd behaved with Clare. She didn't know what was going on between them anyway, if anything. Regardless, she certainly had no reason to mention Jackson to Clare. At this point, Jess was likely just another camper to her.

Until now, Jess had never acknowledged who she was and what she wanted. When would she finally know for sure? It would be so much easier if someone would tell her so she didn't have to figure it out.

"Hi, Pedro." Clare sidled up beside him as they both pulled fresh batteries from the office charging station for their radios. "I'll take the gate tonight. I don't mind."

"Sure." He scratched his head. "It's going to be a busy night up there though. I drove through the campground on my way here, and it's hella cleared out. You might need me up there with you. Have you considered having two lanes coming back in?"

"I'll be fine with only one entry lane. I'm used to it. I'm looking forward to it." She smiled fondly at him. He meant well, but with her seniority, he didn't have room to argue. She didn't feel too bad making sure she was the one at the gate. He was getting the easy end of the bargain in terms of work. "Plus, you'll need to monitor the situation as campers get to their sites. As much as I warn them to keep the noise down when they come through the gate, they'll need reminders."

Most campers would make the trek to the laser show. Patrols until then would be uneventful. That would change when all the drunk and happy campers returned long past quiet hours and rangers had to encourage them to settle down and go to bed. The few who didn't attend the show would likely be fast asleep by then.

Even people who hated mornings and preferred to sleep in found themselves awake and moving around before 7:00 a.m. due to the heat in their tents. It was part of the beauty of camping in a desert. However, that meant if people were partying until 2:00 a.m., arguments would break out between neighboring campers unless the rangers kept a tight hold on the situation. The park rangers strictly enforced quiet hours because they prevented altercations. Their job on such nights was a bit like herding cats. Hundreds of people, many of whom had been drinking, would all be returning around the same time. Many of them wanted to continue having an enjoyable time, but it was the rangers' job to keep the campground a safe and quiet place. This routine would go on until Labor Day, but tonight was a notoriously busy and hectic night.

She walked to the open door of the ranger station and completed her radio check.

"Dispatch, this is Papa Romeo 645. Radio check, over."

Lyn's voice came over her radio. "Papa Romeo 645, this is Dispatch. Read you loud and clear. Over."

She turned the volume of her radio to where she liked it and adjusted her service belt. Pedro checked his radio.

"Ready to do this?"

"Yes, ma'am." He picked up his coffee and followed her out.

Ma'am. Great, like she didn't feel old enough.

Nine years. She'd been doing this for close to a decade. She didn't know if she should feel proud or pathetic. Much like Pedro, she'd been young and fresh-faced when she'd started, full of naivete and optimism. It seemed like a lifetime ago. She'd spent a decent percentage of her life in this park, and what did she have to show for it? She was single, had more baggage than a 747, and she wasn't getting any younger. How many more years would she dedicate to it? At one point in time, she envisioned working this job as long as possible, but things were different now. Now, nine years felt like an eternity.

The drive up to the dam took much longer than it should have due to heavy traffic caused by nearly all the campground's residents and campers from other nearby campgrounds heading to the laser show. Once there, they reclined on a grassy expanse below the dam's visitor center. They were grateful they'd arrived early enough to find a spot to sit. People of all ages packed the area, eager to see the lasers and listen to the music.

They'd all taken hits off the vape before they exited the car. Speakers broadcasted the soundtrack that was also available over the radio for those who couldn't find seats within earshot. An animated laser beam beaver doing his best to educate the crowd on the history of the dam and its workings wouldn't have been anywhere near as entertaining without Tim's chemical foresight. The different colored lasers danced in time to the music across the massive concrete structure with exploding shapes and patterns. It reminded her of a giant kaleidoscope. She couldn't recall the last time she felt so relaxed.

Once the show ended, the place became a mass exodus of people scrambling to be the first ones in their cars and out of the parking lots, so they flopped back on the grass and stargazed while the crowd thinned out. Some forty minutes later, they decided the traffic had dissipated enough to drive back to the campground.

Tim tried to find a radio station that wasn't playing news or country music but failed. Ten minutes down the road and still stuck in traffic, she realized both brothers were out cold. The silence didn't bother her. It never had. She'd grown accustomed to being alone with her thoughts. Plus, the drive gave her time to harness her jittery excitement about seeing Clare again.

Over an hour later, she turned into the park and saw a state park truck's flashing lights at the bottom of the hill. The road had been closed to form a single lane with a metal gate across the opposite lane. A park ranger with a flashlight motioned for her to pull forward. She rolled down her window, exhilarated by the sight before her.

Clare leaned over and shined the flashlight around the front and back seats. She held it above her shoulder like Jess had seen police officers do in movies. Neither Tim nor Ian moved a muscle.

"Hi." Clare pointed her Maglite toward the ground. "How was the show?"

Her left hand rested on the car's door. Jess could see her fingernails, neatly trimmed ovals, even in the darkness.

Jess gave a crooked smile. "Truthfully? It was only okay. I can say I've seen it now, but I don't think I need to go again." They hadn't been this close before, and Clare's perfume scented the air between them, something bright and citrusy, making Jess's brain cells bounce and flash like the patrol vehicle's red and blue lights.

Clare grinned, nodding in agreement. "I had the same reaction, years ago. I haven't been back since. I take it everything's okay?" She cocked her head toward Ian, who was snoring in the back seat.

"Yeah, everything is great. Thank you."

They stared at each other. Sounds emanated from Clare's radio. She straightened. Whatever the dispatcher said wasn't intelligible to Jess, but Clare must have understood because she pinched the mic on her shoulder and spoke, all the while still looking at her.

"Dispatch, this is Papa Romeo 645. Standby." She leaned down again. "I probably don't need to tell you, but it's quiet hours. Many of the campers are asleep, so keep your speed and noise level down as you turn in."

Jess nodded dutifully.

"I'm glad to see you back." She smiled.

Jess returned the smile. "Good night, Clare." She drove toward their campsites. In her rearview mirror, Clare watched her drive away.

Beside her, Tim mimicked her in a high, singsong voice. "Good night, Clare."

She poked him in the thigh.

"Ow!" He rubbed his leg before leaning his head against the window and closing his eyes again. She turned left at the ranger station, now closed and dark.

"You totally drive a Subaru." He chuckled.

When she glanced over at him, he was smiling but his eyes remained closed.

She laughed. "Shut up."

CHAPTER EIGHT

J ess didn't see Clare the next day, or the morning after that. However, when Tim and Ian convinced her to go on a bike ride with them late in the afternoon, she caught her first glimpse of Clare not in uniform.

It was a gorgeous day, hot but not too hot, with a cloudless cerulean-blue sky. Ian suggested a leisurely ride, a circuit to get the layout of the land. Since this would be helpful to her as she chose which spots to study, she agreed to go with them. He suggested riding out to Deep Lake and back, and then continuing around Park Lake if they felt up to it.

It was on the return trip around Park Lake when she saw her. Clare wore shorts and a tank top and pushed a gas lawn mower. Her hair shone golden in the bright sunlight. She mowed the lawn of a small yellow house just off the road. The house bore the same bland color of paint as the ranger station. Was that where she lived?

While daydreaming about the possibility that Clare had been sleeping right there, so close in proximity to the campground, she swerved, her tire coming too close to Tim. He yelped in surprise and called out a warning. The noise of the mower surely drowned out his voice, but Clare looked at them. On a whim, Jess raised her hand in greeting. She passed by too quickly to know if Clare waved back. When Jess could safely glance behind her, Clare stood with one hand on the lawn mower watching them ride away.

❖

Clare enjoyed patrolling the park at night. She loved the unencumbered sounds of nature. It was so different from the loud, hectic daytime.

With the moonlight to guide her way, she walked along at a brisk pace, a cadence in her step that matched the beat in her head. *One, two, three, flip.* On four, she flipped the heavy Maglite flashlight she carried end-over-end and caught it. She always repeated this sequence when she was on foot patrol and had for many years. With her black boots soundless against the asphalt, she walked down the road, only aware of her even breathing and the slap of the flashlight in her hand. This was her meditation.

Jess had been on her mind for most of her walk through the campground. She blamed the distraction for dulling her senses because she was halfway to Jess's campsite when she realized Jess wasn't asleep in her tent. Instead, she perched on top of a boulder near the roadway. She reclined, her legs stretched out before her, her arms propping her up. She faced away from her.

She followed Jess's line of vision to see what held her attention. Near the brothers' campsite, two female mule deer fed on the irrigated grass. The deer had either not seen her or didn't care that she was there, for she sat mere feet from them. Clare knew human interaction had desensitized the deer, but they still grazed closer to Jess than usual.

She tried to walk into Jess's line of sight without startling her or the deer. To her surprise, Jess turned and smiled at her like she'd known she was there all along. As she approached, one of the deer skittered away. The other deer seemed unfazed and continued to eat.

"Hi," Jess whispered.

She looked delighted to see her. Had she been waiting for her, hoping she'd pass by?

"You're up late." Clare stepped closer so they could talk quietly.

Jess shrugged. "I'm a night owl. I couldn't sleep and decided to look at the stars. Then the deer appeared, so I've been watching them."

Clare looked at the sky. She gazed at the long strip of light-colored sky. "You can see the Milky Way tonight."

"Where?"

"Right here." She leaned closer to Jess and traced the path with her finger.

"I thought that was a high cloud." Only a few inches separated them.

"No, you're looking into the widest part of the galaxy. It seems brighter because there are so many stars, stacked on top of one another, layers and layers."

"I like layers." Jess shyly smiled at her.

"I remember. Walk with me?" It came out sounding more like an order than a request, but Jess seemed happy to comply and scrambled off the rock.

They walked in comfortable silence, something she rarely found with others. Most people felt the need to fill the space, to push out the silence like an unwanted intruder. Finding someone who enjoyed simply being with her was refreshing, and she was pleased that Jess seemed content to join her on patrol. Out of habit, she'd begun counting her steps and flipping her flashlight. After a bit, she picked up the conversation like it had never paused.

"I'm a bit embarrassed to admit it, but I think I take the stars for granted." She tipped her head back. Orion looked down at her.

"Why? Because you're used to living here?" They continued to talk in hushed tones, people asleep in rows twenty feet away.

"I suppose so."

"How long have you lived here?"

Jess looked at her intently as they talked, something Clare found she enjoyed, but it also unnerved her.

"Nine years."

Jess's eyebrows shot up. "That's a long time."

"Yes, it is." Clare changed the subject. "I think I saw you today." They turned the corner to complete the circuit. "Did you wave at me?"

"Oh, yeah. Sorry. That was me. I joined Tim and Ian on a ride. You probably couldn't tell it was me at first because cyclists tend to look the same in their gear."

Her rambling convinced Clare that if there had been any lighting other than the moon, she would have seen her blush.

"You looked beautiful," Jess said simply.

Clare missed catching her flashlight, and it clattered to the ground, the sound of the metal housing on the pavement like machine-gun fire. She grabbed it before it stopped moving. Certain that she was now the one blushing, she froze in the middle of the road and listened for any evidence that the clamor had awoken campers, but there were no noises aside from the crickets that would only cease their refrain come daylight and that of the blood pounding in her ears. They began to walk again, slowly, toward Jess's tent. Clare could still feel her pulse racing.

"I thought it was you. I don't know anyone else who would wave at me."

Jess looked stunned. "You must be kidding. Surely your friends or coworkers?"

"My best friend hates cycling, and I knew which coworkers were working and who among them own bicycles." They'd arrived at Jess's campsite.

"I was just riding by and saw you there—" Jess started to offer some sort of explanation.

"I like when you look at me." Clare flipped her flashlight, caught it, smiled, and walked away.

CHAPTER NINE

Clare finished her mid-morning foot patrol of the group camp. The twenty women staying there had been at the park for a few days and had fallen into a routine that needed little attention or effort from the park's rangers. The women were quiet and clean, focused on their reiki retreat and sipping red wine. She wasn't sure how reiki and wine meshed, but they seemed to be enjoying themselves.

When she reached Dry Falls Lake Road, she turned left toward Meadow Lake. It wasn't much of a lake, but more of a marshy area where tule reeds grew in abundance. As she turned to follow the road toward Deep Lake, she realized she was about to awkwardly fall into step with another hiker. Awkwardness turned to elation when she realized who it was.

Jess's face lit up when she noticed her. They stopped on the side of the road.

"What a pleasant surprise." Jess beamed.

"I feel the same. How is your research going?" She removed her sunglasses to better see her.

"It's going well." Jess motioned down the road. "Are you going toward Deep Lake? I can bore you to death with details while we walk."

"I am. Although, I'm not sure you could bore me."

"I'll check with you when we get there. We can see if your opinion has changed." Jess laughed.

Clare reached out, stopping her. "You don't bore me, and no, it won't. Now, why don't you tell me what you've been doing." She saw

Jess swallow as she let go. They started walking again, the sun at their backs.

Jess began cautiously. "Do you remember how I told you I'm interested in rock layers and what they can tell me?"

She hummed an affirmation.

"Well, this area is unique. How do I explain?" Jess paused for a moment. "So, you know that this area was formed volcanically, right?"

"Yes." For the first time, she was grateful for all the shifts she'd worked at the visitor center during her early years. "Did you know it's considered one of the largest basalt-lava formations in the world?"

"I did." Jess looked impressed. "But did you know that the lava is hundreds of feet thick in places?"

"I know it's five hundred feet thick at Dry Falls." Thankfully, some of these statistics had lodged themselves in her brain. Who knew she'd ever use them to try and impress a woman?

"Are you trying to out-fact me, Ranger?" Jess stopped, put her hands on her hips, and smiled.

Clare laughed. Jess looked cute when she was playful.

Jess resumed walking. "So, these flows happened on top of one another. In between the flows, other things were happening, like flooding, erosion, and the deposition of sediment." She pointed up at the striated cliff walls. "Each one of these escarpments represents a different period. You can see the different stratigraphy within the benches along the cliff sides. Each of those benches represents a different lava flow."

"I see." She'd never enjoyed geography this much in her life.

"I suppose you know about Glacial Lake Missoula, too?" Jess gave an exaggerated roll of her eyes.

"I do. A glacier blocked a river and created a big lake, and when the lake breached its dam, it caused the falls here."

"Well, yes, but its magnitude is important. When the glacier blocked the Clark Fork River in what is now Montana, it created a massive lake over two thousand feet deep on average. They think the force of all the lake water caused the ice dam to break. *Or*, all that water caused the ice dam to float, and then it ruptured, or a combination of those two forces breached the dam. They estimate the waves were as high as one thousand feet as they flooded toward the Pacific Ocean. The massive lake emptied in a matter of days in a catastrophic event." She spoke rapidly, emphasizing certain words, her enthusiasm bordering on giddiness.

"How long ago was this?" Clare could listen to her talk for ages.

"Well, it wasn't only one event. Scientists think that happened more than forty times! But, in answer to your question, we're talking more than thirteen thousand years ago." She was breathless.

Clare couldn't help but smile. "Then it stopped? So now the falls are dry?"

"Not quite. Massive waves carrying trees, animals, debris, chunks of ice, boulders, and columns of basalt came through and started eroding the rock, forming a huge waterfall. Originally, it formed twenty miles away from here." Jess pointed. "The face of the falls kept receding and receding until we see what we're looking at now. Each time this happened, the floodwaters deposited debris, and mud covered all that debris."

"Fossils." Clare followed where she was headed.

"Yes." Her eyes shone brightly. "Due to the erosion caused by the water flowing through the area, different geologic periods are evident in the exposed strata." Jess stopped and turned toward her. "For lack of a better analogy, it's like if I cut through a layered cake." She started using her hands to illustrate what she was saying. "From the side, I can see what makes up each layer of cake and what items are embedded in those layers, like nuts or chocolate chips—or in my case—trees, leaves, bones, and fossils. That's what makes this place amazing. It's incredibly unique. Everything is exposed. These geological events have opened amazing doors into the strata, where normally these layers are four to five hundred feet below ground."

"You are fascinating." Clare wanted to say so much more, but she left it at that.

Jess scoffed. "I'm not fascinating. This *place* is fascinating!"

"No, *you're* fascinating, too." Clare reached out and squeezed her arm. Jess awarded her the brightest smile of the day. "So, have you found any fossils?"

"Yes, but don't worry. I know to leave them in place. I had to sign a mountain of paperwork to get approval to be here. I take photos, make sketches, and will sometimes do a rubbing if possible."

"I imagined there was a bit of red tape if you received permission to camp here all summer. So, what have you found?"

"Well, I found a small fern on my second day, a fossil that may be the femur of a small mammal, and a tiny ammonite." Jess glowed, obviously proud of her discoveries.

"You did? That's incredible."

"You just have to keep your eyes open." Jess shrugged in her nonchalant manner, pulled a water bottle from the side of her backpack, and drank. "Most people I know don't think it's incredible. They find it boring. You're nice to listen to me. I'm sure your job is much more exciting."

"I wouldn't be working here if I didn't think this area was amazing, and I like how you describe everything to me. I don't know that *my* job is all that exciting." They were halfway to Deep Lake where she'd left her truck.

"You carry a gun. It must get dangerous."

"Not usually. The rattlesnakes are the most dangerous part of my job. Speaking of which, be careful where you step, especially when you're out here alone."

"What do you do when you run across one? Do you shoot it?"

"No." Clare laughed. "Besides, I'm not sure I'm that good of a shot. I'd use my OC spray if I absolutely had to but backing away slowly is my preferred method."

"OC spray?"

Clare pointed to a canister holstered on her belt. "Oleoresin capsicum aerosol spray. OC spray for short. It's like pepper spray. But I prefer not to be close enough to a rattler to have to use it."

"Have you ever had to use your gun before?"

"No, I've never even had to take it from its holster while on duty."

They arrived at the end of Deep Lake, a long, thin crevice in the basalt that had filled with water. It was a hundred feet deep in some places, and a favorite cliff diving spot. Neither said much as they approached the truck. Clare unlocked it and turned around. Jess stood close to her.

"Thank you for the walk and the conversation. You're easy to talk to." Jess rocked back on her heels, her hands in her pockets.

"I enjoyed it. For the record, I was never bored."

Jess grinned and tipped her head to one side. "Will I see you later?"

"I hope so." Clare opened the truck's door. A furnace of stifling air blasted outward.

Jess gave her a little wave.

While Clare waited for the truck's interior temperature to become tolerable, she watched her walk down the path toward the lake. She hoped she saw quite a bit of Jess over the summer.

CHAPTER TEN

Ican't believe your two weeks here are almost over. What am I supposed to do without my hiking and biking buddies?" Jess had been repeating her lament most of the day.

"Don't forget drinking buddies." Tim paused to take a swig of his nearby beer.

She pouted. "You better promise to come back for Labor Day."

"We told you, we already paid for the site. We're coming back. Tell Clare to reserve us the campsite next to you." Ian crouched by the firepit building a fire, the first campfire the park had allowed them to have. Weather conditions had cooled off a bit, and no winds were forecast for the weekend.

"I'm so glad you had your scissors. I needed a haircut so badly." She felt the ends of her hair.

"I don't go anywhere without my scissors. Now hold still. I'm almost done." Tim steadied her with hands on her shoulders.

She did her best to remain motionless with her legs dangling off the end of the picnic table. Dark locks dotted the towel draped over her shoulders and the ground beneath her.

"Don't take too much off. I like it long."

Jess grinned, unable to see their visitor, but she recognized the sultry voice behind her. Goosebumps spread across her back and down her arms. Sensations even lower surprised her.

"Nah, we're almost done here." Tim came around to the front of her and pulled a bit of hair from each temple together in front of her face, checking to see if the lengths matched. He removed the towel. "Looks good, Sterling. You're free to go."

Jess turned to see Clare in uniform, holding a clipboard.

Clare picked up a length of her hair, grazing her cheek. She let her fingers run to the ends before letting go. "Well, you look nice."

Jess's entire body warmed a good ten degrees from barely a brush on her cheek. Her face felt aflame. She mumbled some sort of thanks, her scalp still tingling on one side. She couldn't drag her gaze away. Thankfully, Ian, who had started a small fire, saved her.

"Are you done with work soon?" Ian took a few steps toward Clare. "You should join us when you're off. We're grilling some kebabs and playing cards tonight. It would be so much more fun with four people."

Clare seemed to mull over the decision, staring at the fire. She turned to Jess when she answered. "I think I could manage that. Sounds like fun."

"There may be some drinking involved, too." Tim grinned and held up his beer.

"I could stand to do some drinking. I don't work tomorrow. I'm on duty until six. I'll change and be over after that." Clare lifted her clipboard as she backed toward the roadway. "I should finish."

"See you soon." Jess waited until she'd walked away before she hissed at them. "What are you doing?"

Ian took a few steps back from his roaring fire. "What? We're trying to help you out. We only have one more day to play matchmaker. Not that it looks like you need it."

"She was just being nice." Or was she? Jess would be happy to be wrong.

Ian batted his eyelashes and mimicked Clare playing with her hair. "Oh, Jess, you look *so* pretty!"

She made a half-hearted attempt to smack away his hand. "You're so bad. Is this what it's like having brothers?" Secretly, she loved it.

Clare answered Lyn's call on the second ring but never had a chance to speak.

"Mushroom demi-glace or bleu cheese crumbles?"

"What are you talking about, Lynetta-Lyn?"

"Wow, I can't even remember the last time you called me that. Someone's in a good mood. I was calling to see what you're doing. I'm craving steak. And toppings—all the toppings. I can't decide between mushroom demi-glace or bleu cheese crumbles. Maybe I'll get both." Lyn finally stopped to inhale and gave Clare a chance to speak.

"I just got home, and I'm about to take a shower, but—"

"Let's head into town for dinner. I'm going to be bad tonight and totally get a loaded baked pot—"

Clare stopped her. "Sorry, but I can't tonight. I made plans."

"Oh."

She could hear the surprise in Lyn's voice.

"You don't usually have plans."

"No, I don't, but I've been invited to dinner." A short silence followed.

Lyn broke the awkward pause. "Is it a date?"

"No. Some people asked if I wanted to join them for dinner and card games, and I said yes."

"Campers?" Derision dripped from the word.

"Yes." Clare wanted the questioning to end.

"I can't imagine what would entice you to want to hang out with campers. That's not like you. It must have something to do with that *girl*."

"Yes, and two of her friends. And she's a woman, for the record."

"So, it's serious then. You like her." It was a statement, not a question.

"It's card games and grilled meat or something. It sounded like fun." Clare felt bad that she could hear the exasperation in her voice, but she hated when Lyn was like this.

"The Clare I know hasn't been into having fun or doing much of anything, so it's a bit strange to hear you making plans with people."

"You should be happy for me. Don't you think it's time?"

"I guess, but it's weird. Anyway, have fun. I'll talk to you later."

"Let's go for steaks another—" Clare heard her end the call. She knew that it wouldn't be the end of the conversation about Jess though. She'd been down this road before with Lyn. Since their college days, every time Clare dated someone, Lyn became frustrated, standoffish, and then learned enough about the woman to insult her or point out her flaws.

They'd once been so close. She didn't know anyone else in her dorm that first day at college, and she and Lyn had hit it off. Their relationship first shifted when Clare began seriously dating a woman in her biology class. She saw a side of Lyn she hadn't known was there. Now, all these years later, she knew Lyn was in love with her, but she didn't know what to do. She worried that having a serious conversation about it might cause her to lose her best friend, and then where would she be? Her social circle might not even be considered a circle anymore.

Despite her flaws, Lyn meant the world to her. She was hilarious, always making Clare laugh with her dry humor. She'd slip in allusions to personal jokes over the radio, sometimes making Clare laugh out loud in her truck. Lyn was spontaneous, the exact opposite of Clare. She had no issue with showing up at any hour with some intrepid plan for having a bit of fun. Socially, she was boisterous and rambunctious, as if the seriousness of her role as dispatcher forced her to release her joyful side like a pressure valve on her off days. She pulled Clare out of her comfort zone with delight. Clare usually protested, then relented, then admitted to having fun in the end. Oh, the stories Clare could tell… She and Lyn had amassed quite the repertoire of hijinks in the years they'd been friends. Furthermore, when Clare needed a shoulder to cry on, Lyn was her rock. Could she risk throwing all that away?

Unrequited love was cruel and heartless. She'd been in Lyn's position before. Yet, she hadn't had to see the woman every day and interact with her at every turn. Eventually, the feelings dissipated with distance and time. Lyn had neither on her side. Selfishly, Clare didn't want to give up her friend either.

Jess could no longer see the sun over the cliffs of the canyon, and the campground had started to hum with evening activity. Ian fed more wood into the fire. She contributed her box of firewood and her s'mores supplies to the evening. She offered to go on a beer run, but Ian said he'd been to the store earlier and insisted they had enough. She shuffled a deck of cards and sipped her beer while he stoked the fire and Tim threaded chunks of sausages and vegetables onto skewers.

She saw Clare walking toward their campsites from the direction of the ranger station. She seemed a bit lost without her flashlight, her hands stuffed in her pockets, her eyes on her black Chuck Taylors. She made a simple T-shirt and jeans look classy. She wore her hair down with one side tucked behind her ear, and the wavy curls bounced with each step. Without her uniform, she appeared less confident, more vulnerable, and more human. The butterflies in Jess's stomach began their Cirque du Soleil routine right on schedule.

Clare looked toward the campsite, flipping her hair from her face with a toss of her head. She found Jess, a smile crossing her face as she did. Jess stayed seated until she came closer, neither of them breaking eye contact. As she approached, Jess set the cards on the table and stood.

"Hi." Jess met her about fifteen feet from where Tim and Ian were busy arguing about whether to cook the kebabs over the fire or on the grill. She wanted to hug Clare in greeting, but the most physical they'd ever been with each other was a hand on the arm. Plus, Clare's hands still were buried in her pockets.

"Hi, you," Clare said playfully. "Miss me?"

She grinned. "Absolutely." It had been less than two hours, but she had. "Can I get you something to drink? Ian has a couple of kinds of beers and some cider."

"Hey, Clare." Tim looked up from the marinade he was whisking with a fork. "Glad you could join us."

"What do you want to drink?" Ian stood over the cooler.

With a beer in hand, Clare grabbed a camp chair and pulled it close to her. They watched Ian, who couldn't leave the fire alone. Tim gave him orders to move the flames to one side so they could grill over the campfire's embers, and he was happy to oblige. He joked about being a self-proclaimed pyro.

Jess was going to miss them. Maybe she'd introduce them to a couple of her friends. She knew a few single women from Portland. It was nice to think she'd developed the kind of friendship that would continue even after they left. She had an inkling that she was about to lose most of her friends once she officially cut ties with Jackson. Molly would always be her best friend, but she was busy with her new job, and they didn't see each other as much as when they were undergrads. It would be nice to have a few new friends. The thought comforted her.

"Do they leave soon?" Clare turned her gaze from the guys to her.

It was like she'd read her mind. "Yeah, tomorrow. I'm going to miss them." Jess couldn't hide the disappointment in her voice.

"You'll have new neighbors tomorrow night. I'm sure you'll like them, too."

"Not like these guys." She watched them interact with each other as they contemplated the best grill arrangement. "They feel like brothers I never had. I can't explain it, but somehow, I know we'll stay friends after this summer."

Clare reached over and held her hand. "I'll still be here. At least you'll know someone." She gave her hand a quick squeeze before letting go. "Now, I seem to recall you promising to show me your rock collection."

Jess's mouth hung open. "Are you serious? I assume you're just being nice. You don't have to."

"I know I don't. I want to see it." Clare looked at her expectantly.

Genuinely surprised, Jess walked to her car with its GEOGRRL license plate, opened the passenger door, and reached under the seat. She came back carrying a thin wooden box. She opened it up and displayed its contents. Small rocks occupied each little square compartment.

Clare inspected the box. "I don't see any fossils in here."

"Oh, please. The fossils are in a separate box."

Clare laughed. "What is this one?" She picked up a purplish rock that looked like dozens of tiny spheres glued together.

"That's purple grape agate crystal. It's found in Indonesia."

Clare's fingers traversed the surface like she was memorizing each little protrusion. If Clare were to touch her, would she touch her the same way she touched the rock—delicately, with purpose? Jess shivered. It wasn't cold.

"It's beautiful."

Ian hadn't left enough embers to cook the kebabs, so they made culinary adjustments over at the fire pit, occasionally glancing at her and Clare.

Clare pointed to another rock. "And this one?"

Jess handed it to her. She caressed the rock's speckled black and blue surface with her fingertip.

"That one is indigo blue covellite in copper ore from Butte, Montana."

She gave it back, her fingers brushing Jess's palm. They were soft and delicate.

"Where did you get this one?"

"That's from Sparta, Illinois. It's called a pyrite sun."

Clare hefted the golden disk. "It's heavy. Did you find it while visiting there?"

"No, my dad got me interested in rocks. He traveled a lot for work. He would always come home and reach into his pocket with a twinkle in his eye. He never failed to bring home a special rock for me. Most of my rock collection is from him." She pushed away the sense of melancholy that rose with the memory. How strange that mere possessions could conjure up such conflicting feelings. This wasn't the time for it.

"What a sweet story." Clare looked at her with a kind smile before picking up another rock. "What is this?" She held a spherical rock. One side had broken away to expose a similar rock inside, like a core.

"That's called a concretion. That one's from Croatia."

Clare asked a few more questions and examined each rock, ending with one of Jess's favorites, the pink rhodochrosite. As Jess latched the box, to her surprise, Clare leaned over and quickly pressed her lips to her temple.

"Thank you for sharing that with me," she whispered.

At that moment, Jess only knew two things. Whatever she felt, she'd never felt before, and if she could bottle the feeling, she'd be the richest person on Earth.

Darkness fell. Empty beer cans and bottles had accumulated at one end of the table. The dinner dishes soaked in a large pan on the grill. The laughter accompanying alcohol and pleasant company had increased through the night. Jess brought over her hanging lamp and lit the card game spread out on the tablecloth. They traded bare arms and sunscreen for long sleeves and bug spray. Clare reluctantly accepted Jess's threadbare Nirvana sweatshirt that had been her dad's as the desert night cooled. Ian kept the fire stoked, and they enjoyed the crackling warmth as they finished another game of hearts. Clare had a competitive streak that surprised Jess. She was a risk-taker and shot the moon, saddling them each with twenty-six points.

Clare seemed to like Tim and Ian, and they, in turn, appeared to like her. It mattered to Jess that her friends liked Clare, even if she'd only been friends with them for a brief time. Ian even joked about whether Clare was going to make him move his tent again before dinner.

Clare had a quick retort ready. "I'm happy you followed my excellent advice, unlike someone else I know." She followed that up by leaning into Jess and nudging her with her shoulder. When their eyes met, they shared a small smile. Clare remained close, their arms touching, and didn't lean away.

Clare won the final card game, the score being too lopsided for the rest of them to have a chance. They moved to sit by the fire. Again, she took the chair beside Jess. Tim handed out the necessities to make s'mores.

"Here." Clare threaded a marshmallow on the metal rod Jess had resting across her thighs.

Jess unwrapped the candy bar. She snapped off a chunk and laid it on top of Clare's graham cracker.

"Who makes s'mores with Cookies 'n' Creme?" Clare looked aghast.

"I do. They're amazing." She raised her chin in defense.

"No, I don't believe it. I'm a purist. You're supposed to use milk chocolate to make s'mores." Clare looked at her like she'd tried to sell Henry Ford a Honda.

"You're going to love it. I promise."

Ian chimed in. "I'm skeptical, too, but I'm willing to give it a try."

"I'm not worried. I'll eat anything." Tim grinned.

Clare narrowed her eyes. "Fine."

Jess watched her roast two marshmallows over dying embers. They toasted to a puffy, golden brown before she pulled them off and placed them on her cookie sandwich.

Jess never could roast a marshmallow without it catching on fire. She torched the first one to a black crisp on one side and ended up sacrificing it to the campfire. Her second attempt didn't fare much better. She blew it out when it flamed. Clare took over.

"This is a good spot. It's not too hot." She took Jess's hand and pulled her closer. She positioned the marshmallow over the same embers she'd used.

Her forearm rested on Clare's knee, and she was so close she could smell her hair, a combination of something floral mixed with woodsmoke.

"Turn it like this, so all the sides get equal heat."

Their hands touched. Their bodies touched. Additional heat wasn't necessary.

Clare took a dainty bite of her s'more. "You're right, this isn't bad at all. I have to admit, I'm surprised."

She smiled. Clare's approval on any matter would have made her happy. With marshmallow roasted, she moved back into her own space with reluctance. She devoured her s'more as she watched Tim roast his marshmallow until golden, pull off the caramelized shell, pop it into his mouth, and roast the remnants again.

Something caught her attention in a stand of trees in the darkness. She tried to focus on a shape behind one of the trunks, but the light from the campfire made it difficult. She was sure she'd seen movement. It looked like someone watched them from a distance. She shivered. It was probably a curious camper.

Clare laughed at something Ian said. Jess couldn't help but admire the pretty crinkles at the corners of her eyes that only appeared with the rich tones of her laughter. The moment made Jess smile and a pleasant warmth poured through her. When she glanced back at the trees, she couldn't pick out the figure she'd seen before. Perhaps she'd imagined it.

CHAPTER ELEVEN

It had only been a few days since they'd left, but Jess felt lost without Ian and Tim. She missed the invitations for impromptu hikes or dips in the lake. She missed Ian's cooking and Tim's jokes. She missed having someone she could talk to about Clare. She should have been used to having no one to talk to, given her pretty solitary existence back home. It's not like Jackson ever wanted to have a real discussion. It had been nice to get close to people for once without worrying whether or not they were going to leave her. She missed them, and technically they'd left, but it didn't feel like a permanent loss, the kind to which she'd become accustomed. Life had taught her that people she loved didn't always stick around, so she tended to hang on a little too tight. This felt different, even if their absence created a hole in her summer. Maybe she was changing.

The couple from Pasco who moved into their old campsite had been cordial, but they told her in their first conversation that they'd been married the month before. They fawned over one another and stayed to themselves.

That suited her fine. She was here for a purpose, and she needed to work on the research for her thesis. She rose with the sun and worked until lunchtime or until the temperatures became too unbearable. In the afternoons and early evenings, she liked to take her laptop to the lake, find a nice picnic table or spot in the shade, upload photos, compile her data and notes, and write. She started to tan, despite her continual use of sunscreen.

She spent the morning surveying the escarpment below the visitor center. The ridge caught the full morning sun, and she covered a decent amount of ground as she examined and classified the area above the talus slope. Now used to the terrain, she felt as sure-footed as a mountain goat. Soon, her keen eyes paid off. Right before noon, she spotted a pair of fossilized ostracods, an aquatic species that was a significant index fossil in biostratigraphy. It had a short lifespan and had been widespread, thus limiting the time in which it could be found in the sediment.

Riding her wave of elation back to the campground, she found her good mood short-lived when she discovered the inverter that she'd been using to charge her laptop via her car's cigarette lighter had stopped working. Without her laptop, she couldn't do anything. She needed to find a solution, fast.

She walked toward the ranger station, hoping Clare would be working. From the roadway, she could see a white truck parked beside the building. Carrying her laptop under her arm, she climbed the steps to the office. The door stood open, and Clare sat at a desk looking at a monitor.

"Hi. Can I come in?" Her heartbeats skittered like deer. Would her heightened physiological functions every time she saw Clare cease anytime soon? She couldn't recall ever being so aware of her body, her breathing, and her heart rate.

"Of course." Clare pushed her chair back from the desk. "This is a surprise."

"I have a fav—Oh! I'm sorry to interrupt." An auburn-haired woman wearing a uniform that matched Clare's minus her service belt was sitting on a corner of the second desk.

"Jess, this is Lynette Weber. We go way back. We've been friends since college, and she's also one of our dispatchers. Lyn, this is Jess. She's the one I told you about who's working on her thesis."

Jess extended her hand.

Lyn shook it and gave her a polite smile. "Nice to finally meet you."

Her voice. Why did she know her voice? Then everything clicked into place. It was Lyn whom Brett had been talking to in the store. Thrown by the knowledge, she stood tongue-tied until Clare spoke.

"You needed something?"

"Yes." She recovered and held out her laptop. "The inverter I've been using to charge my laptop from my car isn't working. Could I plug it in here for an hour or two to charge? I'll order a new one and see if I can have it delivered in the next couple of days."

"Sure. Do you want me to bring it to you when it's done?" Clare took the laptop and charger.

"If it's no trouble. I can come back and get it when I see the office is open again if that's more convenient."

Lyn had yet to move or say anything since the introduction. She simply watched their exchange.

"It's no trouble at all." Clare smiled. "I can bring—"

The radio came to life. "All units, this is Dispatch. Over."

Clare keyed her mic. "Dispatch, this is Papa Romeo 645 at the Sierra Lima station. Over."

A male voice responded. "Dispatch, this is Papa Romeo 699 at the south end of Papa Lima. Over."

"All units, this is Dispatch. Report of brush fire north of lookout. The fire department is on its way. Over."

Clare jumped up and left the laptop and charger on the desk. She grabbed her keys and spoke into the mic on her shoulder. "Dispatch, this is Papa Romeo 645. Copy. On my way. Over."

"Papa Romeo 645, Dispatch. Roger. Out."

The male ranger responded as well.

"Sorry." She pushed past Jess and jumped in her truck. Before Jess knew what was happening, she peeled out, sending gravel flying.

"Don't expect to have a campfire tonight. The restrictions will go back into effect."

Turning back toward Lyn, Jess nodded solemnly. "That makes sense."

Lyn hopped off the desk and picked up the laptop. "She does that, you know." She attached the cable and plugged it in behind Clare's desk. "She's always the first one on the scene of any little fire. It doesn't matter what she's doing, working or not working."

Jess nodded again, getting the feeling she was being told something a little too subtle for her to pick up. The reception she'd received from Lyn felt cool, but maybe she'd misinterpreted it. The overheard conversation in the store still echoed in her head. Was Lyn jealous of her, or was she reading too much into the situation?

"I'll lock the office when I leave. She'll see it on her desk later." Just like that, Lyn dismissed her.

With a quick thanks, Jess left. Unable to work, she made a trip to the general store to stock up on a few supplies. When she came out of the store, she smelled smoke in the air but couldn't see anything. When she returned to her campsite, she made a turkey and cheddar sandwich before digging around in her dirty clothes duffel. She found the paperback mystery she was looking for stashed in one of its pockets. Laundry needed to be done sooner rather than later. The small resort near the general store had coin-operated washers and dryers. She'd need to find her way there one of these days.

She pulled her camp chairs into the small bit of shade at her campsite. She settled into one and propped her feet up on the other. Forty-five minutes later and three chapters in, she was deeply involved in her book when someone parked in front of her campsite. A surge of excitement rushed through her when Clare got out.

Clare was wearing the same uniform she'd worn earlier, but it was now filthy. Dirt and soot covered her from head to toe, and dark smudges marred her cheek and forehead. She carried the laptop.

"Is everything okay?" Jess put her feet back on the ground, dusted off the other chair, and turned it around, motioning for her to sit.

"Yeah, it was a brush fire probably caused by a cigarette butt. People don't realize how dry all this vegetation is." Clare flopped in the chair and handed her the laptop. "It's all charged up. I'm sorry I ran out earlier."

"It was a fire. I understand. Thanks so much. I can't do anything without it. Speaking of which, I can order a new inverter, but I realized I don't have an address to have it delivered." She raised a shoulder, let it fall, and smiled. "Do you think I could have it sent to you at the ranger station?"

"Hmm. No, only because we don't get any mail delivered there. Have it sent to my house. I'll bring it to you as soon as it arrives."

"That's nice of you. Thanks." She jumped up to get a piece of paper and pen on which Clare could write her address. "Can I get you something to drink? I know you're working, but I have water and iced tea."

"An iced tea would be lovely."

She could feel Clare's eyes on her as she moved around the campsite. She prayed that no emergencies would come across the radio for at least a few minutes.

Clare pushed the hair from her face and tucked it behind her ears. She cleared her throat. "Speaking of my address, I was wondering if you might like to come over tonight for a glass of wine."

The unexpected question caught her by surprise. Ice caps melted and formed anew before she could manage a response. She pulled herself together and gave Clare a shy smile. "I'd love to."

"Good." Clare smiled back. "Here. Give me your phone number, and I'll text you when I'm ready. I'm going to need to shower first." She motioned to her filthy clothes.

Jess typed her name and number into Clare's phone.

Clare capped her tea and stood. "So, what kind of wine do you like?"

Jess hesitated, looking up at her. "I don't like wine, but that's okay." She shrugged and flashed an unabashed grin. "I didn't say yes because of the wine."

Clare opened her mouth as if to respond, then closed it and smiled. She tipped her drink in thanks and walked to her truck.

Jess ballooned with satisfaction as she watched her drive away.

Clare wrapped her body in one towel and her hair in another before she picked up her phone. Why did she feel so impatient? She sent a quick text to Jess.

Just showered. Come on over. Remember where?

The response came back promptly.

Yes

She examined her refrigerator. The best she could manage was some cheese and crackers and some green grapes. It would have to do. At least she'd picked up some beer for Jess at the store on her way home. Ever since the charming *I'd love to,* she couldn't concentrate on anything besides seeing her again.

She pulled on some capri pants and a sleeveless, cornflower-blue shirt. She tossed the wet towels and her smoky clothing in the hamper, pulled up her comforter in a meager attempt at making her bed, and ran her fingers through her wet hair. In a rare and unusual move, she turned off her work radio. Tonight, she looked forward to spending time with Jess, and constant interruptions were the last thing she wanted.

The doorbell rang. She took a deep breath and opened the door. Jess, who always wore hiking boots and T-shirts or tank tops, was standing on her doorstep in a green and white spaghetti strap sundress that fell to the tops of her knees. The color of the dress made her eyes even more vibrant. Clare's breath caught in her chest.

"Oh, wow. You look lovely." She hadn't anticipated that Jess might change her clothes.

Jess smiled and tilted her head. "You look…cleaner. But you look nice, too."

She chuckled and ran her fingers through her wet hair. Jess's humor put her at ease. "Come in."

Jess closed the door behind her. She scanned the living room.

"Make yourself comfortable. I bought the beer you like. Can I pour you one?"

"I'm sorry." Jess hung her head. "Wine would have been fine. You didn't have to buy me beer."

"I wanted to." She squeezed her arm before stepping into the kitchen to get their drinks.

Jess wandered over to her bookshelf to look at the books and knick-knacks, then stopped in front of the painting over the couch. "This is interesting. It's so unusual."

The artist had painted the scene looking toward Dry Falls and had chosen to push the color of the rocks toward the pinkish end of the spectrum and the color of the sagebrush toward a cool green. While the artist drew the scene with lifelike accuracy, the color choices were too vibrant, too garish.

"I've had it for many years." Clare poured the beer into a cold glass. She hoped Jess would move on.

She didn't. Jess leaned even closer to the painting and tried to read the artist's signature. "Is that someone famous?"

"No." Clare offered her the beer.

To her relief, the drink distracted her. Jess looked at her instead.

"Thank you." She sipped from her frosty glass. "Fancy. I don't think I've had anything to drink that hasn't come from a can or bottle in weeks." She wore her hair down, something she rarely did. The ends barely danced on her shoulders.

"My duty schedule is so random that I forget normal people eat at normal times." Clare motioned toward the counter. "I can't offer you a decent meal, but I have a cheese plate if you're hungry."

"That sounds great." Jess came closer and popped a grape in her mouth. "I wasn't expecting dinner."

"Let's take it out back." Clare picked up her pint of beer and the plate of cheese and crackers. "Can you get the door?"

Her backyard consisted of the expanse of lawn between the back of her house and the talus slope of the cliff behind it. It was unfenced, but she kept it neatly mowed. It had a barbeque grill, a table and chairs, and a gliding swing with a yellow and blue awning. A low wicker table with a glass top stood in front of the swing. She set the cheese tray on the table and patted the seat on the glider beside her. "Join me."

The sun's rays no longer reached the canyon, but the air remained warm and pleasant. Jess took a seat beside her and kicked off her sandals. Clare moved the cheese and crackers between them and pushed off with her foot on the edge of the table, sending the glider swinging.

"So, tell me. Have you discovered anything exciting?" Clare placed a piece of cheddar on top of a multi-grain cracker and took a bite.

"In life, or work?" Jess's eyes glinted.

Amused, Clare couldn't help but chuckle. "Let's say work."

"Yes, I have. I found a pair of ostracods. They're an aquatic species." Jess tossed another grape into her mouth.

Clare knew she was probably ecstatic but had tempered her excitement. "I'm so happy for you. You must have good eyes. Did you find them separately or together?"

"Together." Jess fixed a cracker. "It's not all about finding fossils though. Most of my research is about documenting the strata itself. Fossils are a fun bonus."

She used the time while Jess chewed to find the confidence to ask the question that had been making her anxious. "So, Jess…"

"Hmm?" She took a drink of beer and waited.

"I have Sunday off. I was wondering if you'd like to spend the day with me. I know of a fossil in the area and thought we could see it together. I could show you parts of the canyon you might not have had time to visit. Would that interest you?" The timid question sounded nothing like what she'd rehearsed. *Damnit.* She ran her finger around the top of her pint glass to steady her nerves.

Jess took her time with her answer. "Did you find out about this fossil when you worked at the visitor center?"

"Yes." The question surprised her.

"So, Sunday would be like a tour because you know the area well?" She sounded cautious, unsure.

Her mind raced, unsure where Jess was going. "I guess so." Clare had the horrible feeling she'd done something wrong.

Jess looked dejected. "Oh." She laughed self-consciously, despite the smile not reaching her eyes. Rosy splotches bloomed on her chest. "I thought you were asking me on a date."

The swing stopped.

Clare's mind reeled, and she quickly tried to steer things back on course. Out of habit, she tucked her hair behind her ear and took a deep breath. She met Jess's gaze, and her smile came naturally. "I would like to spend Sunday with you, on a date, if you would like that."

It took a moment before her words launched a radiant smile on Jess's face.

"I would like that very much." The register of her voice had dropped, but her excitement was palpable. Her eyebrows arched, and her eyes shined bright. "What kind of fossil is it?"

"It's a surprise." Clare scrunched her eyes. "Now, no more fossil questions." She pushed her foot against the table, and they swayed back and forth, life in motion once more.

The night air felt warm and inviting, the kind of night that should be spent outdoors. Purple skies faded to a jet-black backdrop strewn with pin-pricked stars. The moon had yet to rise, and she loved how inky dark the night could be. She could barely make out her house, helped only by its pale color. If her satisfaction resulting from Jess saying yes could put off light, she'd glow in the dark.

They talked on the swing for hours. Between them, they finished a six-pack of beer. Their conversation touched on foods, music, and books they liked, among other things.

"Why do you say Papa Romeo 645 when you're on your radio?" Jess had tucked her legs beneath her on the swing. Her empty glass sat on the table. She leaned on her arm that rested on the back of the glider.

"That's my call sign. PR 645. I'm Park Ranger 645. We use a phonetic alphabet, so the word we use for P is Papa and for R, Romeo."

"I wondered why it was Romeo. I heard the guy on the radio say the same thing."

"Yes, sometimes you'll hear Charlie Delta for Camp Delany, Delta Lima for Deep Lake, Papa Lima for—"

"Park Lake?" Jess grinned.

"Yes." She chuckled. "Now you know our code."

Jess used her feet to feel around for her sandals. "I should get back. This was nice. Thank you for inviting me over."

"Early day?" Clare stopped the swing.

"Honestly?" A tipsy giggle escaped her. "I need to get up early to make sure I do some laundry at the resort. This was the last clean thing I had to wear."

"I like it." Clare reached out and felt the fabric, her fingers brushing Jess's thigh. "The color brings out your eyes." She heard Jess's breath hitch. "Come with me."

Clare moved as if she had night vision, her eyes accustomed to years of night shifts. Jess, blind in the darkness, struggled to follow. Clare flicked on the porch light. Jess caught up and stepped inside.

Closing the back door, Clare pointed behind it to a small alcove where a washer and dryer stood. "Come over and use mine tomorrow. Make yourself comfortable. I'll leave the door unlocked. My shift starts at six."

"That's only a few hours from now. I need to let you sleep." Jess opened the back door.

"So, you'll do your laundry here then?"

Jess bit her lip and smiled. "Yes, thank you. You're sure you don't mind me being here?"

"Not at all. Make yourself at home. Feel free to watch TV, read, nap, or work. Is that all you brought with you?" Clare nodded toward her phone.

"Yes."

"I'll walk you back."

"No, you need to sleep. It only took me a few minutes to walk over here."

Clare appreciated her consideration, but she already had her Maglite in her hand. "Good. It will only take me a few minutes to walk you back."

Jess offered a compromise. "You can walk me to the ranger station. I can see my tent from there."

"I know you can." She flashed her a mischievous grin. "Fine. Ready?"

They walked around the house, along the driveway, and into the middle of the road. Clare had yet to turn on her flashlight.

Jess walked beside her and brushed her arm every few steps. "Is this safe?" She turned around and looked down the two-way road behind them that was nothing but a wall of blackness.

"The gates are locked. There won't be any vehicles on this road for a while. Patrol has already covered this portion."

"How do you see where you're going?" Jess held out her hands in front of her. "All I can see are the stars. I'm scared I'm going to run into something."

"I won't let you."

She took Jess's hand. It was warm and soft, and instead of simply holding her hand, Jess threaded their fingers together. An unexpected wave of emotion washed over her. It made her breathing quicken despite their leisurely pace.

Frogs croaked by the hundreds as they walked past tiny Mirror Lake. Crickets sang by the thousands. Jess stopped and looked up at the millions of stars above them.

"What is it?"

Jess seemed reticent but eventually spoke. "Doesn't it feel like we're the only two people on Earth?" The darkness held her whispered words like a precious secret.

Clare stepped closer. Buoyed by the alcohol and the ambiance, she reached out and touched Jess's cheek and then her jaw before cupping the nape of her neck. She could feel Jess's warm breath, her soft skin, her silky hair caught in her fingers. Her intentions surely were clear by now. Jess hadn't stepped away. She hadn't run. Instead, she closed her eyes. Clare brushed their lips together. Jess gave a little gasp but relaxed and leaned into the kiss, her free hand settling into the crook of Clare's arm. When their tongues met, the thrill of it rushed through her.

Clare could drown in the feel of her. All she could taste, all she could feel, was Jess. Jess, whom she'd dreamed about, Jess who'd permeated her every thought since she'd arrived. She smelled like almonds and tasted even better.

Clare wrapped an arm around her, aware of the Maglite still in her hand, but more aware of her softness and warmth. Jess tipped her head to the side, allowing Clare to deepen the kiss.

Jess had said yes to the date but had seemed so nervous. She gave no further inklings of timidity. She was inviting and eager, matching

Clare's intensity. Was Clare the first woman to kiss her? The thought made her head swim.

Clare's legs, made strong from years of walking and hiking, trembled. She pulled Jess closer, their bodies tight against one another, soft breasts pressed into hers. She didn't know if she'd ever experienced such a perfect moment.

At last, they pulled apart. Her need for oxygen was only slightly greater than her need for Jess. Embracing loosely with soft caresses, she enjoyed a few more precious moments with her, unwilling to sever that special first connection. Eventually, she took Jess's hand and resumed walking.

She began to make out light in the dark. As they passed by the ranger station, a meager 60-watt light bulb above the door attempted to penetrate the darkness. They stopped. The dim bulb helped her see Jess's face in greater detail. They were at the midpoint, the mutually agreed upon place where they would part.

Without breaking her gaze, Jess stepped toward her campsite and tugged her hand. Clare couldn't vocalize all the thoughts swirling in her head. She wanted to follow. Of course, she did. She was human, after all. At times though, two years felt more like two months. This was one of those times. Her wounds still felt fresh, not yet healed. When she took Jess up on her invitation—and she hoped there would be one again—she wanted to be whole. She wasn't ready. So, she stood firm and slowly shook her head.

Jess stepped forward and kissed her again. While their first kiss had been exploratory and sensual, this one wasn't. It heated up quickly, too quickly. At the timid touch of Jess's warm hand beneath her shirt, Clare ended it before it could go further. She broke off the kiss and removed Jess's hand.

"Good night," she whispered. She let their arms stretch out until their fingers slid past each other's, then turned and walked into the darkness.

Chapter Twelve

The dryer buzzed. Jess found a laundry basket to carry her clean clothes to the couch. After switching loads, she returned to Clare's living room to fold her clothing and catch up on *Grey's Anatomy*. As she placed her clean, folded clothes in her duffel bag, she heard a key in the lock. Excited to see Clare, her face fell when Lyn came through the door.

"I wondered who was here." Lyn wore her work uniform and carried an identical shirt on a hanger.

"Clare offered to let me do my laundry." Jess didn't know why guilt nudged at her.

"I see." Lyn stared at her for a few seconds. "I'm going to put this in her closet. I had to borrow it after I spilled coffee on my last clean uniform." She turned down the hall toward the bedroom.

Jess lowered the volume on the television. She transferred folded clothes from the laundry basket to her duffel bag. To her surprise, Lyn didn't leave when she returned but went to the refrigerator. She cracked open a Diet Coke and sat on the arm of an upholstered chair.

"Clare tells me you're working on your thesis."

"I am. I'll be here all summer."

"Then it's a good thing you found a free place to do your laundry."

Laughter on the television sounded incongruous with their conversation.

"I'm doing my laundry here because she offered, but yes, it was kind of her. I've heard the machines at the resort are hard to come by." The tone of the conversation was making Jess's blood simmer.

"So, what is your field of study again?"

"Geology." Jess had a feeling she already knew the answer.

"Are you finding what you're looking for?" Lyn's eyes narrowed.

Jess maintained eye contact with her for a few uncomfortable seconds before answering. "I am."

Lyn took a long swig as she watched Jess arrange the clothes in her bag. She rested the can on her knee. "She's fragile. I hope you know what you're getting into, girl."

"I have degrees in geology and environmental earth science. I'm working on my master's degree. I support myself. I'm hardly a girl." She wondered what made Clare fragile in Lyn's eyes, but she wasn't about to give her the satisfaction she'd probably get from asking.

"You have spunk. No wonder she likes you."

"Have I done something to offend you?" Jess's face grew warm.

"It has nothing to do with you."

Before Jess had a chance to respond, Clare came through the front door. It startled her, and Lyn too, by the way she jumped.

"There's a party at my house, and everyone forgot to invite me." Clare smiled.

Wild emotions stirred inside her as memories of kissing Clare came rushing back like a tsunami reaching shore. Jess almost held onto the sofa cushion for balance.

"What brings you here?" Clare walked to Lyn and took the Diet Coke from her hand. She took a drink and handed it back to her.

"I returned your work shirt. It's hanging in your closet."

"Thanks. What time do you work today?" She glanced at her watch.

"In about fifteen minutes. Who else is working?"

"Pedro. He's out on the boat doing a patrol of the lake. You know he wants the record for the most PFD citations in one summer."

Lyn scoffed.

Clare's expression brightened as she turned to Jess. "How's laundry going?"

"It's going well. The last load is in the dryer." Jess shifted uncomfortably, all eyes on her.

Lyn jumped up. "Well, I'm off. Helen hates it when I'm late."

"As she should. I think it's good to show up on time at least once in your life." Clare playfully admonished her.

"You love my free spirit." Lyn opened the door.

"At times. I'll talk to you soon."

"Good luck with your laundry." Lyn didn't look at her.

Jess felt relieved when the door closed behind her.

"Do you want something to drink?" Clare held her arm out toward the kitchen.

"No, thanks. I'm fine." She set the empty laundry basket on the floor.

"Help yourself to anything if you change your mind." Clare dropped into the armchair on which Lyn had been leaning. "Was she hard on you?"

"I get the feeling she doesn't like me."

"She doesn't like many people I…especially anyone I…well, you know." She sighed. "She tends to be overprotective and a bit possessive. I'm sorry."

"I think she has feelings for you," Jess blurted out.

Clare was so quiet that Jess had already started to form an apology in her head by the time she spoke.

"Yes, I think she has for some time now." Clare moved to sit beside her on the couch, so close that their knees touched, and took her hand. "But I like *you,* and that's all that matters. Right?"

Jess couldn't help but smile. To assume how Clare felt about her and to hear her say it out loud were two different things. Her heart swelled. She'd never had this feeling of intimacy with someone, especially someone she'd only known such a brief time.

Clare squeezed her hand before standing up. "I need to get back to work. Do you mind locking the door when you leave?"

"No problem. Thanks again. I appreciate it."

"Of course." She stopped, her hand on the doorknob. "Oh, and our date? Bring a swimsuit. And boots." She wiggled her eyebrows and closed the door behind her.

It would be the first time Jess had ever needed a swimsuit and boots for a date, but she didn't care. From what she'd overheard, Clare didn't date, yet here she was going on a date with her. Did Lyn know?

Seeing Clare had been an unexpected surprise, but she could've done without Lyn. Next time, she'd use the resort's machines. She didn't need all this drama. The last place she wanted to be was in the middle of whatever was going on between them. Lyn must feel threatened by her because she'd all but peed in the corner to mark her territory. It wasn't Jess's problem that Lyn was in love with her best friend. She'd had ample time to make a move if that's what she wanted. Even if she had, it didn't sound like it would have mattered.

Chapter Thirteen

Clare buzzed around her kitchen, alternating between making coffee and sandwiches. Her excitement had been downright distracting as she waited for this day to arrive.

Errant brown specks dusted over the counter as she measured grounds into the coffee filter, but the mishap didn't interrupt her cheerful whistling. She picked up her phone and composed a quick text to Jess.

Good morning

Minutes passed. After she'd sliced the bread and an apple, she picked up the phone and stared at the message, making sure it went through. Her insecurity surged. Had Jess forgotten about today? She set her phone on the counter and tried to fend off disappointment. As she took mozzarella from the refrigerator, her phone vibrated. She grabbed it.

Good morning! Just showered

Clare smiled, unable to contain her giddiness, even while alone in her kitchen.

How do you like your coffee?

2 creams, 1 sugar

Pick you up in 15 min. Enough time?

Plenty

She finished making their sandwiches and poured them each a to-go mug of coffee, making Jess's to her specifications. She packed their lunches with the rest of her things in her backpack and headed out.

Clare hadn't been this excited in some time. How long exactly, she couldn't even begin to say. Their first kiss had been on constant replay in her mind and amped up her anticipation for today. She couldn't wait to show Jess her surprise. She couldn't wait to show her *everything.*

When Clare arrived, Jess jumped down from where she'd been waiting on the boulder at the entrance to her site. Her hair was still damp, and Clare could see the ties of her swimsuit under the neckline of her tank top. The thought of Jess in a bikini made her heart flutter.

Jess jumped in the truck, beaming. "I'm so used to seeing you in the park's truck that it didn't occur to me that you had your own."

Clare handed her a coffee. "I became used to driving a truck because of my job. They're so practical that I decided to buy one." She drove toward the campground exit.

"Thanks for the coffee. Where are we going?" Jess oozed excitement.

"I thought we could do a little hiking at Blue Lake. Have you been there yet?" Clare glanced at her before turning toward Park Lake.

"I saw part of it on a bike ride."

"I know you hike every day, but it's the only way to see this fossil."

"I don't mind at all. It's so beautiful here." Jess adjusted the vent near her window to direct the air at her face. "It'll be nice to hike with someone. I'm always by myself."

Jess sounded so forlorn when she said it that it made a thick knot form behind Clare's sternum. She'd assumed Jess had been enjoying her summer of independent research. Part of her probably was. Clare had witnessed her excitement firsthand. Still, it hadn't occurred to her that Jess might be lonely.

"I have something for you." Clare reached over and opened the glove box, her arm brushing against Jess's smooth leg. She pulled out a small, padded envelope and handed it to her. "Your package came."

"My inverter!" She dropped her coffee in a cup holder and ripped open the package. "Now I don't have to bother you to charge my laptop anymore."

"It was never a bother. Don't worry. I'll let you know if you're ever a bother." Clare rested her hand on Jess's knee." She was hyper-aware of the silkiness of the skin beneath her fingers. She wanted to glide her hand higher. If the day continued at this pace, she'd be in trouble. She withdrew her hand.

They didn't speak for the next couple of minutes. Jess appeared to be enjoying the scenery. Clare parked at Blue Lake, and they got out.

"Is there anything you want to leave in the car?" Clare dug in her backpack.

"Maybe my beach towel. Will we be swimming here?"

"No. Let's leave the towels in the truck. Do you need a bottle of water?"

"I have one. Thank you." Jess slung her backpack onto her back.

"Okay. Let's do this."

They trudged through some brush to the rocky trail.

"Is this even a trail?" Jess tried to peer around her. "How do you know where you're going?"

"It's not a great trail, but I've been here before. I hear people often have trouble finding it."

"So, this isn't a well-known fossil?"

"I don't know about well-known." Clare turned and spoke over her shoulder so Jess could hear. "People know about it, but few people make the effort to see it. It's difficult to get to. It's high, about three hundred feet above the lake on the cliff's side. We'll take a switchback to make it easier. Once we get up there, we'll need to climb some large rocks. I thought about asking if you have a fear of heights, but I've seen the places you go to do your research."

"You've seen me?"

Clare turned around to find Jess had stopped a few paces back.

"You're easy to spot. Most people aren't hiking where you go." She smiled.

Jess appeared surprised by this bit of information. They resumed walking. Jess's sudden reticence made her wonder if she said too much. Did watching her from afar show her concern or make her sound creepy?

After a bit, Jess spoke in a soft voice. "That makes me feel better. I'm glad that if something happened and I went missing, someone might notice."

Clare studied her. "I think it's brave, what you're doing. You're so dedicated."

"I'm always motivated when it comes to my field and my career. I wish I could transfer that motivation to other aspects of my life." She sounded dejected.

Clare stopped. She pulled her water bottle from the side pocket of her backpack and took a drink. "Some things motivate us, some don't.

It's difficult to force ourselves to do certain things, especially if the task is an unpleasant one."

She must have said something that resonated with Jess because she seemed to glaze over and reflect on something. Clare turned and continued walking. She wanted to ask questions, but also didn't want to pry, at least not this soon. They'd have plenty of time to talk in the coming days and weeks. Right now, she wanted to show her the fossil.

The switchback allowed them to reach a level place on the escarpment, even if it was quite narrow. They stopped and surveyed the ascent. From here, the climb was nearly vertical and would involve scaling slumped basalt pillars whose flat faces provided few handholds or footholds.

"That's where we're going." Clare pointed up to the left. "We'll have to help each other to get there."

Jess returned her phone to a pocket in her backpack and swung the bag back around. She'd taken a photo of Blue Lake, its surface shimmering like a sapphire some two hundred feet below them. "Okay, I'm ready."

Clare formed a basket with her hands and crouched. "I'll give you a boost."

Jess placed her hiking boot in Clare's hands, momentarily using her shoulder for support. When she found a handhold on the basalt column, Clare boosted her. It worked, and most of her torso breached the top of the boulder. She wiggled and pulled the rest of her body up. Clare caught sight of her exposed midriff before she disappeared.

"Everything okay?"

Jess peered over the edge, cocking her head to one side.

"What? Are you hurt?"

She broke out in a grin. "You look happy."

"Do I normally not look happy?"

"Not like this."

Clare *was* happy, and not fleeting happiness like when she heard a good joke or when she found ten dollars in a jeans pocket. It was pervasive, authentic happiness. Everything was beginning to take shape, like her world was slowly righting itself on its axis, and Jess had been the catalyst of that.

"I'm not always happy like this. Now, are you going to help me up there before my neck is stuck in this position?"

Jess grinned. She stretched out on her stomach and reached down. "Grab my hands. I'll help pull you up."

Clare kicked some loose rocks away, found a good foothold, and grabbed her hands. "I'm ready."

Jess's hands felt soft yet strong. Clare used her foothold and pushed while Jess pulled. Her chest ended up right at Jess's eye level as she scrabbled to get her legs over the ledge.

Jess wrapped an arm around her. "I got you." She held her tightly and pulled until Clare made it over the top. They fell onto their backs.

Clare exhaled dramatically. She turned her head and admired Jess's rosy cheeks. "We might need to rethink our tactics."

Jess laughed.

Being with her was easy. She felt comfortable with her, even though they'd only known each other for a matter of weeks.

Jess rolled onto her side. "Can we keep going? It's killing me being so close."

Clare laughed. "I like it when you get excited."

Jess's eyes widened, her entire face flushed, and she looked away. She jumped up, extending her hand to Clare. "So, that's a yes?"

Clare let her pull her up, shaking her head.

Together, they perfected their technique and scaled another dozen basalt pillars. Clare's skin felt sticky with perspiration. A layer of dirt covered them by the time they stopped.

"This is it." Clare could barely contain her excitement, like a kid on Christmas morning.

Jess reached out to the rock face in front of her and ran her fingertips over it as she searched for a fossil. "Give me a clue where to look."

"In here." Clare stepped aside and pointed to a hole low in the rock face behind her.

"The fossil is in a cave? You didn't tell me the fossil was in a cave!" Jess shouted with glee. She dropped to her knees, peering inside.

"You go first. I don't think it's big enough for both of us." She held out a small flashlight.

Jess grabbed the flashlight and turned it on. She crawled in partway, and Clare took in the stunning view. Jess's shorts stretched tight across her backside, leaving little to Clare's imagination. Thankfully, Jess ducked inside because Clare wasn't sure how much more she could take.

Clare knelt outside the opening and watched the light play around the cave's surfaces. It was an oddly shaped cave with strange protrusions. Jess shined the light on the cave's walls, the floor, and then the ceiling.

"I need a clue! How small is it?" Jess's voice, amplified in the small space, burst forth as if from a megaphone.

"I'm right here. You don't need to yell." Clare's laughter echoed in the cave, her head and shoulders filling the entrance. "It's not small."

Again, Jess shined the light around the interior of the cave whose largest dimensions reached four feet tall by seven feet long, if even that. "I don't see it."

"That's because you're sitting in it."

"What do you mean?" Jess turned the light upon her face as if she were telling a ghost story.

"You're sitting inside the fossilized mold of a rhinoceros."

"What?" Her eyes grew huge.

Clare enjoyed her reaction. "I did a little research to brush up on the facts for you. It happened around 14.5 million years ago."

"So Pleistocene," Jess murmured under her breath. Her flashlight's beam darted all around her as she assessed the cave again.

"The rhinoceros was in the shallows of a lake during some volcanic activity, perhaps dead, because he was on his back. When the lava reached the water, the water cooled the outside portion of the lava creating—" She didn't have a chance to finish.

"Pillow lava. Of course."

"Yes, the pillow lava formed around the body of the animal."

"That's why I noticed little evidence of solutional sculpting in the cave." Jess seemed to be murmuring to herself.

"They call this the Blue Lake Rhino. You entered the cave at one of the animal's hindquarters. Hikers found some bones and teeth in here during the Great Depression. Shine your light on the ceiling for a moment."

Jess turned the beam upward.

"Can you see that little round protrusion?" Clare pointed.

"I think so."

"That's the rhino's belly button."

Jess laughed. "Oh, my God. This is amazing. I've never seen *anything* like this."

She turned around carefully and laid the flashlight on the cave's floor. She crawled toward her, took Clare's face in her hands, and kissed her.

Clare leaned into the cave. They were both sweaty. She didn't care.

Jess buried her fingers in her hair, and Clare forgot all about fossils. Her thoughts came in fragmented pieces: soft, delicious, warm, smooth, yes, *more.* Her heart rattled in her chest like a caged monkey. She'd only wanted to witness Jess's excitement. Another kiss, a kiss like this, was more than she'd expected.

"Thank you," Jess whispered.

"I had a feeling you might like it." Clare's lips brushed hers as she spoke.

"Oh, I like it." Her voice, low and throaty, suggested she was enjoying more than the fossil. Jess kissed her again.

CHAPTER FOURTEEN

They sat outside the cave, their legs dangling over the basalt column that served as their seat. Blue Lake shimmered below, the water appearing even more inviting as midday approached. Clare's shoulders heated as if the sun demanded its presence be acknowledged. The lake's glass-like surface mirrored the few fluffy white clouds above.

"If you can wait a bit for lunch, there's an interesting place less than a ten-minute drive from here."

"I can wait. What makes it interesting?"

"More caves." Clare gave a nonchalant shrug.

"Like this one?" Jess looked ready to jump up.

"No. I'm sorry to disappoint you. I think they're regular caves. I'm sure you'll know more about them than I do, at least regarding their formation. But I know a few things."

"Oh, I'm sure someone your age knows many things."

Her comment left Clare momentarily speechless. "Someone my age?" It was the first time one of them had mentioned their age difference. "How old do you think I am?"

"Like, forty?" Jess answered without a beat.

"Oh, my God." Clare shook her head and looked out toward the lake. She'd noticed a few gray hairs and the beginning of some lines around her eyes, but did she look *forty*?

Jess laughed and poked her in the ribs. "Your face! I'm teasing you." When Clare didn't respond right away, she leaned over and playfully bumped into her. "I'm only joking. I'm guessing we're about ten years apart, and you don't look anywhere near forty. I think you're gorgeous, and I couldn't care less how old you are." She reached out and tucked a lock of hair behind Clare's ear.

Clare gave her a wry smile. "You think you're funny, don't you?"

"I'm a little funny. Admit it." She nudged her again.

"A *little* funny." Clare shook her head and nudged her back. "Ready to move on?"

After a short drive, Clare parked at another trailhead. Purple sage sprung up alongside the trail, and rust-colored lichen dotted the flat faces of the rocks they passed on the hike to the Lake Lenore Caves. Bright green Indian hemp provided the only contrast to the otherwise drab landscape.

Above them, towering chimneys of basalt stood apart from the colonnades like soldiers standing sentry. The trail was easier than the one to the rhino, but the terrain was the same. Angular, jagged rocks forced them to watch their every step. They hiked along the entablature, broken rocks of varying sizes creating an otherworldly, stony landscape.

"Who made these steps from the rocks?" Jess inspected them.

"I'm not sure. It might have been a WPA project back in the thirties. The caves are up ahead." Clare turned back toward her each time she spoke, not simply so Jess could hear her, but also because she liked what she saw—Jess's skin shining with perspiration, her eyes bright and lively, a smile always tugging at the corners of her mouth. Clare hardly noticed the strain of her calves or what was probably the start of a sunburn on her shoulders.

As they crested the last leg of the trail, the caves stood in a row. Low, gently sloping, and wider than they were deep, many looked long enough to parallel park a school bus inside. Some caves were only a couple dozen feet apart.

The cuboidal rocks that comprised the walls and ceilings of the caves jutted out in uneven, brick-like mosaics. The floors of the caves looked like someone had upset a box of LEGO bricks.

Clare watched Jess enter the first cave and crouch as she crept toward the back. She ran her hands over the surface of the walls. Clare smiled as she watched her slip into geologist mode.

"These caves are unusual." Jess's voice echoed. "Most caves form when rainwater becomes acidic from the carbon dioxide in the air. Over time, it dissolves the types of rock that are more soluble, like limestone. But of course, this isn't limestone."

She moved to the other side of the cave and continued her exploration. Occasionally, she snapped a photo. Clare watched her with interest, happy to let her take all the time she needed.

"Those kinds of caves have smoother surfaces, and you'll see where calcium carbonate precipitated and deposited to form stalagmites and stalactites." She turned and put her hands on her hips.

"So, how were these caves created? Erosion?" Clare was genuinely curious.

"Basically. At one point, these caves were at water level. The water froze and thawed, weakened the joints between the basalt, and caused further cracking. Then floodwaters and erosion washed the weakened basalt away.

"Long ago, the Indigenous People in the area came here to hunt and forage for food. They used the caves to store their supplies and tools. Unfortunately, that era is over." Clare took a drink from her water bottle. "At some point, people discovered the artifacts, and authorities removed them for posterity."

"I agree. That is sad that way of life is no longer possible and all because of people who look like us." She was quiet for a moment as they reflected. "But see, you do know some things." Jess's eyes sparkled with mischief.

Clare pressed her lips together and shook her head. She tried to ignore the clothes-free ways she'd like to repay Jess for all her teasing.

They explored a few more caves, some wider and deeper than the others. At the last cave, Clare suggested they use the shade to enjoy their lunch. They found a large rock on which to sit. She opened her backpack and handed Jess a sandwich.

"Did you make this?" Jess took another bite. "It's so good."

"I did, but I showed you the extent of my skills with that sandwich. I'm not much of a chef." She'd put some thought into their lunch and was pleased Jess enjoyed it.

"It was a perfect choice for today. The warmth of the sun on your backpack made the cheese melty and soft, and all the flavors come together nicely."

"Melty, huh?" She grinned.

"Mm-hmm. Melty."

Clare reached into her backpack and set a plastic sandwich bag full of potato chips and another filled with apple slices between them.

Jess glanced at her phone. "It's already ninety-three degrees."

"Where do you want to swim?"

"Deep Lake!"

"Okay. Any reason?"

"People were diving off the cliffs the day I was there. Don't you think that sounds like fun?"

Jess's excitement was usually contagious, but Clare had been on top of those cliffs, and diving wasn't her preferred way down. "You're welcome to cliff dive if you want. I'll watch you from below."

"You have to come with me." Jess pouted. "I'm sure you've done it before, having lived here so many years."

"Nope." The nod to her tenure unintentionally made her feel like a fossil.

"Do you have a fear of heights? They're nowhere near as high as we are now, maybe only thirty or forty feet."

"I don't have a fear of heights. I have a fear of *dying*."

Jess laughed. "You're not going to die. Don't you ever need to prove to yourself you can do something? Even the little kids were doing it. We'll jump together."

Clare considered her options. She wasn't often cajoled into doing something, and she wasn't opposed to taking risks. Hell, recently she'd taken a few risks while playing hearts with Jess and the guys, and it had paid off—so much so that she'd been disappointed they hadn't put money on the game. This decision had more at stake, yet a part of her was still interested. She wanted to share the experience with Jess and impress her.

She finally agreed, and they started back. Without any shade, the truck felt like an oven. The steering wheel burned Clare's hands as she drove. She blasted the air conditioning. They needed it after the hike. When they arrived at Deep Lake, the cab had finally cooled.

"Leave anything you don't want to lose or get wet in the truck."

"I only want my towel."

They stuffed their backpacks behind the seats and tossed their towels over their shoulders.

The emerald-green waters at Deep Lake's shoreline turned to indigo in the deepest parts. The vertical-walled cliffs appeared to rise from nowhere and looked even higher than Clare remembered.

She followed Jess this time, who hiked up to the diving spot doing double-time.

The blazing sun made her hairline damp with sweat. She couldn't wait to get into the water. If only she could do it from lake level without disappointing Jess. Maybe it wouldn't look so scary once they got up there.

When they reached the top, she saw two teenage boys, their board shorts and hair dripping from the last plunge. As they planned their backflips and adjusted their GoPros, Clare began to strip to her swimsuit behind them. Jess did the same. A loud yell announced one of the boys had jumped. Clare wrapped her clothing in her towel, slipped her keys into her hiking boots, and tucked it all between some rocks.

When she glanced up, Jess wore a teal two-piece suit that looked like it was custom-made for her slim body. The halter top accentuated her collarbones and petite shoulders, and…well, other areas. Clare couldn't tear her eyes away. A nearby war-whoop announced the second boy had jumped. Her insides exclaimed in a similar fashion.

She refocused. In a matter of seconds, she was going to be hurtling toward the water's surface, out of control. Clare hoped she survived the dive—or the fall. It was all semantics.

Jess looked at her. Clare saw her gaze rake over her amethyst-colored two-piece with white flowers. Their eyes locked. A tremor ran through her. Her nipples hardened against her top. *Jesus.* Would her legs be stable enough to carry her to the jump spot? How could one look dismantle her like that?

Jess tilted her head toward the water. Together they walked toward the cliff's edge. "It feels higher once you're up here."

That exact thought had occurred to Clare, and hearing Jess say it didn't help her anxiety. "So, why don't we go back and—"

"No, we are going to do this. If they can do it, so can we." Jess motioned to the boys who were already halfway back up the trail to jump again. "Ready?"

Clare stared, transfixed on the water's surface four stories below. "Clare?"

She beheld Jess standing beside her on the precipice as her pounding heart threatened to break through her chest, pushed to the max by a heady mix of fear and arousal.

"Do you trust me?" Jess caressed her cheek and took her hand.

Her voice sounded far away. Clare wouldn't do this for just anyone. Her world spun, but it wasn't necessarily a bad feeling. It was kind of nice in an intoxicating sort of way. She looked at Jess and smiled.

Together, they jumped.

Chapter Fifteen

Even though she'd jumped off the cliff with her, Clare was adamant about once being enough. She didn't seem to hold the experience against her though, because she invited Jess to go out on the lake in a boat with her the next day.

"I'll keep it steady while you get in." Clare held the edge of the rowboat against the dock. "Take my hand."

Jess took her hand and gingerly stepped into the boat, but it wobbled, nonetheless. Clare's strong arm steadied her until she found her balance.

"You sit there." Clare pointed toward the simple wooden bench seat.

"What do I need to do?"

"Hold onto the dock until I get in."

Jess held the boat in place. Clare sat on the edge of the dock and swung her legs into the boat. In one graceful, fluid motion, she lowered herself into the vessel and sat opposite her.

"You can let go now." She flashed her an amused grin.

Jess gave up her vice-like hold on the dock and settled for grasping the wooden seat below her as Clare secured each oar into the oarlocks.

"So where are we going?"

"There." Clare motioned with her chin to a small island in the middle of Park Lake. The almost circular protrusion of rock rose from the water with a thin, sloping, and rocky beach. No more than a few stories tall, the island flattened out into a small, round plateau on top. It was unoccupied. Most swimmers and boaters had headed for shore as the sun sank low in the sky.

"Just right there?"

"Just right there?" Clare mimicked her with a laugh. "Do you see a motor on this thing?" She cut the oars into the water with sure, purposeful strokes. They glided over the lake's turquoise waters toward the island, the heat of the day fading with the setting sun.

Jess smiled and dipped her hand into the water as the rowboat skated across its surface. Her trailing fingers left four individual wakes. "Does it have a name?"

"Big Rock Island."

"That's not very original. Why are we going there?" She tried not to notice how each stroke accentuated the muscles in Clare's arms.

Clare glanced behind her and adjusted the boat's trajectory before responding. "It's quiet. I thought we could talk." She smiled.

Talk? What did Clare want to talk about? Jackson flashed through Jess's mind, and guilt washed over her. Surely, Clare didn't want to talk about him, for as far as Jess knew, she didn't know he existed. Although she was curious, she didn't ask any more questions during the short voyage.

They dragged the boat onto the small beach and made the short hike to the top. With an unobstructed view of the setting sun, they sat beside each other on the ground. Clare picked blades of wild grasses and tossed them before her.

"What did you want to talk about?" Wondering had left Jess a bit nervous. Dread felt like a rock in the pit of her stomach. She hated keeping a secret from Clare, but she couldn't bring herself to tell her either. Things with Jackson were clearly over, it just wasn't official yet. Telling Clare might end this dream-like fantasy her summer was becoming, and she didn't want that.

Clare sucked in a deep breath and sighed. She wrapped her arms around her knees and stared toward where the last remnant of the sun dipped behind the cliffs. "I want to tell you some things, things that are important for you to know. That doesn't mean it's easy for me."

Jess focused on the scenery in front of her. It seemed they were both anxious. Maybe it would make Clare less nervous if she didn't look at her.

When Clare spoke, her voice was so low that she strained to hear.

"About six years ago, the park hired a woman who had been a ranger at Lake Chelan State Park. Her name was Dominique. The park assigned her as my roommate. We got along well. We became friends and then more. It wasn't long before we were together."

A pang hit Jess in the center of her chest. The despair in Clare's voice didn't correspond with the words she was saying.

"We fell in love. We were together for years. We talked about our future. We thought we had it all, living here, working the jobs we loved. It was idyllic. I loved her. We even talked about getting married."

She fell silent for so long that Jess turned to look at her. She wasn't surprised to find small rivulets of tears trickling down Clare's face.

"There was a fire in the park two years ago. She was on duty and the first to respond. It was late in the day, dusk, and the wind was beginning to pick up. The fire started right off the road in the northern part of the park. She tried to get a fire line around it, but the winds flared up and changed direction." Clare wept outright, her voice faltering, her sentences broken. "She was trapped between the fire and the cliff. It all happened so fast. By the time the second ranger arrived, it was too late."

"Oh, God. Clare, I'm so sorry." Thoughts and images bombarded Jess's mind from all directions. It was so much information to process.

"Dom had been through training, like me. She knew better. She didn't have an escape route or safety zone, and the wind...You've experienced the wind. It's brutal." She wiped her face with her hand. "That was two years ago. I haven't dated anyone since. I couldn't even imagine dating anyone again, let alone giving myself to someone." She smiled at her through her tears. "But you came along, showing off your rock collection."

She felt terrible for what Clare had been through. It made her heart ache. On the other hand, knowing that sleeping with her was on Clare's mind, that she was considering it, nearly left Jess speechless. When she'd impulsively pulled Clare toward her tent, she'd resisted. Jess hadn't known what to make of that. She knew that she'd never want Clare to do something she wasn't ready to do. Yet, the thought of being beneath her, feeling Clare's weight on her, skin-on-skin wouldn't go away.

"I'm so sorry. You must have been heartbroken." Jess took her hand.

Finally, Clare spoke again. "There's more."

More? "When you're ready." She ran her thumb over Clare's fingers.

"I was heartbroken, but not how you think. I haven't told anyone this except my therapist. Not my family, not Lyn. No one." She stared at the ground in front of her.

Moments passed. Jess stilled her fingers. Was she going to continue?

"The truth is, I lost her before that. I just don't know exactly when." It came out a whisper, barely audible.

"How? What does that mean?" Jess scowled.

"About two weeks before the fire, I found a phone in her pants pocket one night. It wasn't her cell phone, or at least the one I knew about. I saw a text message from someone. She was having an affair."

"No. Oh, God." Jess's head spun and her stomach churned at the word *affair*. Guilt washed over her again. What they had wasn't an affair though. As far as she was concerned, Jackson was in her past. She just needed to tell that to his face. "You had no idea? No suspicions?"

"No. I could only see the notification. The phone was locked."

"Who was the text from?"

Clare shook her head. "It was a phone number I didn't recognize. No name."

"Whoa. Just…wow." Jess blew out through pursed lips and brushed her hair back from her face. Her insides recoiled with guilt, even though technically she shouldn't feel guilty. She hoped her face wasn't flushed. "You didn't ask her?"

"I was stunned and didn't want to believe it. I told myself it wasn't happening. I didn't know what to say or do. I don't even know how I managed to go about life those two weeks before her death. When I managed to get over the shock, my anger replaced it. All these little excuses and oddities in our relationship now made sense. I was figuring out how to confront her when the fire happened. I waited too long. We never…" She gulped. "We never did talk." Tears leaked from the corners of her eyes again. She didn't even bother wiping them away. "I missed the chance to ask her why."

Jess put her arm around her, and Clare leaned against her. Nocturnal life at the park started to stir as the indigo sky darkened above them. Her thoughts ran rampant. "So, you never found out who the other person was?"

"No. Authorities found both phones on her body. I'm sure the few people who knew that had theories on why she had two. That was the only evidence of the affair, and the fire destroyed it." Clare's voice sounded mechanical and hollow.

"Why didn't you tell anyone?"

"It was such a whirlwind. There was an investigation—as there is with any fatality like that—a memorial, a funeral, the media, her family traveled to see the site, and my parents came to stay with me. I was grieving in so many ways for so many reasons. I was helping to pick out flower sprays for her casket with her family when I had to leave. Everyone thought I broke down, when in fact I was filled with rage.

"To be honest, I've felt like a terrible person for some time now. Sometimes I wake up crying because I've lost her, and then I remember that she wasn't mine to lose. It's emotionally exhausting." Clare scooped up a handful of pebbles and let them sift through her fingers.

"I was embarrassed. Everyone thought we were the perfect couple, myself included, but I don't even know how long she'd been cheating on me. I was hurt and upset. I was so angry after I found the phone. There was even a time before the fire when...I wished she were dead. After the fire happened, I wondered if I had somehow caused her death because of my horrible thoughts. I can't even begin to describe my guilt. I thought perhaps the universe was punishing me." She dropped her head to her chest and stared at the ground.

"I don't think life works that way." Jess felt so helpless. "You mentioned a therapist. I'm glad to hear you had someone to talk to."

"Yes, Helen recommended her. She's amazing. She's been an immense help. I used to get terrible panic attacks. At least those have subsided. Unfortunately, Dominique's betrayal affected my ability to trust people. I'm trying to rebuild that after what happened. For a long time, I wasn't sure I could ever trust anyone again."

"That's understandable. She betrayed your trust in one of the worst ways possible." Again, Jess thought of Jackson, and her stomach lurched. She watched the string of taillights crawl up and out of the valley as campers headed to the laser show. A fish jumped, startling her.

"I trust *you.*" It came out softly, a tender admittance.

Nausea swelled within her, a burning sensation rising in her throat. Jess forced it down with a swallow. She wished Clare hadn't said it. Under different circumstances, she would have been thrilled to hear Clare admit it, but now it only made her feel terrible. She had to say something.

"I trust you, too." Even though it was true, she felt terrible saying it, as though their trust in each other was equal. It wasn't like Clare *shouldn't* trust her, she'd just feel a whole lot better if the Jackson issue weren't there.

"Was that a falling star?" Clare squeezed her hand.

Jess thanked all heavenly beings for the distraction and looked toward where she pointed. "I missed it. I love meteors."

"Did your parents take you to watch meteor showers when you were a kid? You mentioned your dad got you started on rock collecting. After all, aren't meteors falling rocks?" Clare wiped under her eyes with her thumb, more composed now.

Jess hadn't expected to go there, not tonight. What choice did she have now? It seemed to be the night for sharing. The prolonged silence must have alerted Clare that the answer wasn't a simple one because she turned to study her.

Jess ran a hand over her face. "My dad raised me by himself. My mother died giving birth to me."

"Oh, Jess. I'm so sorry. I've spent so much time talking about me and my life, and I neglected to even ask you about yours. I didn't even know women still died in childbirth."

"Have you heard of placenta previa?"

Clare shook her head.

"It's when the placenta covers the cervix. It sometimes causes bleeding. The mortality rate of mothers with placenta previa is around one percent, and my mom happened to be in that unlucky percentile."

Clare squeezed her hand.

"I always wondered if not having a mother was worse than having a mother and then losing her. When my dad died during my first year in college, I realized it was apples and oranges. Both ways hurt." Jess stared straight ahead.

"Oh, Jess." She swatted a bug away from them. "May I ask how he died?"

"He was riding his bike on Mercer Island and a car turning right hit him. It happened two weeks before the end of my first quarter in college. They said he never regained consciousness and didn't suffer. At least there was that." Even through her sadness, Jess couldn't help but smile as she remembered him. "He was always so encouraging, always so proud of anything I did."

"I'm sure he would be so proud to see you now, his daughter the geologist." Clare smiled at her.

She had no idea. He would have been ecstatic. Rocks had always been a special love they shared. For Jess to come this far, to earn multiple degrees in a family where college degrees were rare, would have made him burst with pride. For her to do it on her own, with little to no support, would have pleased him, too, but also filled him with sadness. The last thing he ever wanted was for her to be alone.

They couldn't stay on the island too long because the rowboat didn't have lights. Clare was grateful that she didn't have to row them back. Jess wasn't as confident with the oars or as strong as she was, so it took longer, but Jess seemed to realize that she was emotionally and physically exhausted. They leisurely walked toward her house as darkness fell.

"Can I ask you something?"

"Sure." Clare wasn't certain she had much left to say after pouring out her heart over the last hour.

"Was Dominique the only casualty in the fire?" Jess's voice seemed higher than usual.

"Yes. Why do you ask?" She hadn't been prepared for the unexpected question.

"The plaque at the scenic vista, is that for her?" Jess stopped.

"Oh, you saw that? The State Park Department had it installed as a memorial to her."

"Can we sit?"

"Okay." Clare scowled. Why was Jess asking all these questions?

Jess pulled her toward a wooden bench, and they sat facing the lake.

"Is something wrong?" She grew more concerned by the second.

"I don't know how to say this. You know what they say about shooting the messenger." Jess wrung her hands.

"Now you're scaring me. I'm not like that. Please say whatever it is." Clare hadn't seen Jess this anxious.

"As I processed what you told me, something clicked into place. I don't know how to say this, or even if you want to know at this point, but I know whom your girlfriend was cheating on you with." Jess hadn't made eye contact with her the entire time she spoke but instead stared out toward the lake.

"Who? Of course, I want to know. How could *you* possibly know?"

Clare had been in love with Dominique and expected they would have a future together. Of course, she wanted to know. Why was Jess, of all people, the one who was telling her? She broke out in a sweat.

"On my first day at the park, I pulled into the scenic vista. I was reading the plaque that explained what happened, and a ranger approached me." Jess looked like a deer in headlights.

"If you don't give me a name right now, I think I'm going to explode." She was emotionally exhausted and out of patience.

"Your boss. Brett."

Clare froze, absorbing the information, trying to make it make sense, trying not to let her mind conjure up unwanted images.

"He told me they'd been dating when she died, and the last couple of years had been hard on him, but he was beginning to venture back into dating. Then he asked me out." Jess scoffed.

"Jesus Christ." Disgust enveloped her, and she worried she was going to be sick. She leaned forward, elbows on knees, and held her head. Images took form, images she never wanted to imagine. Part of her wished she could go back in time twenty seconds and change her answer. Her stomach revolted. "Dominique. What the hell?"

"Maybe I shouldn't have said anything."

Clare sat up, flipping her hair back. Her eyes were probably bloodshot by now. "No, you did the right thing. I wanted to know. How do you think it's been the last few years of being suspicious of everyone around me? This damn park is worse than a small town. I figured it was someone I knew."

"I'm so sorry."

Clare stood. "I'm afraid I need some time alone. I don't feel well, and I should sleep. All of this has worn me out."

"Are you upset with me?" Jess sounded frightened.

"No, of course not. Even though I knew there was someone, it was shocking to find out it was him. I never expected to hear the news from you. What are the chances?"

Jess stood. "Let me walk you home."

"You don't have to."

"I know, but I'm going to anyway."

They walked the rest of the way in silence. To her credit, Jess didn't ask to come in, and she didn't extend an offer. She wanted to crawl into bed and dwell on it alone. It was nothing against Jess. It was a prior chapter of her life that needed closing. Having Jess there wouldn't allow her to do that. She needed to shed a few tears in private and then move on with her life. It remained to be seen what she'd do now that she had a name.

Chapter Sixteen

Clare asked Lyn to meet her for dinner the next day. She wanted to talk, to share some of the stuff that was going on in her life. After she told her, maybe Lyn could help her decide what to do about Brett. Clare knew Lyn wasn't a fan of him at baseline. It was a good thing the restaurant served drinks.

She arrived a few minutes late to the steakhouse. Lyn had texted that she'd already been seated. The host, young enough to still attend high school, showed her to the table where Lyn waited. She slid into the wooden booth.

"Did you find the shoes you were looking for?"

"No." Lyn motioned for their server to come over. "I went to two stores and gave up."

"I'll have what she's having." She didn't bother looking at the drink menu.

"Want any appetizers?" He sported an electric-blue faux hawk, black nail polish, and an uninterested attitude that gave him the appearance that he would rather be working anywhere besides a steakhouse.

"We haven't looked at the menu yet." Lyn stared at him.

"I'll come back."

She rolled her eyes as he left. "I can't imagine he makes much in tips."

Clare placed her napkin on her lap and fiddled with its hemmed edge.

"So, you mentioned you wanted to talk about something." Lyn stirred her martini with the toothpick-skewered olive and took a sip.

"Do you mind if I get my martini first?" She knew that bar drinks took time to make, and she'd have a few minutes to compose her thoughts. "Shall we get an appetizer?"

Lyn didn't budge but continued to stir and sip her cocktail. "Pick two that you like, and I'll make the final choice."

She studied the menu for a minute. "Spinach artichoke dip or shrimp cocktail."

"Ugh." Lyn made a face. "Maybe I better take a look." She reached for a menu, and then changed her mind. "No, never mind. The spinach artichoke dip is fine. I'll consider it my serving of vegetables."

"Why did you tell me to pick if you're going to complain?"

"I don't know. I assumed you would choose something I liked."

The server took this as his chosen moment to interrupt them again, bringing Clare's drink. His crooked name tag said his name was Theodore. Lyn ordered their appetizer.

"What do you want for your meals?" He shuffled from foot to foot.

"We haven't gotten that far yet." Lyn smoothly switched into bitch mode. "We're not in a rush and from the looks of it, Theo, you don't need to turn our table, so why don't you come back when we're finished with our appetizer?" She gave him a saccharine smile.

He mumbled something about the kitchen making fresh chips as he retreated.

"Is that necessary? He's just doing his job."

"Not well, he isn't. Now, besides delicious, warm, nearly raw slabs of beef, why are we here?" Lyn leaned on the table.

"I need to tell you something." Clare took a sip of her drink for courage. "You're not going to be happy I haven't told you this, but it's something I'd like to share with you now because I'm finally ready."

"You sound serious. Is this about *her*?"

Lyn's derisive tone was offensive. "No. Can you let that go for a minute?" She took a deep breath and smoothed the napkin on her lap. "This precedes Jess."

"Please tell me. You know I can't handle the suspense."

Clare sighed and studied a deep ridge in the surface of the wooden table where grime had accumulated. "The last few years have been hard on me."

"They would have been difficult for anyone. Grieving a loved one is a terrible thing to have to go through." Lyn reached out and gave Clare's hand a quick squeeze.

"That's the thing. I haven't been honest with you. I haven't been honest with anyone."

"What's going on?" Lyn pushed her martini to the side.

"The chips are hot and fresh." Theo interrupted by delivering their appetizer. He'd received Lyn's not-so-subtle message because he departed right away, the appetizer sliding to a stop in the middle of the table.

"While you thought I was grieving, I wasn't *just* grieving." Clare looked up.

They ignored the bubbling dish sitting between them.

"What the hell are you trying to say?" Lyn looked confused.

"Well, yes, I was grieving, but I was also angry. Everything was so confusing. There were so many people around who loved Dominique, and I didn't know what to do." Clare took a deep breath. "Two weeks before she died, I found out she was cheating on me."

Lyn's mouth hung open. "What? I can't believe she'd cheat on you. With whom? How do you know?"

Theo approached their table again, starting to ask if the appetizer was satisfactory, but Lyn put a palm up. "No!" He did an about-face and slinked away.

"I found her burner phone and saw a text."

"Who sent it?"

"It was a number I didn't recognize."

"Did you call it?" Lyn leaned back against the booth's seat.

"No, I was so shocked that it didn't occur to me. I put it back in her pants pocket. I was going to confront her, but the fire happened. I was so angry. I was angry at her, angry at whomever she was sleeping with, angry that she'd been taken from me, angry with God, angry that my entire life had been flipped upside down." Clare stopped to breathe. She was shaking.

Lyn leaned forward to say something, but their server approached their table again.

"Theo! I swear to God if you come over here right now…"

He stood frozen like a deer in headlights.

"It's just…uh…if there's something wrong with your food, I can tell my manager." He tugged at a corner of his black apron.

"The food is fine." Lyn scooped up some dip with a chip and shoved it in her mouth. "See?" She exaggerated her chewing and waved him away with her hand. "We're talking. Scram."

Wide-eyed and nodding, he backed away.

"Damnit, that's hot." She reached for her glass of water.

Clare splayed her fingers on the wooden tabletop.

"So, you never talked to her about it or found out who the other person was?" Lyn reached for her martini. She stirred the drink but didn't take a sip.

"She died before I could talk to her about it. Strangely enough, I just found out." She took a breath and exhaled. "Brett."

"Brett?" Lyn scoffed. "How do you know?"

"Jess told me."

"How the hell would *she* know? You only met her this summer. You're going on her word?"

"On the day she arrived, she had a conversation with him. He told her he'd been dating Dominique." Clare took a drink, trying to drown the mental image.

"Maybe he was talking from his ass trying to impress her or somehow trying to win her sympathy."

"I believe her." Clare didn't want to get into Lyn's issues with Jess. She'd deal with that another day.

"Well, he does have a reputation for not being able to keep his pants zipped," Lyn said drolly. "Unbelievable. He's an asshole. They're both grade-A assholes."

"You know what else is strange? He tried to get close to me after she died. I always felt like he wanted in on my grief or something. Months later, he asked me out a few times, so I assumed that's why he was being so friendly. Maybe he thought we had a connection because we both grieved for her. Of course, he had no idea that I knew she was having an affair. No one did."

"Who knows why he does what he does? I'm so sorry. You've been dealing with all this by yourself. I can't believe you didn't tell me." Lyn's shoulders drooped.

Clare didn't know how to respond to that, so she pulled a small plate in front of her and took some dip and chips. "It's taken me a lot of therapy to get to this point. It's hard to see yourself as a good person when you wish someone dead, and then they are."

Lyn shook her head and took the other small plate. "Cheating. I still can't believe it. I never got the inkling anything was wrong between you two."

"You and me both." Clare reached for the salt.

"So, Jess found out about the cheating before I did, so that must mean you're sleeping together."

"That's none of your business."

"That's a yes if I ever heard one." Lyn raised her eyebrows for effect.

Clare pushed her plate aside. "I need you to be supportive of me. If you can't be supportive, then I don't know how I can share things with you." She took a sip of her martini, already warmer than she preferred.

"Well, obviously you can't. You've been keeping a huge secret from me for more than two years." Lyn stared at her.

"It wasn't *you* that I didn't tell. I didn't tell anyone. For all I knew, she could have been sleeping with you." Clare heard the sentence exit her mouth and regretted it at once. "I didn't mean that." She reached across the table, but Lyn pulled her hand away.

"Wow. I thought you knew me better than that."

"I didn't mean it. My emotions got the best of me. I'm sorry."

"Forget it." Lyn picked up her glass and finished her drink. "You know, I would support you if I thought you were making the right decision."

"I don't know what you have against Jess. I've always found these conversations about whom I'm dating to be difficult with you." Although frank, the statement still left mountains unsaid between them, and Lyn looked away, clearly unwilling to fill the space. "I suppose we should talk about that soon, too, but this isn't the place. This should cover the bill and tip. I'm not hungry anymore. And please tip him even more. You were rude." Clare opened her wallet, laid four crisp twenties on the table, and left.

CHAPTER SEVENTEEN

Clare drove back to the park as the long rays of the sun slipped below the horizon. Her residual anger slipped away too as her thoughts turned from Lyn to Jess. She found it difficult to stay angry when thinking about Jess.

The drive afforded her time to organize her thoughts. It occurred to her that there was a difference between feeling alone and feeling incomplete. She didn't mind being alone. She often enjoyed it. On the other hand, for a long time, she'd felt incomplete. However, even when she wasn't with her, Jess made her feel whole. The simple thought made her smile. Did Jess feel the same?

Her mind took an unwanted hairpin turn back to Lyn. It annoyed her that she couldn't begin to understand her feelings for Jess. Lyn probably did understand, she simply didn't want to give them credence. After years of unhappiness, Clare was happier than she could ever recall being, but the fact that she couldn't share that momentous occasion with Lyn frustrated her. Instead of being pleased that Clare had found someone, Lyn's jealousy and possessiveness had only grown. Frankly, she was tired of it.

She knew she needed to have a long-overdue, serious conversation with her. Lyn's jealousy annoyed her. If Lyn couldn't find it within her to be supportive, was she her best friend or even her friend at all? Clare loved her and valued their friendship, but she'd never felt the romantic spark with Lyn that she had with Dominique or Jess. Even if she'd been single, Clare wouldn't dream of entering a relationship with someone she didn't think about each morning before opening her eyes. As much as Lyn desired a romantic relationship with her, their relationship was destined to remain platonic or become nothing at all. The mere thought of losing her friend depressed her, but she needed to get through to Lyn. She also needed to ask for her spare key back.

She hadn't expected to return to the park so early, but the turn dinner had taken caused her to end it prematurely. While she was disappointed that she and Lyn couldn't reconnect over a nice meal and drinks, coming back early allowed her to see Jess. She turned into the campground.

She smiled when she saw Jess's features light up at her arrival. Her cooler stood open on one of the picnic table benches near where her propane stove burned. Jess stopped what she was doing and waited for her. Her gaze made Clare's insides ripple.

"Would you happen to have enough for two?"

Jess's smile faded. "Of course, but why are you here? I didn't expect to see you tonight." She touched her arm. "I thought you had dinner plans."

Jess read her like an open book, a feeling to which Clare was unaccustomed. Jess made her feel stripped bare, vulnerable. While she recognized some discomfort in the newfound feeling, she also welcomed it. She'd been lost, and Jess had found her.

Clare took her in her arms, bending to bury her face in her neck. She breathed in the scent of her hair products, fresh and familiar. Jess didn't question her further, but held her, her hand making small circles on her back. Clare's stomach growled.

Jess chuckled and pulled away enough to look into her eyes. "I felt that rumble. Let's get you some food."

"I can help. What are you making?"

"Spaghetti and salad. Nothing fancy. The marinara is from a jar, but I have real Parmesan. You can't cut corners with certain things."

"That sounds delicious."

Clare glanced at the neighboring campsite. Two older men played chess at their picnic table, neither even glancing up from the game. They had one tent and not an exceptionally large one at that. How nice it would be to spend the night close together, snuggled in a tent with someone special.

Jess slid a small cutting board and paring knife toward her. "You can cut the tomato and cucumber for the salad. I already washed them."

Together they made dinner with little said that didn't involve food preparation. They moved in harmony around each other. Jess seemed aware of Clare's need to focus on the task at hand and not on whatever had preceded her arrival.

"Taste this." Jess blew on a spoonful of marinara before offering it to her. "I added some basil that I found in my little bag of spices."

Clare hummed her approval.

"Enough salt?"

"It's perfect, simply delicious."

"Good." The answer pleased her from the way her eyes sparkled. "The pasta is almost ready. I'm glad you're here." Jess squeezed her shoulder.

Clare leaned into her. "Me, too." It wasn't the filet mignon and dry martinis she imagined her evening would entail, but the simple meal with Jess felt wonderfully domestic and comforted her in a way no dinner with someone else could.

Jess turned to walk away, but she stopped her with a hand on her arm.

"Speaking of delicious food, I'm supposed to go to dinner at Helen's house on Monday. She's our other dispatcher, and both of us have the night off. She and her husband have me over for dinner every couple of weeks. They own land near here that's been in their family forever. She told me to ask you to come along so she can meet you, if you want, if you're free…if you want to go with me."

Jess appeared amused by her nervous spiel. "Of course. Of course, I'll go with you." She touched her cheek before returning to the small stove.

When it came time to eat, Jess sat beside her. They watched other campers as they enjoyed their meal. Jess had cooked the pasta perfectly, and Clare told her so. She ate with an appetite equivalent to the noise her stomach had been making, even indulging in a second helping.

"Do you want to talk about what's going on?" Jess rubbed her hand up and down her thigh.

Clare pushed her plate away and began tearing her napkin. Jess's hand on her leg sent shivers running up the opposite side of her body.

"Lyn is…I don't even know anymore. I miss my best friend. I miss whom she used to be. She's become so different over the years, but especially lately. I've always thought that eventually, she'd get the hint that I'm not romantically interested in her, but now we're into our second decade of knowing each other, and it seems worse than ever." She slapped a shred that threatened to fly away in the light breeze. "When Dominique and I got together, I thought Lyn finally understood our relationship was, and always would be, platonic. Then, after she died, Lyn started in again, maybe worse than before."

Jess reached over and gathered the scraps of the napkin, both from Clare's hands and from the tabletop. She wadded them together and placed the ball on her plate before taking her hand. "What did she say?"

"She's mad at me for keeping secrets from her. Dominique's cheating came as a surprise, though that isn't the real issue." Clare paused and looked at their hands. "She thinks I'm making poor decisions."

"So, I came up."

She gave a small laugh. "Of course, you came up."

"She doesn't like me."

"No, but she wouldn't like anyone in your position." Clare squeezed her hand and tried to communicate that it wasn't personal. The chess players broke out in laughter. She watched them start another game, arranging pieces on the board like they'd done it thousands of times before. "How long would you guess they've been playing?"

"Oh, I would say they've been playing a long time." Jess wiggled her eyebrows up and down and dragged out the word *playing*. "They're cute. Their names are William and Stan. They introduced themselves earlier."

Clare smiled and studied them for a moment. Would she have someone to share the little pleasures of life with when she was their age? She turned back to Jess and resumed the prior conversation. "The part that makes me the angriest—no, I suppose the saddest—is that she can't be happy for me. Her selfishness won't allow her to see that I'm happier than I've ever been."

"You are?" Jess's voice squeaked.

"Yes. Why?"

Jess blushed, the scarlet splotches even appearing on her neck and chest. "Well, you were considering marriage, weren't you? With your girlfr—with Dominique?"

There was no denying that Clare had loved Dominique. Yet, she'd been young, and in hindsight, the relationship had all the earmarks of first love. This felt different, and she was older and wiser. She placed her hands on Jess's shoulders. "I am happier with you than I've ever been."

Jess's dimples flickered into sight before erupting into a full-blown grin. "I'm happy, too, happier than I've ever been." Her eyes shone bright, her smile brighter.

Clare caressed her neck with her thumbs. Jess closed her eyes right before Clare kissed her.

As they cleaned up, Clare wondered what it would be like to make dinner together, not over a camp stove, but in a real kitchen, in a real home. The image she had wasn't the small house the park provided for her, but somewhere she'd never been. She imagined them cooking together after they returned home from work, laughing as they told each other about their day, nudging and teasing each other in the kitchen they called theirs. The problem was that she didn't know where this scene existed or how to get there. Or if Jess would even want that. Jess said she was happy, but for how long? What if this *was* a summer fling? Clare held her tighter, refusing to entertain the thought.

CHAPTER EIGHTEEN

Clare and Lyn hadn't talked since the steakhouse. Granted, they'd spoken in brief spurts over the radio while working, but not face-to-face. It left Clare feeling strange and unsettled. She knew walking out of the restaurant had been harsh. Lyn was her best friend, and she missed their frequent chats and funny texts. So, to ease the tension, she picked up two iced coffees from the concession stand right before the end of their shifts—an olive branch of sorts—at least until they had a real conversation. She was uncertain what might transpire after that.

Carrying the drinks into the visitor center, she greeted the volunteers out front before heading to the dispatch office in the back. Based on the low-volume crackles coming from the speaker clipped to her shoulder, she knew that Lyn was on the radio before she entered the room. Clare took a seat and waited. Lyn glanced at her, but her expression didn't change.

"Papa Romeo 621, please confirm when the road is open again. Out."

Nicole responded. "Dispatch, roger. Out."

Lyn typed something on her keyboard before pushing the monitor aside and looking at her. "Hi. We're still waiting on the tow trucks."

Clare had heard about the non-injury accident while driving over. It wasn't unusual to wait a good amount of time for a tow truck to make its way from town.

"I brought you an iced coffee." She pushed the drink across the desk.

Lyn accepted it with a small smile. "Thanks. I needed this. It's been a long day, and every time I get two spare seconds to run to the kitchen, I find an empty coffee pot."

Clare grinned, all too aware of her rants against the young people who staffed the visitor center. "Well, you only have ten minutes left before you're finished. At least your day will end on a good note."

Lyn sipped the cold, sweet beverage and rolled her eyes with exaggerated pleasure.

Both of their radios came to life. "Dispatch, this is Papa Romeo 676. Please call me before you sign off. Out."

Lyn shook her head as she spoke into her microphone. "Papa Romeo 676, this is Dispatch. Roger. Out."

"What does Brett want?" Clare scowled. "Isn't he off today?"

She shrugged. "Who knows? There's been some talk about getting us some part-time help or an intern so one of us doesn't have to take a radio home every night. Maybe that?"

"My ears are burning." Helen entered the room. "Oh, hi, dear." She squeezed Clare's shoulder before dropping her tote bag beside her desk.

"Brett wants to chat with me. We were trying to figure out if it was about the interns." Lyn swirled her cup of coffee before taking another sip.

Helen went through her routine of flipping switches and pushing buttons as she brought her workstation to life. "Let's hope. There's not much activity at night, but it would still be nice to be free of the radio more often than we are. Maybe he wants you to train them." She turned to Clare. "I've been doing this almost as long as he's been alive, but he treats me like I'm incompetent when it comes to technology."

Everyone in the room knew that she was anything but incompetent.

"I should leave you." Clare stood up. "She has a phone call to make, and you need to settle in."

"Okay, dear. I look forward to having you and Jess over tomorrow night. We can't wait to meet her."

Clare caught Lyn's head jerk out of the corner of her eye, and Helen did too, or she was being kind, consistent with her personality. "Lyn, we'll have to have you over for dinner the first night we get an intern to cover for us."

She gave a half-smile and nodded. "Sure."

Clare dropped her empty cup in the garbage. "See you tomorrow, Helen. Bye, Lyn." She felt Lyn's eyes on her back as she exited the room, and discomfort clawed at her. Whatever inroads the iced coffee made had melted when Helen had mentioned having her and Jess over for dinner.

❖

"Are you sure this dress is fine?" Jess adjusted the straps of her sundress.

Clare glanced at her. "You look gorgeous, as gorgeous as I said you looked when I picked you up."

She hadn't been fishing for a compliment, only wanting to arrive wearing appropriate attire, but Clare's words still sent a lovely warmth through her.

They left the park and drove for about fifteen minutes. Despite it still being light out, the full moon hovered just above the horizon in front of them.

"Helen lives out here?" Bone-dry dirt and shrub-steppe vegetation covered the ground.

"Yes, they live on a ranch that her husband, Hank, runs. They have quite a few acres. You'll have to ask him how many." Clare turned onto a dirt road that someone had recently graded. Still, the truck bounced and bumped along. "I wouldn't be surprised if most of the land between here and the park is theirs."

Impressed, Jess enjoyed the scenery. Ranching had to be difficult in the arid, desert climate surrounding the park. Modern inventions like irrigation and the ability to purchase hay or grain grown elsewhere must make it possible, otherwise, she couldn't imagine how cattle could find enough vegetation to survive. Clare broke her reverie.

"I think you already know this, but you need to move campsites soon."

Jess sighed. "Yeah, I knew the date was approaching. It was part of the agreement to let me stay the entire summer."

"It's because they don't want people taking advantage of prime locations for extended periods. Campers usually can't occupy a space for more than two weeks. I guess you're special." Clare glanced sideways. "But I already knew that."

She smiled. "How do I get a new campsite?"

"I took the liberty of reserving you one of my favorite spots. It's on the edge of the campground, so you won't have campers behind you as you do now. You'll have more space at the rear of your site to pitch your tent. It's nice and private. It's not across from the lake or anything, but it's a great spot. If you want a site somewhere else, I'd be happy to change the reservation." Clare reached over and took her hand.

"That was kind of you. It sounds nice. Should I stake down my tent again?" Jess smiled sweetly and tried to look innocent.

Clare rolled her eyes and shook her head. "I'm not coming to look for you if you don't."

"Yes, you would." Even Jess was surprised by the low, suggestive tone of her voice.

"You're right." Clare cleared her throat. "I would."

Jess hadn't expected Clare to sound so serious or her voice to tremble as it did. They quietly held hands.

The dirt road turned out to be a driveway. They passed beneath a wooden sign welcoming them to the Rocking G Ranch. Clare pulled up beside a dusty, white Ford F250 and parked. As they exited the vehicle, Jess smelled the telltale scent of ranching in the air. Did ranchers ever become immune to the scent of manure?

An older man stood on the porch and called out to them. "I saw your dust coming up the road. Come on inside, ladies. Helen has cold drinks for you."

Clare led her up the steps with a fleeting touch to the small of her back. A lingering spot of heat remained where Clare's hand had been.

He embraced Clare and kissed her cheek. His weather-worn face looked like he'd spent many summers outdoors.

"Hello, Hank. It's been too long." Clare slipped her arm around Jess's waist. "This is my girlfriend, Jessica Sterling."

Girlfriend. Jess might have expected Clare to introduce her as her girlfriend if she'd thought about it, but she hadn't. Was it too soon to be thinking in those terms? It didn't matter. She was probably grinning like an idiot.

He shook her hand. "So, this is the geologist. I've heard so much about you from Helen."

"You can call me Jess. It's nice to meet you." How had he heard so much? Clare must be close to his wife. The screen door opened.

"Ladies, I'm so glad you're here. Henry, let them come inside out of the heat!" She ushered them into her home. Before Jess could take in her surroundings, Helen enveloped her in a warm hug. "We're so happy to have Clare's someone special join us for dinner."

Jess caught Clare smiling and blushing.

"I brought this for you." Jess offered her the bottle of wine she carried. "Clare said you liked reds."

"Oh, it's lovely. Thank you." She examined the label and gave her a conspiratorial wink. "I do like a little glass every night before bed. It helps me sleep. You're so sweet to bring something, but that wasn't necessary. She should have told you."

"I did. She's stubborn." Clare put her arm around Helen's shoulders and hugged her. "I thought I should at least give her advice on which kind to bring if she's going to bring one anyway."

"Make yourselves comfortable in the family room. I only have a few things left to do."

"Do you need some help?" Jess breathed in the delightful scent of something warm and sweet.

"No, darling. I only need to know what you'd like to drink." She spoke to them over the half-wall that divided the kitchen and family room. "I made some of my special spiked lemonade, or I can open the wine if you prefer. If you want something stronger, Hank would be happy to mix up something for you."

He had settled into a well-loved, leather recliner that was his favorite spot to sit based on the television remotes lined up on the table beside him. She sat next to Clare on the sofa.

"I'll have some of your lemonade, please."

"It's not traditional lemonade, dear. There's alcohol in it. Is that okay?" Helen hesitated, holding a glass and ladle.

"Even better." A little alcohol would help her relax.

"I'll have the same." Clare crossed her long legs. "It smells amazing in here. What are you making?"

"Clare said you weren't a vegetarian, dear. Otherwise, I don't know what I would have made. We tend to be beef eaters around here. Hank smoked tri-tip for us earlier today. I'm warming it up in the oven. I made some twice-baked potatoes and a zucchini gratin with some of the vegetables from my garden. There's a strawberry rhubarb pie in the oven and homemade vanilla ice cream for dessert." Helen handed them their drinks.

Clare laughed at Jess's huge eyes. "It's like this every time. I leave ten pounds heavier."

Hank had reclined, propping his stockinged feet up. His cowboy boots stood by the door. "I knew I wanted to marry her the first time she cooked for me." He smiled and watched Helen return to the kitchen.

"You know what they say, 'The way to a man's heart is through his stomach.'" Helen donned checkered potholders, pulled a pie out of the oven, and set it on the stove. She focused on them, one red and white potholder held in the air. "I suppose it's probably the same for women. Is it?"

Clare smiled at Jess. "I suppose it is. She does make a mean spaghetti."

The way Clare looked at her made her face warm. Even her ears felt hot. She'd never been in a relationship with a woman before, let alone discussed it with people she'd recently met, but to her surprise, she didn't feel uncomfortable having her relationship with Clare be the topic of conversation. She could tell they adored Clare. Relaxing in this situation seemed unimaginable to her earlier in the day, but calmness suffused her. She'd initially agreed to come because she knew it was important to Clare, but to her surprise, she found she was enjoying herself.

After dinner, Clare and Hank retreated to the family room while Jess helped Helen fix dessert. She heard them discussing the current count of his head of cattle in the other room.

"The ice cream is in the freezer, dear, and the scoop is in the second drawer. If you run it under hot water, it will make the job easier."

Jess retrieved both items as Helen set out four dessert plates. She turned on the tap.

"Have you known Clare long?"

"Why, probably close to ten years now. I knew she was special from the day we met." Helen used a sharp knife to cut the pie into six large slices. "Clare loves this park as few rangers do. Others complain about the heat or the aridity." She waved the knife in the air. "They use the park to get a year or two's worth of experience under their belt and move on to greener pastures. Everybody wants to work in Yellowstone or Yosemite. She sees how extraordinary it is. Sometimes, I think she needs the park as much as the park needs her." She pushed two plates of pie across the table so Jess could add scoops of ice cream and lowered her voice. "She's like a daughter to me. We were never able to have kids."

"I'm sorry." It sounded trite and didn't begin to convey how sorry she felt. Here stood two women, one who wanted a child, and one who wanted a mother, yet life had had other plans for both of them.

"What she went through a few years ago was heart-wrenching. It was like watching my child grieve." Helen pulled dessert forks from a drawer. "Do you know about what happened?"

Jess nodded.

"I was working that night. Everything happened so fast. It was over before it started. No one saw it coming. These terrible messages kept coming over the radio. It's one thing to deal with emergencies and disasters daily, but when you know the people involved, it's different."

Helen tried to tuck imaginary strands of hair behind her ears, a habit from when her hair must have been longer. Realizing her error, she adjusted the glasses on her nose instead and lowered her voice. "I don't know how much she told you, but she was on duty that night."

"I didn't know that." Jess's heart sank imagining how catastrophic it must have been for Clare.

"She was already responding to another incident, so she was the last ranger to arrive on the scene, thank God. Barry, a ranger who used to work here, had to intercept her near the road as she got out of her truck. He held her back. Barry quit after what he went through, what he saw that night. I think the thought of continuing to work here with the memories haunting him every time he drove by the site was too much. Such a tragedy. She was a sweet girl."

What could she possibly say? Thankfully, Helen didn't seem to expect anything from her. Helen took the ice cream container from her and returned it to the freezer. Laughter came from the other room.

"She blames herself for not getting there sooner, but it wouldn't have mattered. It all happened so fast."

"Have you told her that?"

"I've told her many times, but I'm not sure she believes me." She pulled out a tray.

Jess looked at Clare as Clare glanced toward the kitchen. Their gazes met. As Hank flipped through a magazine looking for an article, and Helen added napkins to the tray, Clare smiled and winked at her. Their wordless connection across two rooms was enough to take Jess's breath away. They stayed like that until Hank handed Clare the magazine.

Her insides still awhirl, Jess helped load the tray with plates and forks. Helen reached out and held her wrist.

"The reason I'm telling you all this is not to gossip. I'm telling you because she hasn't been the same since." Her brown eyes brightened, appearing more amber than walnut colored. "Until you. You might not realize the difference you've made because you didn't know her before, but there's been a wonderful change in her ever since you came into her life."

Exhilaration rose within her. Jess smiled, hugging Helen to her. "Thank you for telling me that." Knowing she'd affected Clare in that way meant everything. She knew how much Clare meant to her, but to hear from someone else that she'd had an impact on Clare made it more meaningful than she could admit. Maybe they were meant to come into each other's lives.

Clare offered to help load the dishwasher after dessert. Jess stood to help clear plates, but Hank stopped her.

"Come with me to the garage for a minute, kiddo. There's something I want to show you." He went to the front door and slipped his feet into his cowboy boots.

Clare shrugged. Jess followed him through a nondescript door in the kitchen into the garage. He flipped on the lights, and she saw a Toyota Corolla parked next to a riding lawn mower. Tools of all kinds hung on pegboards, and paint cans and boxes sat neatly on sturdy shelving.

"She made me wait until after dinner." He pulled a couple of old cigar boxes from one of the shelves and set them on his workbench. "Forgive the handwriting. I was only seven, not that my handwriting has improved much over the years. Here it is: my rock collection from Ms. Warble's second-grade class."

She studied the open boxes. Each contained a piece of cardboard on which grids had been drawn in pen. Different rocks had been glued within each gridded box and labeled in a child's handwriting. She turned to him and grinned.

"This is amazing." Her fingers ran over calcite, beryl, carnelian, citrine, obsidian, and alabaster, among others.

"Why do you think so many people are fascinated by rocks at one time or another in their lives?" He lifted one of the boxes to peer at it.

"Oh, I don't know. Maybe we're captivated by how beautiful they are in their different ways. They're all rocks, but they're so wonderfully unique."

"Well put, kiddo. I was going to ask you if you wanted them, but she thought I should hold on to them for some odd reason. She's sentimental like that." He walked back to the shelves and pulled another small box from one corner. "Did you know that this land has been in my family for four generations?"

"No. Clare mentioned you had quite a few acres, but not how long you'd owned them."

"My family has been ranching on this land since the late 1800s. Imagine how different life must have been back then." He handed her the small box. "As a young boy, I used to roam all over the place. I often found these."

She lifted the lid and gasped. It contained dozens of arrowheads of assorted sizes and colors.

"I don't find as many as I used to, but I'm not running around like a young, wild thing like I once did, either. I'm riding around in my truck these days, not out forging trails by foot as I did in my youth." He gave her a rueful smile.

"Can I touch them?"

He nodded, so she set the box on the workbench and lifted a few to inspect their chiseled sides and pointed tips.

"They're a sad remnant of times that once were. I suppose my ancestors played their part in that. I do my best to protect and respect these pieces of history that I find on my property. It's not often that I meet someone who has that same kind of respect, but from everything I've heard about you, you do. I'd like you to choose one to keep. You should have a memento of this area to take with you."

"Mr. Greenberg, I couldn't possibly." She shook her head.

"It's Hank, and you choose your favorite. Maybe it will inspire me to get out of my truck and look for more."

She smiled and acquiesced, choosing a sand-colored, medium-sized point with a wide body. It fit perfectly into the palm of her hand. "Thank you, Hank. I'll treasure it."

"The pleasure is mine." He replaced the lid on the box and held out his arm. "After you. Let's see what our girls are up to."

CHAPTER NINETEEN

Clare waited until she knew Lyn had finished her shift and called her.

"Do you have time to go for a walk? I think we should talk." Clare dreaded the conversation that had been years in the making, but they couldn't avoid each other forever. She needed to stop skirting around the issue and deal with it.

"Can we do it on Saturday instead? I wouldn't mind getting a shower and changing out of these clothes."

"I work on Saturday. I traded shifts so I can take Jess to Coeur d' Alene for her birthday in a few weeks."

Clare was excited to stay with Jess at what her parents referred to as their cabin, but the large lakefront home with a boathouse, landscaped gardens, and ninety-foot cedar T-dock looked like a resort-level property minus bellhops and a concierge desk. It did, however, include a resident housekeeper and groundskeeper who took care of the gardens, as well as the lap pool and hot tub.

She didn't want to take Jess there because of its extravagance. Entertaining was more her parents' style. The lake was one of her favorite places, deep blue and gorgeous, with plenty of places to boat. Mostly, she wanted to spend time with Jess away from the park. Why shouldn't they stay at the cabin while her parents traveled? It would be empty otherwise.

Lyn had been to the cabin and knew all this. Before she could say something negative about Jess, Clare spoke again. "Please? Why don't you change now and then you can shower after we walk?"

Lyn sighed. "Fine. What time?"

"Come over when you're ready."

"Okay, I'll see you soon."

Twenty minutes later, Clare heard a key in the lock. "Back here! I'm almost ready. I need to put on my shoes." She sat on her bed and loosened the laces. Lyn appeared in the doorway.

Clare had never walked out on Lyn before. Their few interactions since had been strained. Asking for her key back on top of the forthcoming conversation might make things worse, but this talk was long overdue.

"Which way do you want to walk around the lake?"

Lyn thought about it. "Counterclockwise. The sun won't be in our eyes as long."

They headed out. Now and then, Clare swung her ring of keys around her index finger and caught them in the palm of her hand.

"Even though it's probably uncomfortable for both of us to some degree, I think we should finally talk about it, don't you?" Clare had suggested a walk thinking it might be easier to have the conversation if they didn't have to face each other.

"Probably."

"So, you know what I'm talking about?"

"Yes, I know. It's not like I chose things to be this way." Lyn sounded dejected.

"Neither did I. When I first had an inkling of how you felt, I thought it might eventually pass, but that hasn't happened, so I think we should address it." Clare genuinely felt for her friend.

Lyn cleared her throat. "It's just…You were the prettiest girl on campus. I don't think you have any idea how pretty you were, and you only grew more beautiful. On top of that, you have an amazing personality. You're kind and you're generous. You're funny as hell. I didn't know what to do. Before I knew it, I was in too deep."

"I'm flattered, but—"

"Please, let me finish. You know I tried dating other women. I never felt as much for them as I did for you. There were times I considered asking you…well, every time I thought I had worked up the courage, you ended up in a relationship. My timing was never right. Once you met Dominique, I told myself that was the end of it. I didn't stand a chance. You'd never leave her. I convinced myself I needed to move on. That's when I downloaded that dating app and joined that women's softball team."

While Clare appreciated her honesty, she needed Lyn to understand it wasn't an issue of timing. They weren't right for each other.

Lyn went on. "Then Dominique died. As sad as I was for you, and as much as I grieved my friend, her death reignited that sliver of hope. Of course, I never intended to do anything while you were grieving. I'm not heartless. But I hoped that when you stopped grieving and started to heal, you would notice that it's been me beside you all this time."

"Oh, Lyn. I don't even know what to say." Clare squeezed her hand. "The years have been hard on both of us, haven't they?"

She didn't answer, and Clare didn't look at her. Lyn was crying, and she wanted to give her the space to do so without any added embarrassment. Clare gave her time by talking.

"I care about you. I always have. You're my best friend, and you deserve happiness. You deserve so much more than I could ever give you, even if that's difficult to see right now." She cast a glance at Lyn and noticed Lyn had bowed her head, her gaze focused on the ground at her feet.

"Waiting for me to stop grieving and hoping I'd see you there shouldn't be good enough for you. Waiting for someone to notice you is settling, and you're too big of a catch to settle. You need someone who thinks you hung the moon, and I know you'll find them. You should want someone who can't stop thinking about you, who can't tear their eyes from you. We aren't the right fit." She watched a flock of birds fly low over the lake. "I'll be honest with you, though. You may not find that person here. Maybe you should think about transferring. You could live in a more populated city and date in a place where you have options. We'll always be friends, no matter where we are."

A boat slowly motored past them trying not to create a wake, but still loud enough that Clare waited to speak until the noise faded. She couldn't gauge Lyn's reaction since she'd remained quiet and focused on the ground. Clare pushed up her sunglasses and took a cleansing breath before saying the most difficult part.

"I need you to let me live my life, even if sometimes I make choices you don't like. Lately, I feel like you're on the verge of organizing an intervention for me. I'm an adult, and I need you to let me make my own decisions. I need you to let me live life as I choose to live it. If I choose to be with Jess, that's my choice to make." When silence met her, she glanced at Lyn.

"I'm sorry." Lyn sniffed and straightened her back. "I'm not sorry for falling in love with you. I didn't mean to, and honestly, it's cost me years of my life. But I am sorry for how I've treated Jess and your other girlfriends. I was selfish and jealous. I apologize for that. I do want you to be happy."

"Thank you. That means a lot."

Lyn shook her head, as if in disbelief. "I forgot how beautiful you are when you're in love. I hate to admit it, but you've had that look lately. Even I can see it."

Clare stopped and hugged her. They stood on the side of the road like that, the lake stretched out beside them. Was Lyn right? Was she in love? Was that what this was? Did Jess feel the same way? Clare had been through such a traumatic ordeal. She wasn't sure falling in love with someone she'd met a handful of weeks before was even smart.

Clare didn't know what to say to make things better, but perhaps that wasn't her place. Lyn needed time to adjust, to work through things, to grow accustomed to the fact they would never be more than friends. Maybe Lyn just needed to know she was there for her. It was Lyn who pulled away.

"I need my spare key back, please. It was different when I was single." Clare fiddled with her keys. "Here's yours."

Lyn wordlessly pulled her keys from her pocket. She removed Clare's key, and they exchanged them.

"You understand, right?"

"Sure." Lyn didn't sound convinced.

They walked in silence for a few minutes. Clare could see her house again. The end was in sight for the walk and the difficult conversation.

"What did you decide to do about Brett?" Lyn seemed ready to change the subject.

"I don't know what I want to do yet. But don't worry, I'll deal with it."

He had slept with her girlfriend, and she didn't intend for him to get away with it. She couldn't wait to see his reaction when she informed him that she knew. Did he remember that it was Jess he'd spoken to at the lookout or was she just another pretty face? Would he be shocked or apologetic? Would he deny it? Clare didn't know and wanted to find out. Once they were back from Jess's birthday weekend, she'd talk to him.

CHAPTER TWENTY

Jess unfolded her tablecloth and gave it a shake. The afternoon sunlight poured through the red-and-white-checked fabric as she spread it across the picnic table at her new campsite. It amazed her how much her old site had begun to feel like home, but she had to admit that the new site was so much better. It was spacious, and she didn't have to pitch her tent mere feet from other campers. It had been fine when Tim and Ian had stayed next to her, but a bit awkward at other times. Still, most of her neighboring campers had been friendly, and problems few.

Tires crunched on gravel. Car doors slammed as she bent and chose a few fist-sized rocks from the rubble behind her tent. She carried them to the picnic table and used them to weigh down the corners of her tablecloth. She was a veteran now, and she wasn't going to let the wind get the best of her this time.

Strong arms encircled her from behind and lifted her into the air. She squealed as she tried to see who had her in a bear hug.

"Can't a couple of friends get a hug or are you too busy playing with rocks?" a familiar voice asked. He put her back on solid ground.

She spun around, and Tim and Ian stood before her, grinning widely.

"You're back! What are you doing here?" She hugged them and noticed Ian's car parked at the campsite beside hers.

"We came back to see you." Ian gave her a playful push. "We closed the shop. It's not like anyone gets their hair cut this weekend anyway."

"Labor Day seemed too far away. You would have forgotten us by then." Tim gave her a crooked grin.

"I will never forget you. Is that your campsite?" She pointed to the adjacent site.

Ian grinned. "We had a little help."

"We couldn't reserve a site this late, but Clare put us on top of the list for cancellations and then shuffled things so we could camp next to you." Tim made himself comfortable at the table. "Otherwise, you would have had us as your beloved guests."

"She didn't say a word to me." Clare's surprise made her quite happy.

"She's good at keeping secrets." Ian winked.

"How are things with her?" Tim picked up one of the rocks on the table and turned it over.

"I mean, good, I guess." Jess almost tripped over the fire pit as she took a step backward. She regained her balance and tried to appear nonchalant.

"Head over heels, huh?" Ian grinned.

"We drove halfway across the state to see you, and all you're going to give us is *good*?" Tim pretended to be hurt.

"Do you want a beer?" She opened the cooler.

"Always." Tim held out his hand.

"Hit me." Ian sat next to his brother.

She handed them each a cold can of lager and sat across from them. "It's complicated."

"Let's play a little game. I ask you questions, and you answer them because you're super bad at this." Ian slid his beer to the side, folded his hands, and leaned forward, the picture of seriousness. "Now, have you seen much of Clare since we left?"

She nodded and Tim grinned, happy to be an entertained spectator.

"So, it's safe to say you two are friendly?"

"Yes." She rolled her eyes.

"Have you kissed?" He arched his eyebrows.

Jess squirmed. "Yes."

"Good girl." Ian extended his fist.

She returned the fist bump and added an eye roll.

"Where?" Ian narrowed his eyes.

"On the mouth."

Ian covered his face with his palm. Tim snorted.

"Oh, by the lake." She wanted to crawl in a hole.

"Who kissed whom?"

"She kissed me."

The brothers exchanged glances.

"How many times have you kissed?"

"I don't know. Who keeps count?" They were beginning to annoy her.

"So, more than once." Ian grinned.

"I don't think I like this game." She stole a drink of Tim's beer.

Ian wasn't dissuaded. "Have you had sex?"

She choked. The beer came out of both her nose and mouth. Ian jerked his upper body away from the table to avoid being hit.

"No! Game over!" Jess used the sleeve of her T-shirt to wipe her face.

"I'm surprised she hasn't slept with you already. That was totally sexy. I *really* want to drink this beer now." Tim wrinkled his nose. He dangled the can between his finger and thumb and pretended to examine it.

She burst into laughter and looked at them fondly. "I missed you two." Spending time with Clare had been wonderful, but they'd left an unexpected hole in her life when they left. It felt good to have them back. It was kind of them to surprise her and so like Clare to help them find a campsite at such a late date.

Jess pulled out her cell phone to see if she'd missed any texts from Clare. While looking at her recent contacts, she realized she still hadn't heard from Jackson. It was clear she mattered to him as much as he mattered to her. She didn't care she hadn't heard from him in over a month. It was just a kind of limbo she didn't like. In her mind, it was over. She didn't consider her relationship with Clare—if that's what it was—cheating on him because he no longer played a role in her life. There was no reason to tell Clare about him since he wasn't in the picture. Technically.

"So, what are we doing for the Fourth of July?" Tim rubbed his hands together eagerly.

"They're having a fireworks show at the lake. We could watch and get drunk like any sensible people, and not necessarily in that order." Jess shrugged.

"I like how you think. We should spend the entire day at the lake." Ian elbowed Tim. "I'm sure it will be packed with women in bikinis for us to admire." He nudged Jess. "For you too, Subaru."

She laughed, happy to be included, not that she'd be checking out any women. She still had plenty to think about with the image of Clare in her violet bikini seared into her mind ever since the cliff diving episode. Still—their friendliness, their teasing, their banter—she'd missed them more than she realized.

Her life that had felt so empty at times over the last half-decade felt rich and full, even if it was only temporary. She vowed to enjoy it while it lasted.

❖

Jess was pleased to see that Independence Day had been honored with picture-perfect weather. Clear blue skies and sunshine seemed to ignite the celebratory mood among the people at the park. Children raced around waving small, hand-held flags, and patriotic colors abounded. The occasional solitary scream and blast of a rogue firework marred the day, despite the sun being high in the sky and fireworks banned in the park. The resort situated outside the park's boundary had scheduled the display tonight over the lake.

Carrying a blanket, she and Tim walked past the ranger station to the lake. Ian was going to use the facilities before he drove the cooler of beer and the grill over. As they neared the grassy area near the lakefront, they saw hundreds of people sunbathing, grilling, and swimming. Shade was hard to come by, so they settled for a nice spot with an unobstructed view of the dock across the lake where the fireworks would be set off once darkness fell.

She spread out her blanket, stripped to her bathing suit, and began applying sunscreen. Tim grabbed his T-shirt near the nape of his neck and pulled it off in one swift motion. He ran to the swimming area and jumped in. She watched him swim out and tread water for a while before swimming back. He paused to speak to a young woman dangling her legs off the dock. Her bikini had white stars on a blue background on one breast and red and white stripes on the other.

Jess felt her cell phone vibrate. She wiped the remaining sunscreen onto her legs and pulled it out. Her heart sank when she saw the text was from Ian, not Clare. After giving him directions, she resumed applying the lotion.

"Can I use some of that after I dry off?" Tim motioned to her bottle. He picked up his towel and vigorously rubbed his hair.

"Sure. Ian texted me. He's in the parking lot. He wanted to know where we were."

"I'll go help him." He dropped the towel and took off barefoot in the direction of the parking lot.

Her cell phone vibrated again. Ian needed to relax. She pulled out her phone to text him that Tim was on his way to help, but saw the text was from Clare instead.

I was hoping to watch the fireworks with you after work. If you're busy, I understand.

Jess grinned at her phone and texted back.

I want to watch with you. We're at the lake.

She waited for a response.

My shift ends at 9. I'll need to change.

She texted back.

I'll come get you. You'll never find us. Ppl everywhere

Something heavy hit the ground beside her as Ian dropped the cooler of beer.

"Here." Tim approached her from the opposite side carrying six hot dogs.

"Where did you find these?" She took two off his hands.

"I was talking to a woman from Olympia down at the lake. She's here with some friends, all of whom are women, I might add. When we were coming back with the beer, we ran into them, and they gave us these. They have a ton of food." He took a big bite, and a third of the sandwich disappeared into his mouth.

"That was nice of them. I saw you talking to her. She's pretty."

"Oh, and by the way, you're our cousin from Seattle." He winked at her and wiped mustard off his lip with the back of his hand.

She rolled her eyes, but the comment made her happy. She'd fake being their cousin. Too bad they weren't her cousins. Friends could grow apart, but cousins were always cousins. She missed having a family she could call hers.

The hot dogs hit the spot, but swimming and sunbathing made them ravenous again by late afternoon. They'd planned to get the propane grill from the back of Ian's SUV to make burgers, but once more, the women from Olympia came through.

Melanie, the owner of the patriotic bikini, visited them with her raven-haired friend Britney in tow. After quick introductions, Tim and Ian accepted the invitation to come and share in their barbecue and leaped up to follow them. Jess agreed to join them only after some coaxing.

She followed behind the foursome as they headed toward the smoking grill surrounded by young people under the shade of one of the trees. A second table had been set up to hold all the food that wouldn't fit on the picnic table. A three-layer cake sat in the middle, small paper flags and unlit sparklers decorating the top. Someone had piped rings of red, white, and blue icing up the sides. Feeling a bit alienated, "Cousin" Jess gratefully filled a paper plate from the overloaded picnic table and found a place to sit.

She dived into potato salad, macaroni salad, baked beans, and a veggie burger she'd chosen from the array of choices on the grill. It was the perfect food for a day like this. Tim flirting with Melanie and Ian awkwardly chatting with Britney provided entertainment for her.

As usual, her thoughts drifted to Clare. Summer was flying by, and no matter how much Jess wanted to stall the inevitable, she knew her time remaining would pass quickly.

What would happen when it came time for her to leave? She didn't doubt Clare's love for her job and the park. A fool could see that. Jess also loved her chosen field, and while she found Dry Falls fascinating, the area didn't hold any employment opportunities for her. The population was too small to support the kind of jobs in her field. She needed to be in cities at least the size of Olympia, Yakima, Spokane, or anywhere in King County if she stayed in Washington. Clare lived here, and she lived on the other side of the state. Was there no way around the distance? How would they handle a relationship involving that kind of separation? An eruption of laughter interrupted her melancholy thoughts, and she shook them off. Those were heavy thoughts for later.

After dinner, they enjoyed less swimming and more beer. With the sky nearly dark, Jess pulled her clothing over her swimsuit and left the foursome on her blanket. Fireworks would be starting any minute. Hundreds of people filled the large grassy area, their eyes to the sky in eager anticipation. She weaved through them to her destination and tried not to stumble in her tipsy state.

Clare opened her front door and watched her approach. She didn't seem to care that Jess could see her gaze roam from her face to her feet and back up again, and Jess found she didn't mind her appreciation in the least. It made her tingle all over.

"You're a welcome sight. I've been looking forward to spending time with you all day." She wrapped her arms around Jess's shoulders and briefly hugged her. Jess thought she felt a kiss on her hair.

"I missed you today. The guys met some women, and I've been the odd one out all day."

They stood in the open doorway. Clare hooked her finger under the strap of Jess's swimsuit visible at her neckline and ran it over her collarbone. "I remember this suit. I like the way it looks on you."

Multiple alcoholic beverages, the subtle tug, and Clare's honey-like voice sent a twinge of arousal through her that left Jess weak-kneed. She put her hand on the doorframe and tried to breathe normally.

"Are you a little drunk?" Clare gave her a sly smile.

"A little. Are you tired after working all day?"

"A little, but I want to watch fireworks with you."

"We should go. They'll be starting soon." Yes, going back now was best. Standing here with Clare, with her flirting and little touches, was a bad idea.

"I'll follow you." With an amused look, Clare picked up a folded blanket from the end of her couch.

"Do you need to bring your radio in case there's a fire?" Jess knew people might set off illegal fireworks, not caring they were within a state park.

"No." Clare held her head higher. "I'm all yours."

She grinned. The gesture meant a lot, especially on a night like tonight.

Taking Clare's hand, Jess led the way back to the group and introduced Clare to Melanie and Britney. Clare spread out her blanket. Jess sat next to her and leaned back. She propped herself up with her arms, their shoulders touching.

"Do you two want beers?" Tim opened the cooler.

They both accepted, and Melanie passed cold beers to them.

"I'm happy you had tonight off." Jess lowered her voice so only Clare could hear.

Clare nestled her beer in the grass. Her smile lit up her eyes. "I traded shifts."

"Everybody needs a sparkler!" With plenty of exuberance, Britney handed a small metal rod to each of them and lit Ian's with her lighter.

They passed along the flame. Clare lit Jess's sparkler, cupping her hand while she did. The sparklers sputtered and flashed, the crackling and spitting sound creating a symphony of sizzle. Jess waved her sparkler in wide arcs above her head. She wrote *Clare* in the night sky like a lovesick teen with a massive crush. The singular word floated above her, emblazoned on her retina or in her mind's eye, she couldn't be sure. Maybe it was all the beer she'd had throughout the day. She glanced at Clare to see if she'd been too obvious, but Clare was busy spinning circles with her sparkler with a happy smile on her face.

A piercing cry foretold of the red burst that exploded above them, showering fiery flashes of light outward in all directions. Somewhere, "America the Beautiful" began playing. The fireworks show had begun. With her sparkler's life extinguished, she lay back on the blanket, and Clare did the same. Jess reached over and intertwined their fingers.

She liked how Clare held her hand tenderly with little squeezes or caresses. It was so different from Jackson, who crushed her fingers in his grasp. Anyway, she didn't want to think about him now. Or ever. She noticed a uniformed ranger on the outskirts of the crowd, and she recalled what Clare had said.

"Thank you for trading shifts." She smiled, looking at Clare. Flashes of colored lights lit up the sky, and Jess saw the reflections in Clare's eyes.

"I didn't want to miss the fireworks." She leaned so close to Jess's ear that her breath tickled. "I couldn't imagine not spending at least part of the day with you."

Jess's heart felt like a firework, careening through the sky, ready to burst. She knew there was no more precious gift than someone's time and attention, and she gave Clare's hand a little squeeze in thanks.

People exclaimed loudly as a particularly large white firework exploded right above them, its trailing debris-like fingers reaching for the ground. Beside them, the foursome oohed and ahhed. She glanced over and noticed Tim had his arm around Melanie.

"All day long, I felt…" How could Jess explain what she had a sudden desire to express? Lonely in a crowd? Alone among friends? "Well, I just wished you were with me."

"Come here." Clare welcomed her into the crook of her arm. "I'm here now." She kissed Jess's temple. They watched the brilliant display above them.

When it was all over, she gave Clare a long, lingering kiss before she got in the car for the short ride to her campsite. Although she wanted nothing more than to spend the night in Clare's arms, she respected that Clare wasn't ready. Considering what she'd been through, and all that she'd shared with Jess about her past, it made sense she needed some time. When they eventually had sex, Jess wanted her to be ready.

Maybe it was the alcohol, or maybe she was braver than she thought, but Jess was ready. It didn't mean she wasn't nervous. It didn't mean she had confidence in her skills. She didn't even know if she had skills. The thought of Clare teaching her things made her entire body tingle. She wasn't sure she'd be any good or would be able to give Clare what she needed, but she certainly wanted to try. To share something so incredibly intimate, to show Clare how she felt without words, to touch Clare and to have Clare touch her in return.

Yes, Jess was ready.

CHAPTER TWENTY-ONE

C lare rolled up to Jess's campsite on her bright yellow-and-black striped bicycle.

"Did you steal that from a construction zone?" Jess looked amused.

"I want the idiots driving on these roads to be able to see me." She dismounted.

"Oh, they'll see you. I think I'm getting dizzy." Jess swayed, her hand pressed to her head.

Clare rolled her eyes. "Did they leave?" She referred to Tim and Ian. Clare had enjoyed getting to know them. They'd taken Jess under their wings like a little sister, and that scored them big points in her book.

"About an hour ago. I need to take this amazing piece of machinery for a spin." Jess took the handlebars from her grasp. "Every little bulldozer-loving child in this campground is going to be jealous." She pedaled off.

This time, Clare laughed aloud as she watched Jess pedal to the end of the row and make a wide turn. Clare liked when she teased her. Jess rode back and circled her twice. Clare tried to grab the handlebars.

"I'm a bumblebee!"

Clare laughed and shook her head. "Now you're making *me* dizzy. It's a good thing I find you amusing. Grab your bike. I want to show you something."

"Okay." Jess returned Clare's bike and righted hers from where she'd propped it against the picnic table. "Do I need anything?"

She shook her head. "Follow me." Clare swung her leg over the seat and pedaled away.

Jess followed her into the park as the sun dipped below the rim of the canyon. Cars and cyclists passed them going in the opposite direction. The last sliver of sunlight split the steel-colored clouds and glinted off the top of Umatilla Rock.

"Slow down. We're stopping here." Clare braked and jumped off her bike. She walked her bicycle over to a Volkswagen-sized rock about forty feet from the road. She leaned it against the boulder and motioned for Jess to do the same.

"Are we leaving them here?" Jess looked around.

"Yes, can you lock them together? I'm sure they'll be fine, but if something happens to them, I'll replace your bike."

Jess bent and unwound the lock beneath her seat. She passed it through tires and frames and spun the combination closed.

"We need to walk a bit." Clare took her hand.

"Then why did we leave the bikes?"

"They're too visible. Especially mine."

"Why do we have to be covert?" Jess looked confused.

Clare stopped and faced her. "I haven't shown anyone else what I'm about to show you."

Jess raised her eyebrows, her eyes wide. "Oh."

"I know it's a strange request, but will you promise not to tell anyone? I know I'm asking you to give your word without giving you much information, but it's important to me."

Jess nodded. "I promise."

"Thank you." Clare smiled.

Over the last few weeks, she realized she trusted Jess, maybe more than she'd trusted anyone in years. Jess was sincere, had a good heart, and she seemed to reciprocate Clare's feelings. So, under the ashen sky, on a midsummer July evening, she'd give her a gift.

They walked another five minutes. Jess seemed to be admiring the darkening dusky-purple clouds in the distance when Clare spoke.

"Do you know what geocaching is?"

"Sure, I used to do it all the time as a kid."

"Well, about four years ago, I started doing a bit of geocaching to entertain myself, especially in the off-season. I was looking for one that I had read about online. It was supposed to be right about here." Clare stopped. A large pile of rocks stood before them. Various-sized basalt pillars slumped against each other, partially buried under dirt and soil deposited by the elements. Where wind, water, and wildlife had lodged dirt and seeds between them, sagebrush and other local vegetation had grown. "I eventually found the cache under that rock." Clare pointed to a horizontal basalt pillar about the size of a kitchen table. "However, initially I thought it was over here." She turned and pointed to much larger pillars and boulders, their edges rounded over time.

"Okay." Jess seemed unsure of her point.

"I'm going to show you where I had been looking, and what I found." Clare winked at her. She felt the same burst of excitement as she had that memorable day.

They climbed over the first couple of boulders on the eastern edge of the conglomeration. The larger pillars and rocks blocked their view of the visitor center and the western edge of the canyon. Where two large pillars came together in a V-shape, Clare sat against one pillar and planted her feet against the other. Doing a makeshift crabwalk, she moved farther into the crevice. Jess followed her using the same method.

"I was right about here, and I wanted to get up there." Clare pointed at a little crevice at the top of the tallest rock. "I was sure it was up there. It was in the high nineties that day, and I stopped here to rest and drink some water. That's when I noticed a cool breeze on the underside of my legs." She continued to scoot into the crevice. When she reached what looked to be the end, she dropped over the edge into a low space that hadn't been visible. Only her head showed from where Jess remained. "The cool air was coming from this bush."

Jess inched closer. Clare held out her hand and helped her down into the tiny space mostly occupied by a large sagebrush.

"Oh, I do feel the breeze."

"Look." Clare yanked the sagebrush to the side to show her a dark hole between the rocks slightly larger than the mouth of a kitchen garbage can. It extended both backward and downward from where they stood, a rocky chute heading into darkness.

Jess's mouth hung open. Clare released the brush, and it sprang back into place, obscuring the hole.

"Are you up for it? I can hold it back for you. Slide yourself in and wait for me. There's a horizontal pillar that extends for a few feet before it drops off. You can take this." Clare pulled a small flashlight from her pocket.

"You're kidding me." Jess had yet to move.

"Are you saying you don't want to see it?" Worry crept in. Had she guessed wrong? Was Jess not interested?

"I absolutely want to see it. You found a secret cave!" Jess jumped in place, excitement written all over her face.

Clare's heart swooped. "Let's get inside before someone spots us. I always try to come at twilight to hide my activity."

"The park doesn't know about it? What about your colleagues?" Jess knelt in front of the brush.

"Not that I know of."

Clare pulled the bush to the side, and the spicy, bitter smell of the crushed leaves surrounded them. Jess slid her feet into the hole and took the flashlight. Her head disappeared. Clare followed her, entering the cave as she'd done so many times before. The brush snapped back into position behind her.

Once inside, her eyes adjusted. Jess had made room for her, so they sat side by side on the basalt bench. The air inside the cave was cooler, and the organic, musty scent of the interior of the cave replaced the smell of sagebrush.

"I left a small notebook on my second visit, but to date, the only name in it is mine."

"Not even your girlfriend's?" Jess shined the flashlight's beam in front of them. It wasn't strong enough to reach the end of the cave.

Clare contemplated her answer. "No, I never told her about it. It never felt right for some reason. I used to come here when I wanted to be alone or when I was upset. I've spent a good deal of time here the last few years."

Jess reached out and squeezed her hand.

"Give me a second." Clare swung her legs over the edge of the pillar and dropped to the floor of the cave. Jess followed her with the flashlight's beam, but she didn't need it. She could make her way around the cave blindfolded.

The scratch and hiss of a wooden match became a bright flame. Warm light followed as she carried a long taper from one votive to another. They glowed along the cave's walls, the flames illuminating wax that had sagged and dripped over time. This wasn't the first time she'd used the candles.

Smiling, Jess dropped to the cave's floor. Clare watched as she examined the interior. Almost identical to the Lake Lenore Caves, this cave was longer than it was wide and about twenty feet long. They'd entered near one end. Jess reached up, running her hands over the sharp rocks comprising the walls and ceiling. The ground was less angular. Water had deposited soil in the cave, creating a fairly even surface for them to stand, though it was strewn with occasional rocks.

"You're smiling." She'd been watching Jess explore, her flashlight-free hand never resting, always touching and assessing the rocky surface.

Jess came toward her. "I'm smiling because I'm happy. Thank you for sharing this with me. It means a lot." The candlelight flickered over her cheekbones.

Clare couldn't remember if she'd ever looked so beautiful. Her hair appeared almost black, her eyes, too. Her gaze dropped to Jess's lips, slightly parted. Jess leaned forward and expressed her gratitude with her mouth, tantalizing her with each sweep of her tongue across her lips until Clare gave her access. The kiss was arousing, stirring her into a frenzy of want and need. Jess shoved the flashlight in her pocket. Her hands seemed to be everywhere.

Clare felt herself losing control. With restraint she was unaware she possessed, she pressed her forehead to Jess's. "Wait." Her voice sounded husky and strange.

A sharp clap of thunder came from the entrance and echoed through the cave. They both jumped.

"I want to show you one more thing before we leave, and we better do so soon. I thought the rain wasn't supposed to start until around midnight." Clare pulled her toward the far end of the cave.

Jess followed her. The end of the cave tapered until the ceiling met the floor. Where they could still stand upright, an outcrop of rock jutted out above their heads. Clare aimed her flashlight's beam into the crevice. She reached in and pulled something out.

"That better not be a spider or snake." Jess's warning was filled with fear.

Clare laughed. "It's inanimate. Here." She pressed a small woven basket no bigger than half a grapefruit into Jess's palm. Someone had woven the delicate basket with two types of thin reeds, their mahogany and chestnut colors creating concentric stripes. No spaces existed between the fibers. It looked like it could hold water. It was a work of art.

"Am I holding what I think I'm holding? Is this Native American?" Jess ran her fingers around the rim of the basket and along its sides.

"I think so. They found artifacts like this in other caves. Someone hid it or put it on that ledge for safekeeping." Clare watched her pick up one of the tiny contents of the basket. "Do you know what those are?"

Jess examined the three cream-colored items. They were rough-hewn and shaped like a checkmark. "Are they fishhooks?"

"That was my guess." Clare picked one up. "I think they're bone or maybe shell."

"I'd guess antler or bone. I think it's too porous to be a shell." Jess felt one between her thumb and forefinger. She grinned. "I wonder how long ago the last person touched this before you found it."

Clare shrugged. "With your knowledge, you could make an educated guess before I could. A long time ago, that much is certain." She accepted the basket from her and returned it to its hiding place. "Do you want to sign the notebook before we leave?"

"Of course, I do."

A clap of thunder punctuated her sentence, the noise louder than the first one. Near the entrance, Jess picked up the notebook and pen. She opened to the first page and signed her name and the date below Clare's entry more than four years prior. It felt special to see their names together on the page.

They stood facing each other, only looking, not touching. Clare knew she shouldn't, not here. The air felt heavy, like it might ignite if one of them moved. It seemed like Jess felt it, too, her chest visibly rising and falling with each breath.

"We should go."

Jess nodded.

Clare made a circuit of the cave, blowing out candles as she went. They exited the cave sans flashlights so as not to draw attention. She made sure the sagebrush covered the entrance behind them.

Rumbling thunder, sheet lightning, and a vicious wind accompanied them on their brisk walk back to the bikes. By the time Jess unlocked the bicycles, larger droplets pelted her from above as her hair whipped and stung her face.

Before she could right her bike, Clare pulled Jess against her and kissed her like the world was ending. "Stay with me tonight."

Her passionate plea made her voice sound an octave lower than usual. Raindrops soaked and trailed along the strands of hair plastered to her forehead before they ran down her face or the wind whisked them off. She saw the answer in the spark of desire in Jess's eyes even before she spoke.

"Yes."

They held flashlights against their handlebars as they rode, the slate sky above rumbling and foreboding. The shrill sound of the wind through the canyon raced them.

They dropped bicycles in the driveway without a second thought. Their muddy shoes landed on the small porch with soggy-sounding thuds. They hurried inside as the storm began to rage.

CHAPTER TWENTY-TWO

L arge drops pelted the windows with the sound of a hundred Trojan arrows bombarding Achilles' shield. Outside, the wind howled. Tree branches screeched and scraped against the siding. Thunder boomed.

The storm, despite its ferocity, was not Clare's focus.

Jess stood on the threshold of her bedroom, her drenched clothing clinging to her body, wet hair stuck to her forehead and neck.

"Come here."

Jess took a few tentative steps. "I'm a mess." She pushed her hair from her face. She was breathing heavily, though they hadn't biked far.

"You're gorgeous." Clare held her by her hips. "I've never wanted you more."

Jess's eyes grew dark, a darker green than Clare had ever seen them. Her gaze fell to Jess's parted lips, full and soft. Clare touched Jess's cheek, barely grazing the tender skin below her eye where her blush always appeared first. "Have you ever been with a woman?" She presumed she knew the answer, but she had to ask.

Jess shook her head, breaking eye contact. "Does that bother you?"

"No." The magnitude of the affection she felt for Jess was ridiculous. Her chest felt like it might burst. "No."

Clare would go slow, let *her* set the pace. Jess's comfort and pleasure were paramount, especially this first time. She wanted to show Jess how beautiful being with a woman could be. It had been quite some time for her, too. She hoped she remembered how. Had things changed? Maybe she should have googled it.

Clare had never wanted anything, anyone, so much. It occurred to her that it wasn't only sex she wanted. She wanted intimacy, to share things with Jess, to experience things together, just the two of them. She wanted to fall asleep every night counting Jess's eyelashes and wake up to her warmth pressed against her. Her emotions overwhelmed her. Yes, what she felt for Jess was more than just about sex.

Clare leaned in, their lips a breath apart, not quite touching. Rocking onto her toes, Jess pressed against her. Their mouths met, warm and soft. Despite her skyrocketing arousal, the kiss was so sweet, so languid, and so unhurried that it brought tears to her eyes. They tentatively tasted and tempted, and their tongues moved together with unpracticed ease. When Jess moaned into her mouth, she tugged her until their bodies pressed firmly against one another.

Clare needed to touch her, peel off her wet clothes so she could feel the warmth of her skin, revel in its softness, and feel every rise and fall as her hands glided over Jess's curves. She lifted Jess's shirt and spread her hands over her ribs, the skin thin and taut there, not baby soft like her stomach where Clare's brushing thumb made her gasp. Clare reached higher and traced the curve of her breast. Jess jumped, her fingers digging into Clare's arms.

She tasted like rain as Clare kissed along her jaw. Clare gently sucked at the delicate skin of her neck. "Oh, my God. Your pulse is racing." She pulled back and saw the alarm in Jess's eyes.

"I'm sorry. I can't catch my breath." Jess shook her head and gulped air.

"You're shaking."

"I don't know what's going on." Jess paced back and forth.

"You're hyperventilating. Take some slow, deep breaths." Clare sat on the bed and urged Jess to sit beside her. They stayed like that, Clare gently rubbing her back until she breathed easier.

"I'm going to leave you for a few seconds to get you some water. I'll be right back." Clare dashed to the kitchen. She didn't understand why this was happening when they'd been so close. Still, her concern for Jess far outweighed any disappointment she felt. She needed Jess to be all right before anything happened. Clare needed her to feel safe. She hurried back and handed her an opened bottle of water.

Jess drank. Her eyes watered. "I'm so sorry."

"Shhh. Don't be. Let's make sure you're okay." She sat beside her, unsure what to do, tentatively resting her hand between Jess's shoulder blades.

"I don't understand what's happening. I want this. I do." Jess's hand still clutched at her chest.

"Are you in pain?" What if it was a heart attack and not a panic attack?

"No, not pain. More like…anxiety."

"There's no pressure, okay? I'd never pressure you. Making sure you're okay is all I care about. Nothing else matters."

"I wanted to be with you tonight." It came out like a whimper.

"You are with me." Clare tried to console her. "I'm not going anywhere. Whatever happens, you can stay here with me tonight." She gave her a buoyant smile and felt her neck. Jess's pulse was quick but no longer raced. Clare brushed back her damp hair and kissed her cheek.

Jess leaned against her shoulder. "I'm sorry I ruined everything."

Clare kissed her forehead. "You didn't ruin anything." She rose and switched off the light, turning on the soft light of her bedside lamp instead. She lay on one side of the bed and patted the spot beside her. "I won't touch you if you don't want me to."

Jess reclined, then turned and faced her. She gave a short laugh. "That's the thing. I *do* want that."

Clare chuckled. Jess's breathing sounded normal, but she still had a bit of a deer-in-the-headlights look about her, and her hands still trembled.

"I suppose I'm a bit more nervous than I thought." Jess's skin looked pale, almost translucent. Her gaze darted around the room. "I don't…I don't have any experience with this."

Clare ran her fingers through Jess's hair before settling her hand on her waist. "It's okay to be nervous, but I want you to feel safe. We don't have to do anything you don't want to do. I'm happy simply being with you. You can borrow some pajamas and stay here tonight." She paused. "We could talk. We could talk about…rocks." Clare winked.

Jess laughed. "No, I do not want to talk about rocks." The color came back to her face. "I love rocks as much as the next person, but—"

"You love rocks *more* than the next person." Clare grinned.

"Yes, I suppose I do." She became serious once again, her gaze traveling over Clare's neck and chest. "But I would much rather talk about how irresistible you look with this shirt clinging to you." She reached out, her fingers tracing the vee of Clare's shirt to where it ended between her breasts.

Clare's breath hitched at her touch. Jess's fingers felt cool against her warm skin, and when Jess raised her head, she looked at her with huge, hungry eyes. Her gaze dropped again, and she cupped Clare's breast. Her thumb brushed over her taut nipple through the thin fabric.

Clare's breaths came in short little gasps. The sensation of Jess's hand on her breast was more intense than she expected. Clare looked at her, her gorgeous face aglow in the soft light. She knew if it were to go further, the ball was in Jess's court. *Her* body hummed with enough energy to power the freaking dam, but she'd rein it in, if necessary.

Jess traced Clare's lower lip with her finger. "So soft," she murmured. Her eyes fluttered close. She hovered close, and then their lips met. It was unlike any other kiss they'd shared. It was Clare who moaned. There would be no turning back now.

Clare grasped her hip. Jess rolled on top of her, the weight of her welcome, a small pleasure that Clare hadn't realized she missed. She felt like she'd been floating through life for more than two years, but Jess anchored her against the outgoing tide that threatened to sweep her away. Everything was different when she was with Jess. She slid her hand up Jess's smooth thigh and only stopped at the hem of her shorts. Jess reached under her shirt, her hand working its way under the cup of her bra. Clare blinked, her mind trying to reconcile what her body was finally feeling. Jess was touching her, at last.

Kissing Jess was a surreal experience. Clare couldn't get enough. She wanted to consume her and be consumed in return, but she couldn't succumb so quickly. Not yet. She had plans. Her first order of business was ridding them of their wet clothing.

Clare rolled them so she was on top, loose curls partially obscuring her vision. "Is this okay?"

Jess nodded, her eyes bright and welcoming.

Clare kissed her again, then sat back and removed first her shirt and then Jess's. She left kisses across her chest, over her bra, nudging her nipples with her lips through the material, loving how Jess pushed up into her and skimmed her hands over her sides.

Their mouths met again before she moved her lips to Jess's neck. Clare turned her over on her stomach without her lips ever leaving her skin. She undid Jess's bra and slid her hand around to cup her breast as she licked and sucked the delicate skin of her neck. Jess moaned, and the simple sound did things to her. Clare turned her over again.

The sight before her was stunning. Jess's breasts rose gently, creamy white in contrast to the rest of her sun-kissed skin and tipped in pink. "You're so beautiful."

Jess sat up, tracing where Clare's skin met the edge of her bra. She felt intoxicated by Jess's gentle, timid touches, by the kisses atop her breasts.

"You can take it off." The words came out hoarse and needy. Arousal coursed through her like the waters that once cascaded over the falls at breakneck speed, but she needed to slow things. No one had touched her like this in over two years, but if it meant assuring that Jess felt safe and comfortable, she'd happily go as slow as needed. She wanted to make sure Jess's pleasure remained high and her anxiety low. Clare would do most anything for her.

Jess leaned forward, trying to work the clasp at Clare's back. Her brows furrowed. "This is harder when it's not your own."

"Got it?" She chuckled and tried to help as they fumbled like teenagers.

Jess pulled her bra off slowly, her gaze roaming from breast to breast. Her hand and tongue replaced the fabric of the discarded garment. Jess touched her gently, with reverence. She took a nipple into her mouth and sucked.

It was too much. Clare closed her eyes, lost in the sensation. Shockwaves shot through her. Jess's nimble fingers on her other breast forced her to extricate herself.

She stood and removed the rest of her clothing. She watched Jess's eyes widen as she slid her underwear over her hips. Kneeling, she peeled off the rest of Jess's clothing, too. She stretched out atop her, both now naked, their skin bathed in the soft light of the lamp.

"Are you okay?" Clare searched her face for any signs of panic. Jess's eyes, usually bright and clear, now appeared hazy and dark.

Jess smiled and nodded. "More than okay. I'll let you know if… if I feel anything different than what you're doing to me, what I'm supposed to feel." She looked at where their breasts pressed together.

Clare wasn't the only one feeling the desire, the need, the ache for more. Jess surged upward again, searching for her mouth. This time, Clare didn't hold back when she kissed her. She touched the soft curve of her breasts, such a stark contrast to her nipples, tight and hard. She felt Jess press into her, her hands on her back pulling her closer.

She'd thought about their first time more than once, and the beginning stages of their actual lovemaking lacked the frantic, tearing-off of clothing Clare had always imagined it would entail. Instead, it possessed a steady tempo all its own, in part due to her desire to assure Jess's comfort, but also because she wanted to savor every second of their first time together that they could never quite re-create.

Clare dragged her lips and her tongue, over Jess's neck and chest. She kissed the swell of her breast, soft yet firm. Clare learned what Jess liked based on the little sounds she made. She kissed and touched her until Jess writhed with pleasure and anticipation.

Between breathy gasps, Jess urged her lower, hands on her shoulders. "I need you." Desire laced her voice. "And don't ask me again if I'm okay."

Clare smiled against her breast. She licked a wet trail as she slid downward and reached her hand between them. When she touched her, Jess closed her eyes with a soft moan.

Based on the warm slickness that greeted her, she seemed more than ready. Clare shifted between her legs. Jess cupped her face, then tucked errant strands of hair behind her ear.

Clare took a moment to look at her, truly look at her. Jess was gorgeous, naked, and spread out beneath her looking more stunning than she could have ever imagined. She wanted to make her feel everything, give her everything, all night long. Clare closed her eyes and tasted her. Jess's warmth, wetness, and scent surrounded her.

"Can I be inside you?" She kissed Jess's hip bone and waited for her answer.

Jess nodded, then smiled.

When Clare filled her, Jess's eyes closed. She released a soft, "Oh," and pressed her hands into the mattress. She began to move. When Clare curled her fingers, she heard the gasps, the breathy moans, the expletives, and the prayers Jess cried out. She'd never been so aroused or filled with so much affection. It was Clare's body that clenched when Jess cried out for more. This was how it was supposed to feel. Through her touch, Clare hoped to convey the love that ran like an undercurrent through their intimate act.

Clare could feel Jess's muscles tense and her breathing quicken as she got close. Jess writhed and squirmed, clutching at Clare's shoulders, her hair, and the sheets.

Clare raised her head and waited until Jess looked at her. "You can let go now. I got you." She found Jess's hand, laced their fingers together, and lowered her head again.

That was all Jess needed. Like the great lake breaching the dam, her orgasm appeared to sweep through her with tremendous force. Jess arched, a cry caught in her throat. Clare took her high, let her ride it out, and then brought her down.

Sticky with perspiration and breathing hard, Jess sagged into the mattress. Clare left a kiss on her inner thigh and climbed up to lay beside her. She kissed her softly.

"Beautiful, just beautiful," Clare whispered. Lightning lit up the room.

Jess smiled, looking happy and sleepy. A great boom of thunder shook the windowpane.

Clare pulled her close, wrapping her arms and legs around her. Jess nuzzled her face into her neck. Her hair smelled like rain. It had been perfect, so perfect. If Clare had known how she'd feel at this moment, she wouldn't have waited so long. Her body hummed with arousal, but the emotional high she rode was far more powerful.

She'd often felt like a husk, so fragile that her shell would disintegrate in the wind like an insect's molted carcass. The events of the last two years of her life had left her as empty as a honeycomb, her wax caps scraped off by life's cruel beekeeper. Her ability to trust and her ability to love had oozed and drained with every tear shed until nothing remained except the stickiest remnants clinging to paper-thin walls, a reminder of her once-full existence.

Yet when she was with Jess, Jess filled her. Jess held her together. Jess, her anchor, her well, and her stores. She made Clare feel whole again. She made her unafraid. With Jess, she felt loved. With Jess, she loved again.

Jess rolled on top of her and sat up, tossing her hair from her face. Her knees rested on either side of Clare's thighs. She openly gazed at all of her.

Clare didn't usually like being the object of scrutiny, but this felt different. She let Jess look, unhurried. Then Jess used her delicate hands on Clare's damp body just as she had on the sides of the caves, her fingers brushing over Clare's skin as if trying to memorize every contour, her lips and tongue worshiping every dip and curve.

It usually took Clare some time to reach orgasm. It wouldn't tonight. It had never felt like this, like she might combust at any moment if Jess didn't touch her. She didn't have to wait long. Looking at her, Jess reached between her legs.

"Yes. Yes, just like that." Clare's gasps filled the room. She understood then that she stood in Jess's spotlight, bathed in the light that Jess shined only for her. She was Jess's sole focus, and nothing else existed.

What sense of timing and control Clare had somehow managed until then vanished. She was unprepared for Jess's eagerness and enthusiasm. Jess went about her beloved task with fervor, the actions of her inexperienced fingers and tongue wonderfully chaotic and erratic, causing Clare to hurl out of control. It was entirely unexpected. She couldn't have slowed it if she tried. The powerful orgasm left her calling out against the wind.

Chapter Twenty-three

C lare smiled as she pushed the lawn mower, recalling the long night and morning; Jess on top of her, head thrown back, her body illuminated by lightning. Jess, sitting on her kitchen counter in her robe, Clare standing between her legs, both eating from a single pint of ice cream at four in the morning. Jess, standing with her hands behind her back, leaning on the shower wall with a look that made them run out of hot water. Jess in her bed, legs wrapped around her, hands in her hair a half hour later.

They hadn't slept much, but at noon, they agreed to get up. They each made it through half a piece of toast before leaving a trail of clothing back to the bedroom. Abandoned cups of coffee grew cold on the table.

Midafternoon arrived, and responsibilities called. As much as Clare hated to be away from Jess for a single minute, maintaining the lawn on the state park's house was part of her contract, and she needed to mow it before she returned to work. She'd neglected it too long.

Sweat collected between her breasts. She turned the mower around and saw the end in sight. She had one more strip of grass to mow before she could get out of the heat. Halfway to the end, a state park truck pulled up beside her on the wrong side of the road. Her stomach plummeted.

Brett leaned out the truck's window and called out to her.

She cut the lawn mower's motor. She was annoyed at having to stop when she was so close to finishing. Her unadulterated distaste for him had grown exponentially after she learned that he'd been having an affair with Dominique. She wiped the sweat off her brow.

"Hey there, gorgeous."

"What do you need?" She regarded him coolly as she stood with one hand on the mower, one hand on her hip. Living within the park took its toll on her work-life balance. She found it difficult to get a break from her coworkers on her off days without having to leave the park. With colleagues she was friendly with, it wasn't a problem. With him, it was.

"You were out late the other night." He winked like they shared a secret. "I was wondering what you were up to."

"What do you mean?" She scowled, not in the mood to talk to him, or at least not until they had the serious conversation they needed to have.

"I saw your bike up in the park. I looked around for you and your little bike buddy, but you were nowhere to be seen."

Her scowl deepened, but either he missed it, or her sunglasses hid it. "How do you know what my bike looks like?"

He laughed. "A bike like that? I'd remember."

"What I mean is, I haven't ridden my bike in almost four years. It's been in storage. And you've worked here for what? Three years? I'm not certain how you would have seen it." She studied him as confusion started to creep into his expression.

"Oh, uh, you showed me your spare room that one time, and that's when I saw it." He yawned in an exaggerated fashion. It appeared to be a nervous tic.

"I see." She froze, considering what to do.

Jess burst out her front door holding a glass garnished with a lemon wheel and tinkling with ice cubes. "I brought you a lemonade. It's ninety degrees out. Are you finished?" The screen door swung and banged shut behind her. When she saw Brett, she slowed but continued to walk toward them.

"I didn't realize you had company." He grabbed his cell phone that hadn't made a sound and glanced at the screen. "I need to go take care of this." He slipped on his sunglasses and took off, leaving divots on the edge of her lawn.

"Thank you. I didn't know I had lemonade." She sipped the refreshing drink and tried to calm her nerves as she watched his truck recede.

"You didn't, but you had lemons and sugar." Jess shrugged and glanced down the road. "What did he want?"

"I'm not sure, but you won't believe what happened." Clare offered Jess some lemonade, but she shook her head. "He commented on seeing my bike in the park the other night."

"Are we not allowed to bike in the park that late?"

"That's not the interesting part. As far as I know, he's never seen my bike, yet somehow, he recognized it. I remember the last time I rode it because I hit a rock and went over the handlebars. I fractured my wrist. That was four years ago. I've been hesitant to ride it ever since."

"Could he have seen it before your accident? You must admit, it is…" She giggled and searched for a word. "…unique."

"He didn't work here four years ago. When I told him that it had been in storage—which means I keep it in the spare bedroom that used to be Dominique's—he told me that I had shown him the room once. The room contains a bed, bikes, some winter clothes, and my suitcases. I rarely ever go in there. I promise you that I can recall every instance he's been in my house for any reason, and I've never shown him that room or even opened it in front of him." She watched Jess process the information.

"Dominique."

"Yes." She stared at the ice cubes in her glass. "In my own damn home."

"What did you say to him?" Jess trailed her fingers down her arm before taking the empty glass from her.

"I didn't have a chance. He saw you and drove off."

"I'm sure he realizes he said too much to me that first day. It probably never occurred to him that we might become friends."

Something in the air changed as if a high-pressure system blew out and a less oppressive system took its place.

"Friends?" Clare raised one eyebrow above the frames of her sunglasses.

Jess blushed. "I mean…"

Clare leaned close, cocked her head to one side, and asked in a low, sultry voice, "Do you do those things with *all* your friends?" She grinned and pulled the cord to start the lawn mower.

Jess tilted her head and gave her an amused smile.

Later that night, they lay in bed, Jess half sprawled on top of her. It was late and they hadn't eaten dinner, distracted by other activities. Clare lazily ran her fingers through Jess's hair.

"I want to take you away for your birthday. What do you think?"

Jess raised her head and grinned. "Away? Where?"

"My parents have a house on Lake Coeur d'Alene and a boat. They'll be in New York. I traded shifts with Nicole. I thought it might be nice to get away for a weekend if you don't mind missing a few days of work on your thesis. If not, we can spend the weekend together here."

"A real boat?" That seemed to pique her interest.

"It even has a motor." Clare laughed. "I won't make you row this time."

"It's just a birthday. You don't have to—"

"Do I seem like someone who does things I don't want to do?" If Jess only knew to what extent she'd go for her, how completely enamored with her she'd become. She wanted to give Jess everything, whatever that meant.

"I could stay an extra day or two at the end of the summer if needed." Jess smiled. "I have a few days before starting classes."

"Nicole asked me where I was taking my rock lady." Clare chuckled.

"So, your coworkers know about us?"

"Some do. I explained to her why I wanted to trade shifts."

Jess rested her chin on Clare's chest. "We could take my car. It's a better road trip vehicle than your truck."

She shrugged. "It's your call. We're going to look uber-lesbian in either one."

"Is that a thing? Lesbians and Subarus?" Jess wrinkled her nose in the most adorable way when she was skeptical. "I never knew."

"Well, you weren't a member of the women-loving-women club until recently, were you? You'll probably be getting your certificate in the mail any day now. We can go frame shopping." She wrapped her arms around Jess and squeezed her. It was the wrong move.

Jess's fingers playfully dug into her ribs, right where she knew Clare was the most ticklish.

Clare squealed and squirmed but couldn't get away with Jess on top of her. "I take it back. I take it back!"

Jess stopped tickling her. "That's right. There's more where that came from." Her eyes glimmered with mischief.

She liked this devious side of Jess she hadn't seen before. More than that, she liked that Jess had agreed to go away for her birthday and seemed excited about it. A weekend away was exactly what they needed. However, the reminder that Jess's time was ending made her ache, and she wasn't sure what to do about it.

CHAPTER TWENTY-FOUR

As they crossed over from Washington into Idaho, Jess gazed out the window at the Spokane River meandering alongside the interstate. What would Clare give her for her birthday? The trip would have been plenty, but she'd hinted at something. Jess assumed it would be a rock or small fossil like those found at ubiquitous roadside shops. From her past experiences with friends and family, they were safe, go-to gifts for a budding geologist. Perhaps Clare would take her on a hike to see a cave in the area. Regardless, Jess would be spending it with her, and that's what mattered.

Only a few small clouds dotted the sky behind them. Dry roadside grasses and scattered bunches of evergreens whizzed by. In the distance, pine-covered mountain ranges stretched in every direction. Clare drove since she was familiar with the winding road that edged the lake, and she encouraged Jess to enjoy the scenery.

It felt good to leave the park. Jess hadn't expected to find that she needed a reprieve, but the farther they got from Sun Lakes, the freer she felt. They could be together without worrying about other people, like Lyn or Brett. Although she'd been spending plenty of time with Clare, she'd also been working hard on her research, especially with the end of the summer looming. Any time Clare was busy at work, and even times she wasn't, Jess had thrown herself into the research for her thesis. She couldn't come this far and fail because she'd gotten sidetracked by a beautiful woman.

Clare wore her hair down, something she did more often. Jess loved how her gentle waves oozed femininity. With an elbow resting on her car door, her golden tan, and her oversized black sunglasses, she looked like a movie star who should be cruising in a convertible under a strip of palm trees, not road tripping through northern Idaho in an Outback.

"I can feel you looking at me."

Caught, Jess grinned. "I like looking at you."

Clare switched hands on the wheel and put her hand on Jess's thigh.

They entered the town of Coeur d'Alene, and Jess gasped when she saw the shimmering blue lake dotted with kayaks and motorboats. "It's gorgeous!"

"That's one small part. The lake is twenty-five miles long."

"It is?" She eyed the natural beauty outside her window. "How far are we going?"

"The cabin is about a third of the way down the lake, but we can take the boat as far as you like. It's your birthday."

She grinned. "I'd like that."

Clare turned south on Highway 97. The road curved in and out, following every jut and cove of the lake. Evergreens blanketed the landscape. Jess rolled her window down, and their fresh, earthy smell wafted inside. Clare slowed for hairpin turns that often gave some of the best views. They turned down a paved driveway.

"Shit. Why is the gate open?"

"Do they usually close it when they leave?"

"Always."

An elaborate house situated near the water's edge came into view. Built with more glass than wood, decks and balconies extended out from each side. Other outbuildings Jess assumed were part of the property stood nearby. Thick woods on both sides separated the home from its neighbors. As they came around the house, one set of double garage doors stood open, a black Range Rover parked inside.

"You have to be kidding me." Clare pulled in beside it and parked.

"What's going on?" Jess didn't know if she should be worried. She couldn't tell if Clare recognized the vehicle or not.

"My parents, who are supposed to be on a flight to New York, seem to still be here for some reason. I'm sorry."

"Oh." Jess stayed glued to her seat. "Does that mean we can't stay?"

"No. It means my mother is curious and wanted to meet you. Again, I'm so sorry." She gave her a wry smile. She led Jess through the garage into the cabin's spacious kitchen. "Hello?"

"Darling!" A striking woman resembling Clare flew around the corner with her arms spread wide. Gray hair replaced blond, but the stylish cut indicated the same wavy inclinations. Impeccable in her fashionable clothing, she was apparently one of those people who still dressed up for a flight.

Clare hugged and kissed her. "Mom, why are you still here? I thought your flight was at eleven."

"Your dad and I are leaving tonight. We haven't seen you for months and didn't know the next time we might have the chance, so we decided to catch a later flight." She turned away from her. "You must be Jess." She hugged her just as she had Clare, then held her at arm's length. "She didn't tell me how beautiful you are."

"It's nice to meet you, Mrs. DeVere."

"Call me Elizabeth, darling. She doesn't tell me much, but I suppose that's how it is with mothers and daughters." She gave Clare a disapproving glance. "So, Gregory and I didn't mind postponing our flight to meet you when you have her so enraptured."

"Mom." Clare rolled her eyes.

"Don't worry, darling. We just wanted to say hello. I know you want to get on with your special birthday weekend. We'll be gone in a few hours." She turned to Jess. "Let me wish you a happy early birthday. Would it be rude to ask how many years you'll be celebrating?"

"Mom!"

Jess laughed. "No, it's fine. I'll be twenty-five."

"Hmmm. Twenty-five." Elizabeth looked wistful as she studied her. "Oh, to be that age again." She squeezed her shoulder. "I hope you have a wonderful birthday. We think this is a little slice of heaven. I hope you enjoy being here."

"Thank you for letting us stay. Your home is stunning." Jess looked at the gleaming kitchen, the elaborate rockwork on the large, custom fireplace, and the exposed wood of the vaulted ceiling in the living room. Beyond that, the sparkling blue waters of Lake Coeur d'Alene glimmered through a wall of windows.

"Clare and her friends are always welcome here. We're here in the summer and sometimes in the winter now that Gregory is retired. Why don't you give her a tour and settle in? I have a few more things to pack so your dad can bring my suitcase down. Let's meet on the lower deck for light bites in, say, twenty minutes. I'll ask Bernice to lay things out."

"Sure. Thanks, Mom." Clare hugged her again.

Jess could tell Elizabeth was reluctant to let her go.

When she pulled away, she cupped Clare's cheek. "You look well, darling." She planted a kiss where her hand had been and left the room with the same flourish with which she'd entered.

Clare gave her a half smile and raised an eyebrow. "One down, one to go."

They retrieved their bags from the car, and she gave Jess a tour on their way to her old room. Located on the middle floor, it had a view of the lake and an en-suite bathroom. A hot tub sat on the deck outside.

"It's a queen bed. I hope that's okay. My parents have a king bed, but I think sleeping in my parents' bed would creep me out." She wrinkled her nose in disgust as she put her hands on Jess's hips.

Jess giggled. "This is great. I'm fine sleeping anywhere you want."

"We could always sleep on the boat, too." Clare brushed her lips along Jess's jaw.

"The boat? Didn't you say your dad uses it for fishing?" She pulled away, scowling.

"Yes, he does." Clare looked bewildered.

"I think I would sleep in your parents' bed before I had to sleep in a boat covered in fish guts."

Clare laughed and pulled her toward the sliding glass door. They stepped out onto the deck. At the edge, she let go of her hand and pointed toward the water. "That's my dad's fishing boat."

At the lake's edge perched a large, wooden boathouse. A long dock ran out into the sapphire-blue water. Moored at the end was a yacht. The white and black double-decked vessel was at least forty feet long. It read *Clare Elizabeth* in script across the stern. A man walked up the dock toward the house.

"That's not a fishing boat."

"That's where my dad escapes from my mom. Occasionally, he brings home a fish." Clare leaned on the rail with a smile.

"How sweet. He named the boat after you and your mom."

"Well, Elizabeth is my middle name."

"I didn't know that." They still had so much to learn about one another. "You two must be close."

"Hi, Dad!" She waved.

He looked upward, searching for her. When he spotted them on the deck, he smiled and waved back.

"We can sleep on it?" Jess couldn't believe the size of the boat.

"Yep. It has two staterooms. We can spend all weekend on the boat if you want. It's your birthday."

Jess turned to her. "I'm so happy being with you. This is all nice, but I don't need anything besides you."

Clare smiled and kissed her, one hand holding the back of her neck. She ended it with a quick peck. "Summer isn't going to last forever, you know. We need to talk about that."

Jess rested her forehead against her shoulder. "Not this weekend, please. Can we just enjoy being here and not worry about the future?"

Clare kissed her temple. "We should talk about it. Ignoring it won't make it go away."

"I know." Her voice came out muffled. "But I don't want to be sad or stressed this weekend. It's my birthday. I just want to enjoy being here with you."

"Okay, but let's do it soon though." Clare stayed silent for a moment. "We should go and join my parents. Our time is almost up." Releasing her, she went back inside, and Jess followed. She stopped in front of the mirror and ran her fingers through her hair, and then Jess did the same. "Ready?"

Clare's dad sat at a glass table, opening a bottle of wine. His hair may have been salt-and-peppered, but it was still thick. He wore shorts and a golf shirt. "Liz, they're here!" He stood and enveloped Clare in a giant hug. His blue eyes, reminiscent of hers, sparkled with adoration. "How's my girl?"

"I'm fine, Dad. This is Jess."

"Jess." He extended his hand. "Greg. Nice to meet you. We're so happy she brought you to the cabin. It's too big for only Liz and me to be enjoying it, especially when young people like you can make the most of it."

"It's lovely. I'm excited to spend the weekend here." She sat beside Clare.

"She saw your boat, Dad. I think she's in love." Clare teased her with a little squeeze of her leg.

Jess knew she must be blushing. She also knew it wasn't her love for the boat that made her cheeks red.

"Ah, my *Clare Elizabeth*." He turned to gaze at his boat. "One of my three favorite ladies. Vessels are always female, you know. I fueled her up for you. It should get you through the weekend. I asked Oliver to stock her with some food and beverages, too." He turned his head as Liz swept out onto the deck.

"So sorry." She took the last chair. "Bernice found all the items you asked for. You'll find everything except the…" She mouthed the word *cake*. "…in the dining room."

"Thanks, Mom." Clare caught Jess's eye and gave her a little wink.

Gregory poured them wine, but only poured himself a small amount. "I'll save my drinking for the plane. I have to drive to the airport soon."

Three plates of hors d'oeuvres sat in the middle of the table. They each filled small plates with chilled shrimp, deviled eggs, and crostini with bruschetta.

"Oliver will be around if you have any problems with the boat. So will Bernice. I'm sure they won't mind if you need anything. They'd love to see you." He turned to Jess. "They're our housekeeper and handyman, although they're like family. They live here on the property and keep it running, whether we're here or not. They've been with us since she was little."

"Do you need anything else?" Elizabeth smoothed down her shirt front.

"I don't think so, but if we do, we can drive into town or take the boat." Clare reached for another deviled egg.

They chatted and most of the food disappeared. When Gregory excused himself to load the luggage into their vehicle, Elizabeth began to clear the dirty plates. Jess stood, too.

"Here, let me help."

"Do you mind if I run and tell Bernice hello?" Clare rose. "I'll be right back."

"Of course not." She watched Clare descend the deck stairs.

Jess followed Elizabeth into the kitchen where she helped consolidate the remaining food for snacking on later. Elizabeth's hand on her arm stopped her.

"My daughter has been through a lot, as I'm sure she's told you."
Her eyes misted over.

Jess nodded and held the box of plastic wrap against her chest.

"The last couple of years have been so difficult for her. It's been
difficult for Gregory and me. She's been so far away." She gazed at the
lake over Jess's shoulder.

"You don't get to visit her often?"

"We try." She sighed. "I don't mean far away in terms of miles,
sweetheart. She's been so distant. Unreachable even." Her eyes
searched Jess's. "Do you understand?"

She nodded again, realizing what Elizabeth was trying to say. She
saw how the sadness that surrounded Clare affected those around her. It
gave her a bit of déjà vu after her conversation with Helen.

"I'm always the one to call her. When she called me—" Elizabeth's
voice cracked, and tears glistened in her eyes. "When she called and
first told me about you, I heard something in her voice that I hadn't
heard in an awfully long time. When she called me the second time and
asked if she could bring you here, well, you can ask Gregory, I cried for
an hour afterward."

Jess covered her hand with hers.

"When she walked in, I thought I was seeing things. She doesn't
even look the same as she did when we visited her. She's vibrant and
lively. I didn't know if I'd ever see her happy again. When I see her
look at you, I don't know if my heart can take it."

Jess embraced her. "I feel the same way." Her heart often felt like
it would burst when Clare was involved.

"I just wanted to thank you." Elizabeth kissed her cheek.

"I didn't really do anything." Jess gave her a small smile.

"You're there for her. That's everything. Now, give me that,
sweetheart, and get out of here before she catches me crying." She took
the box of plastic wrap and shooed her away.

The conversation left Jess feeling conflicted. On one hand, she
was thrilled to have made a difference in Clare's life. To be the cause of
any amount of Clare's happiness filled her with joy. It ranked up there
with fuzzy kittens and Christmas mornings.

On the other hand, she had no parents concerned about her well-
being or her happiness. Molly cared, but her best friend was the only
friend she'd brought up to speed on the summer's events. Since most of

her friends were also Jackson's friends, she couldn't update them when she and Jackson were in this state of limbo. She wondered if they'd still be her friends after the official breakup.

There was also the issue she and Clare avoided talking about. The fact that the hourglass was quickly running out of sand terrified her. She'd go back home, to her one friend, her empty apartment, and finish her degree with no one there to celebrate the accomplishment with her.

At times, the world felt like a large and lonely place.

Chapter Twenty-five

A fter her parents left for the airport, they headed to the lakefront so she could give Jess a tour of the boat. They passed by the boathouse on their way to the shiny, five-year-old Meridian yacht. Upon boarding the vessel, she saw Jess look up at the enclosed pilot's cabin.

"We'll save that for last." Clare loved riding up there. The views of the pristine lake were spectacular.

"Do you know how to drive the boat?" Jess ran her hand along the shiny rail.

"Yes, I can pilot it." Clare dropped her overnight bag at her feet and gently corrected her terminology. "Do you want a crash course in boating terms?"

"Sure."

She moved behind Jess and rested her chin on her shoulder. "This is the bow, and this is the stern." She pointed to the front and back of the boat, respectively. "Port," she pointed to one side and then the other, "and starboard. Let's go below."

Inside, Jess admired the polished dark wood accents. "I can't believe how spacious it feels."

Clare tugged her by her hand. "This is one of the berths. We can sleep here." Nice linens and pillows decorated the large bed.

"I feel like we're in a fancy hotel."

She chuckled and showed Jess the salon and dinette areas.

"It even has a kitchen!" Jess ran her hands over the gleaming counters and stainless-steel appliances.

"That's the galley." Clare gave her time to open doors and peer inside at stocked cupboards and refrigerator. "And this is one of the heads." She opened a skinny door to reveal a small shower and toilet.

Jess followed her into the second stateroom. There wasn't as much room as there had been in the first berth due to the curvature of the boat's hull at the bow. "Is this where your parents sleep?"

"This is where my dad sleeps if he sleeps on the boat. My mom says it makes her feel seasick. Let's go up."

Up in the pilothouse, Jess smoothed her hands over the supple brown leather seats that sat side-by-side. "They're like recliners."

"Yes, they're extremely comfortable. Try one out if you like."

Jess sat in the pilot's chair, and Clare sat beside her. Out on the lake, sunlight glinted off every wave and ripple. She turned back to Jess, who examined the console with all its screens and buttons.

"It even has a phone." Jess grinned and grasped the shiny chrome wheel in front of her.

"I guess we know who will be piloting the boat this weekend." Clare enjoyed watching her take everything in, be it a cave wall or ridiculously large boat.

"Your dad won't care?"

Clare shook her head. "Not at all. If you scratched it while docking it, he would gladly use it as an excuse to upgrade to the latest model." She meant it as a joke, but he might.

"Your parents have a lot of money." Jess stated the obvious.

She shrugged. "I guess so. They worked hard and were lucky enough to do well."

"Do they help you out?"

Jess brought up a touchy subject, and Clare lifted her chin as she answered. "They try. My parents paid for my education, something they always said they planned to do and something I appreciate. However, I've been independent ever since." She turned from Jess to the view outside. "Of course, I'm welcome to stay here and use the house and boat whenever I like. I'm sure they wish I would come up here more." She faced her. "I make decent money, and the park provides my housing. That enables me to save most of my paycheck. I paid off my truck, so I don't have a lot of expenses. My independence is important to me."

"I didn't mean to insinuate anything." Jess let go of the boat's wheel. Her jubilance had faded, like a child who'd been scolded.

"I know you didn't. I just wanted to explain." She smiled. "What do you think about a sunset tour of the lake?"

The look in Jess's eyes was everything she'd hoped.

Jess drifted from her dreamy state to semi-awake. The boat rocked gently, reminding her of where she was, but it was the hand caressing her upper thigh that held her attention. Behind her, she could feel Clare's warmth and her breasts pressed against her back.

She opened her eyes. The LED clock in the stateroom read 3:17 a.m. She was officially twenty-five years old. She closed them again and enjoyed the hazy sensations of Clare's fingers.

Clare buried her nose in her hair, and her fingers moved higher, reaching the junction of her legs. Jess gave her more access, giving up any pretense of being asleep, and Clare made an approving sound. It wasn't long before she ached with want. She needed more.

On the drive to the lake, Jess had reflected on their lovemaking. They'd started to find their groove. They quickly learned what the other liked, and the newness of their relationship heightened each instance. She'd never experienced anything like it in her previous relationships. There was something about Clare. She made every cell in her body sing. Jess needed her now.

She felt the heat of Clare's mouth on her neck, and her hand caressed Jess's breast. Sweat gathered where their bodies touched. Jess gasped each breath, fast and uneven. She was close.

Jess tried to make it last. She wanted to prolong Clare touching her, keep them moving together in synchrony, keep them connected, but everything happened so fast. Her body clenched and spasmed. The pillow muffled her cry.

Clare kept touching her, barely moving her fingers. She dropped gentle kisses on her spine, then turned her over in her arms and brushed sweaty strands of hair from her forehead and cheek. Jess didn't know which one of them was more breathless.

Clare kissed her tenderly. "Happy birthday, baby."

Jess wanted to stay like that forever, spent and content, wrapped in her lover's arms. She didn't want to figure out what they were going to do when she went back to Seattle.

❖

They spent most of the weekend on the boat. When they weren't cruising the lake or diving off the back of the Meridian into the refreshing waters of Lake Coeur d'Alene, they spent time in the gorgeous stateroom, tangled up with each other.

Clare brought the items she'd asked Bernice to purchase. They celebrated Jess's birthday with a tiramisu cake, a bouquet of fresh lilies, and an expensive bottle of champagne before falling into each other's arms. Jess shouldn't have bothered to pack extra clothing. She'd spent the glorious weekend in her swimsuit or nothing at all. Every time she put it on, it wasn't long before Clare nimbly pulled it off and dragged her to the berth, the couches in the salon, the upper deck under the stars, or wherever they ended up in their frantic need for each other. What opportunities they might have missed earlier in the summer, they made up for at a frenzied rate.

Tiny aftershocks still made her insides tremble as she sat on the edge of the bed and tied her swimsuit behind her back. Clare already wore her suit, so Jess didn't know why she was rummaging through her overnight bag.

"What are you looking for? The sunscreen is in the salon." She adjusted the straps over her shoulders.

"I was looking for this." Clare turned, holding a small white box with a simple green bow. "It's not much. I wanted to give you something meaningful for your birthday."

She took the box. Clare sat beside her.

"You've already done so much for me." Jess pulled off the bow. Would it be a rock or a fossil? She lifted the lid. A solitary item gleamed against the cotton batting. She picked it up and looked at her with surprise and adoration. "It's a key."

"Yes, to my house." Clare smiled, then laughed in surprise when Jess threw her arms around her neck.

Jess kissed her, their lips already swollen and chafed, but she didn't care.

While the key was such a thoughtful gesture, she didn't know how to tell Clare that every moment spent with her was just as meaningful. How to hold on to those moments like these and have more to come was the problem.

"It's so you can do your laundry." Clare's joke earned her a playful swat.

"What laundry? Every time I put on clothes, you take them off me."

With impeccable timing, Clare tugged at the bow, and Jess's swim top went slack.

CHAPTER TWENTY-SIX

The escape they enjoyed on Lake Coeur d'Alene ended too soon. On the drive back to the park, she and Jess discussed what to do about Brett. Clare didn't want to be around him until she'd had a conversation with him about Dominique. The scene in front of her house had left her rattled enough. She didn't want to have to avoid him either. Jess agreed that she should find time to talk to him soon.

Unfortunately, it happened sooner than she anticipated.

One of the taillights on her work truck was out. Clare needed to take care of the issue before her next shift. She parked in the empty lot outside the service shed that doubled as a supply room. When she opened the door, she noticed lights inside the building.

"Hello?"

Brett stepped out from between two shelves. He held a cardboard box, and similar boxes lay on the floor around him.

"Aren't you off today?" He seemed surprised to see her.

"I need a bulb. My taillight is out. I didn't see your truck."

"Gordon dropped me off. I need a fan belt. Mine is trashed. Somebody needed a gate unlocked, so he responded."

Clare would have known all of this if she had her radio with her. Since meeting Jess, she'd been able to wean herself from it more.

She found the spare bulbs hanging on the pegboard and took one, signing it out on an inventory clipboard. She was about to leave, but he opened his mouth.

"Where's your hot little girlfriend today? I can't blame you for liking that. Damn, those little shorts she wears…"

Clare reacted, the question flying from her mouth before she could stop it. "Wasn't sleeping with one of my girlfriends enough?" Her icy voice rang out in the cavernous warehouse. Silence followed.

He stepped out into the aisle, his eyes cold and dark. He clicked his tongue and took a few steps toward her. "You shouldn't pay attention to every rumor you hear. People gossip all the time. That doesn't mean there's any truth behind it." His voice lacked any of the humor from before.

"It's not a rumor. You weren't careful and gave yourself away." Her voice remained confident although fear seeped through her. A line of nervous sweat trickled down her spine. It dawned on her that an isolated service shed wasn't the best place to have this conversation. She realized the gravity of the situation too late, and snippets from her training came back to her. *Always be aware of your surroundings. Don't get cornered. Men are almost always bigger, faster, and stronger.*

"I don't know what you're talking about. I should sue you for slander." He stepped around the pile of cardboard boxes.

Clare moved toward the closed door, her only means of escape. "Go ahead, but you'll be too busy explaining yourself to the state park's director. The policy against supervisors sleeping with a subordinate is in the handbook for a reason."

She chastised herself for venturing into such a dangerous position. He carried a gun, and she was keenly aware of his larger physique. She wore a T-shirt and shorts and only had her keys and a miniature light bulb in her hand. She glanced around for anything she might be able to use as a weapon should she need to protect herself. There was nothing substantial within reach.

His demeanor changed. He smiled, but even in the fluorescent lighting, the smile didn't reach the dark, unreflective pools of his eyes. "Hey, there's no need for that. We're friends, aren't we? How about we talk and figure things out? I'm sure there's an explanation. Why don't you come here?" He shot forward and reached for her arm. She spun away from his grasp and lunged for the door.

Someone yanked the handle from her hand, and the door flew open. She lost her balance, falling toward the sunlight.

Gordon caught her and helped her regain her footing. "Hey, easy there! What are you doing here on your day off?"

She squinted. "I needed a bulb." She held up the packaged bulb. Her hand was shaking. He looked between her and Brett.

"Sorry, if I interrupted som—"

"You didn't. I was leaving." Clare pushed past him without looking back.

She hurried back to Jess. When she relayed what had happened, Jess abandoned the bagel she'd been making. Irate, she paced back and forth in the living room.

"That man!" She gesticulated with a knife covered in cream cheese. "You should have *actually* talked to the state park's director before you said that. What if something had happened to you?" She put her hands on her hips.

Clare might have said something about how adorable she looked had Jess not been so upset.

"I simply reacted. I thought that if perhaps he thought I had, he would realize threatening or hurting me was useless, and he would back down."

"Should we call the police?"

"To tell them what? He didn't threaten me. He didn't even touch me, although he tried. It would be his word against mine. I'm not sure it would do any good."

Jess continued to pace.

Clare stood and put her hands on Jess's hips. "Calm down. I'm fine. I knew that even if something happened to me, you knew, and you would have made sure the information reached the correct people."

Jess scoffed and looked away, her eyes watery. "That's a terrible way of thinking."

"But you would have, wouldn't you?" She craned her neck to make eye contact.

"Yes." Despite her grumbling, Jess put her arms around Clare's neck. "I don't want anything to happen to you."

She looked even cuter when she pouted. Clare squeezed her waist. "Good, me either. I promise I won't put myself in situations like that again." She wouldn't. It made her feel helpless and vulnerable, and she'd neglected to heed her training and good sense. She vowed to stay safe in the future for them both.

Jess's eyes widened. She scowled, then looked sheepish.

"What?"

"I got cream cheese in your hair."

❖

"I am so glad to be done with this shift!" Nicole barged into the ranger station, releasing her hair from the bun at the nape of her neck. It exploded into a mass of red curls. She undid the top two buttons of her uniform and flopped into a chair. "Why is Brett being such an asshole?"

Clare looked at her. "What did he do?"

"He's being more *Brett* than usual—citing motorists for doing seventeen miles per hour in a fifteen-mile-per-hour zone, sniffing the contents of every teenager's soda can, and writing noise ordinance citations like he has a quota to fill. Campers don't have any respect for us when we go around acting like jerks." She signed her timesheet and dropped it into a bin on the wall before she flopped into a chair and crossed her legs. "I'm more like you, the catch-more-flies-with-honey type. We have a nice little chat with folks, and they comply. He's taking this job to the extreme. Why do men have to flaunt their power?"

"Maybe because he has none."

Her answer made Nicole laugh.

"I'm not sure any of the rangers respect him." Clare didn't usually gossip, but her recent altercation with him seemed to have turned off her filter.

Nicole shook her head, her hair swinging free. "Gordon might because of his military background. Even then, I think it's more of an ingrained habit than actual respect, instilled deference to the hierarchy and all that."

It gave Clare a small amount of satisfaction to know the stress was getting to him. It served him right. "You reap what you sow." She hadn't intended to speak the words aloud.

"What?" Nicole looked confused.

"Oh, nothing."

"When does your girlfriend leave?" Nicole ran her fingers through her hair, making it look like a fiery halo.

Clare didn't want to discuss Jess and her imminent departure. She glanced at her phone so Nicole wouldn't see the moisture springing to her eyes. "Right after Labor Day."

"Do you know what you're going to do? Are you going to try to do long distance? You two seem serious. You planned a special birthday weekend for her and everything. Plus, I don't think I've ever seen you so happy. You sort of glow when you talk about her. I like her. She's pretty. You two make a gorgeous couple. Plus, you've been through *so* much already. You deserve to be happy. It makes me sad to think about you two being apart." Words slid from her mouth like drops of water down a Seattle windshield. After purging her thoughts on the matter, Nicole mimicked a sad face, more akin to an emoji with a pink, pouty lip than actual sadness.

The conversation made Clare feel ill. She didn't need Nicole's verbal vomit for Jess's departure to be on her mind. Were her feelings for Jess so intense that others could see them? She knew that Jess made her happy, but did she glow?

"Maybe you'll decide to move to wherever she's from." Nicole pulled her shirttails from her waistband and slouched again.

"My job is here." Clare picked up a large paperclip she found sticking out from beneath her keyboard.

"You've been here a long time, haven't you?"

"Nine years." She unbent the paperclip into an S-shape.

Nicole groaned. "I don't know how you've done it. I can't stand the heat here. I wanted a position at the San Juan Islands, but I ended up with *this*. I shouldn't complain. It pays the bills."

Clare had always felt the opposite. "I decided I wanted to work here when Lyn and I were still in college. A group of us camped here one summer, and I fell in love with the place. I dreamed of getting a job here, and I did. Lyn ended up working at Craters of the Moon in Idaho, but when a dispatcher position opened here, I recommended her. We've worked together ever since."

"She had a job in a national park? She must like you a lot to give that up."

If Nicole only knew. That was the understatement of the year. Of course, Clare would never divulge that out of respect for Lyn. Instead, she bent the paperclip back and forth.

Nicole prattled on. "Everybody I know wants to work in a national park. Brett would kill for a gig at a national park." She giggled, oblivious to overstaying her welcome. "Can you imagine him in the hat? At least we don't have to wear those." She referred to the iconic National Park Service's broad-brimmed ranger hats.

Clare managed a cursory laugh and wished for an incident that would need her attention. Thankfully, Nicole decided to leave.

"I need a nap." She tucked in her shirt for the walk to her truck. "I'll catch you later."

Clare tried to bend the paperclip back into its original shape. She believed in her heart what she'd told Nicole. She loved the park. It was her home, even if some memories caused her to lose sleep at night. Still, she didn't understand why she should have to choose between her life here and the possibility of a life with Jess.

What if she quit her job and moved to Seattle? It was such a U-Haul move, so typically lesbian. They'd only been together a brief time. Jess often spent the night at her place, but they hadn't lived together. While Clare had shared extremely intimate details of her life with Jess, there was still so much they didn't know about one another. Could they manage to coexist? Would they be happy? Something else bothered her. What if she quit her job, and they broke up? Then what? She couldn't expect to have a job here waiting for her in that scenario, especially if Brett continued to be in charge. Plus, the competition was stiff.

The realization hit her like a ton of bricks. If that happened, it wouldn't be the loss of her job that broke her heart. Clare gave up on the stubborn paperclip that refused to return to its original shape and hurled the bent clip into the trash can, metal-on-metal making a loud ping.

Chapter Twenty-seven

They sat on the dock, Jess's head in Clare's lap. Jess found the gentle rippling of the waves against the pilings comforting.

"You need to move campsites again. I'll help you." Clare's fingers sifted through her hair.

"Okay. Do you have any ideas where?"

"I've already secured a site, but if you don't like it, we can look at others." She brushed the hair from Jess's forehead.

"I trust you to know the best spots. You did an excellent job choosing the last one." Jess smiled at her. Darkness had fallen. It wouldn't be long now.

"A penny for your thoughts?" Clare leaned back.

Her mind had drifted while Clare played with her hair. She sighed and looked away. "You know what I'm thinking."

"Yes," Clare said with a straight face, "but I don't think the Mariners have what it takes to win the World Series this year."

Jess giggled, but her smile faded. "Shall we talk about it?"

"I think we should."

"It makes me sad. I don't want to leave."

"I don't want you to leave either." Clare looked at the sky. "Here's how I see it. We can be depressed and mope around your last few weeks here, or we can make the best of the time we have. It's only a few months until you finish your degree. It won't be easy, but we can manage. Once you've graduated, let's see where you land a job and go from there."

Clare continued to run her fingers through her hair, the action threatening to lull her into a false sense of peace and security.

"There isn't a better option, is there? I wish things weren't so uncertain, or you didn't have to be so far away. I wish we could be together." Jess pressed her cheek into Clare's abdomen.

"I want that, too."

Was Clare as frightened about the summer ending as she was? How would they manage the fall? Autumn playfully hid around a corner like a young child in the classic children's game, toes peeking out from beneath a curtain and readily seen by anyone seeking. Leaves had started to fall from the deciduous trees in the campground. She heard them hit her tent, the brittle plop and scratch as they slid, a reminder of what the future held. The sound was like nails on a chalkboard to her ears. Nights had become cooler, forcing the use of her sleeping bag on the rare night she spent in her tent and not in Clare's bed. The sun set earlier now, too.

"You know, there's a chance you'll feel differently when you get back home, surrounded by your academics and your friends."

Jess's stomach churned. "I won't. I know I won't." She didn't know how to be more adamant. She might be younger than Clare, but she knew how she felt. "Do you think that might happen to you? After I leave?" She almost didn't want to hear the answer.

Clare spoke softly. "No."

Beneath the cloudless sky, they waited to spot the evening's first falling star of the Perseid meteor shower. Jess wished bravery filled her like stars filled the sky. She wanted to ask Clare to come with her. Her apartment was small, but the two of them could manage. Even so, she knew how much Clare loved her job and the park. How could she ask her to leave that behind? What if she said no? Jess wasn't sure she could stand the rejection. She didn't know if there were jobs like Clare's in Seattle or if Seattle even had state parks. Could she ask Clare to give up everything—her job, her home, her friends, her career—for her, when Clare had already lost so much? What did Jess even have to offer? She had little money since she'd used most of what her father had left her to pay for her education. She hadn't finished her master's degree. She didn't even have a job. Other than a shabby, one-bedroom apartment and her affection for Clare, she had nothing to offer.

While Dry Falls had been the perfect place to do research for her thesis, it didn't offer her any options in terms of employment. The park was in the middle of nowhere. She couldn't live here, not if she intended to have a career. It was difficult enough finding a movie theater or a gas station, let alone a college or university nearby at which she could teach, not that she'd ever had the inclination. If she were to work in her field, it would have to be elsewhere.

Her insecurities rose like an incoming tide. Had this already occurred to Clare? Despite her suggestion to wait until her degree was finished, maybe Clare already knew it wasn't meant to last. Maybe it has been a summer fling to her after all. Did Clare prefer the comfort of what she knew over the frightening idea of uprooting her life to live elsewhere? Did Clare think it would be easier to break up with her after she left? Maybe what they had, the fire between them, burned too bright, destined to flame and flash before fizzing out like a Fourth of July sparkler. Jess felt the stinging urge to cry.

"There!" Clare pointed. "Did you see it?"

"I did." Jess welcomed thinking about something else.

Soon they spotted more and watched the streaking orbs fall from the sky, burning up in the Earth's atmosphere in bright, glowing arcs. After twenty or so, they stopped counting.

Clare turned to her. They dangled their legs off the dock. "I'm so happy you're here to share this with me. There is no one in the entire world I'd rather be with right now."

Overcome by what they'd witnessed together, Jess looped her arms around Clare's neck, her eyes now searching for contact and connection, not shooting stars. What she felt with Clare was far more exhilarating.

They may not have reached any definite conclusion during the conversation concerning their future, but even that couldn't put a damper on her spirits on such a night. The stars might have twinkled above them, but they were no match for the beauty in Clare's eyes. She found it difficult to breathe. Clare leaned in, so close she could feel her warm breath on her lips. Jess closed the gap. Their bodies became soft and pliant, and the gentle kiss soon had them abandoning the dock for the comfort of Clare's bed.

Chapter Twenty-eight

Once again, Clare made it possible for Tim and Ian to camp next to Jess for Labor Day weekend. They arrived late Friday night. Jess played a few hands of gin rummy with them, and they drank some Portland microbrews that Ian brought. Tim updated Jess on his ongoing long-distance relationship with Melanie from Olympia. Clare had to work, and Jess missed her. The knowledge that this would become a familiar feeling brought tears to her eyes.

The next day, after Clare grabbed a few hours of sleep, she met them at the lake where they spent the rest of the afternoon. That evening, with everyone sun-soaked and buzzed from day drinking, they played a round of mini golf at the resort. Ian convinced everyone to toss back shots of tequila beforehand. Jess came in second place. Ian won, and Clare and Tim both blamed their poor performances on too much sun and alcohol. As they drank and played cards in Clare's backyard until late, someone would inevitably ask, "Do you remember the time Clare lost her ball in the pond?" or "Do you remember when Clare lost her ball inside the windmill?" to raucous laughter.

The next morning, Jess got up early and spent a few hours at Red Alkali Lake taking notes and photos. When she returned to the campground, Ian and Tim appeared a bit hungover but insisted they were starving. She suggested they eat at the concession stand near the general store.

The line at the order window was a dozen people deep, but soon they became the happy recipients of fried food and milkshakes. They found an unoccupied picnic table, spread out their empty calories, and ate like they hadn't seen food since spring.

"I'm glad we got here when we did." Ian looked around. "The line is twice as long now."

Jess and Tim barely glanced up, line lengths unable to distract them from hot fries and cold milkshakes.

"I forgot to ask you. How did the Seattle situation go?" Tim took a bite of his corn dog.

"Seattle situation?" Her brows furrowed.

"You know, your boyfriend." He slurped his milkshake.

"Oh." Jess lowered her gaze. "I haven't dealt with that yet."

Ian piped up, surprise in his voice. "It seems like you might not want to have a boyfriend right now."

She refused to make eye contact with either of them. "Trust me, I wish the situation were different. It's not like I want a boyfriend, but there's not much I can do about it right now. I can't break up with him if he's avoiding me. Breaking up with him by sending a text seems a bit too junior high, and although I've called a couple of times to do it over the phone, he hasn't answered or called me back. I don't want to stoop to his level, so I need to do it face-to-face."

Tim opened two ketchup packets at once. He squeezed the ketchup over his fries. "You know you have to find a way to deal with that, right?"

Little did he know, it had been on her mind ever since Clare had confided in her about Dominique's cheating. Jess was ashamed to be in the situation she was in, but thankfully, Clare would never have to find out. She'd take care of it as soon as she returned to Seattle. Still, guilt consumed her.

"I'll deal with it when I get home. I can't do anything about it right now."

"Why is he avoiding you?" Ian gave her a strange look.

"Because he's a jerk? Because he has better things to do?"

The guys looked at one another. "I'll bet he does," Ian said with a knowing tone.

"Has he cheated on you before?" Tim reached for a napkin.

"Not that I know of." She pushed her food away from her. Had he? Was he? Did she care? The fact it hadn't crossed her mind spoke volumes.

Tim picked up her remaining fries and dumped them on his. "You know we have your best interests at heart, right?"

"Yeah, I know."

"The longer you wait, the worse it will be." He shoved some fries into his mouth.

Ian elbowed her. "Get rid of him. You deserve better, and so does Clare."

She nodded. "Can we change the subject now?"

Ian slurped the dregs of his milkshake.

Someone behind them spoke. "I see you met some friends."

Shit. Jess knew that voice. She raised her eyes to see Lyn come around the table. Lyn looked casual in her rolled-up jeans and T-shirt and held a container of tater tots and a milkshake. She took a sip while staring at her. Jess fervently hoped she hadn't been within earshot of their conversation.

"Lyn, this is Tim and Ian. They were here for Memorial Day and came back for the Fourth. Lyn is Clare's best friend."

Lyn greeted them. "You must like it here a lot. Do you come every year?"

"Nope, we came back to see Jess." Ian leaned into her.

"I see." Lyn smiled, but it lacked friendliness or warmth.

"Would you like to join us?" Jess made the polite offer.

"No. I'm just grabbing some food before my shift. I couldn't resist stopping to say hello."

She and Lyn assessed each other silently while the brothers focused on their food. Something caught Jess's attention. Clare walked toward them and spotted her in the small crowd. She paused and slowly smiled. Jess was thrilled with the unexpected encounter but tried to curtail her excitement in front of Lyn.

"Look at all of you." Clare appraised the small group. "Hi."

Jess thought she looked especially sharp in her uniform, always so crisp despite the heat.

"Why aren't you dressed for work?" Clare motioned at Lyn's clothing.

"I'm heading home to change right now." Lyn watched as Clare stole one of her tater tots.

Jess had the feeling Lyn would have swatted Clare's hand away had she not been holding something.

Clare sucked air into her mouth to cool the hot bite. She walked around the table to stand beside Jess and discreetly brushed her arm with her fingers.

"I figured I wouldn't have time to eat later. I'm sure it'll be busy." Lyn seemed to take note of the lack of personal space between Clare and Jess.

"Well, don't piss off Helen by being late again." Clare took a sip of Jess's drink.

"Right. I'll see you around. Nice to meet you." She walked toward the parking lot.

"Are you still on duty?" Jess tilted her head to look at her.

"Yes, but not for much longer. I stopped for an iced tea and saw you sitting here. I better get in line, or I'll be here forever." Her body went ramrod straight, her nose high in the air, a serious look on her face. "Does anyone else smell smoke?"

They sniffed the air, looked at each other, and shook their heads.

"Maybe someone made a campfire." Ian crumpled his cheeseburger wrapper into a ball.

Clare turned around and scanned the horizon. "There are no campfires allowed this weekend. We expect high winds. That's also not a campfire smell."

On cue, her radio came to life announcing another brush fire. She relayed her intent to respond.

"I'm sorry. I have to go. I'll text you later." She squeezed Jess's shoulder.

Jess silently cursed. Ideally, Clare could have sat with them for a few more minutes. Jess wanted every minute she could with her. Their time was limited, and as much as she didn't want to admit it, the clock was ticking. Jess only had a few days left.

Later, after she'd helped extinguish the small brush fire and finished her shift, Clare insisted on one last barbecue at the lake before Ian and Tim headed home. While they'd taken the weekend off, the barber shop would be open on Monday. Jess admired the dedication they showed toward their business, even if it meant spending less time together.

Ian offered to help Clare with the grilling. Jess and Tim deposited the briquets and bags of ice on the picnic table.

"You two should go relax." Clare shucked an ear of corn, the silk clinging to her hands and covering the table.

"Don't you need our help?" Jess dumped the ice into the cooler.

"We can manage it." Ian unwrapped a rack of ribs. "There's not that much to do. You can clean up."

"Okay, then." The cleanup looked like it might be worse than the preparation as she surveyed the corn husk mess. She turned to Tim. "Are you up for a swim?" The sun was scorching, and the lake looked refreshing.

"Yeah. I need to cool off." He stripped off his T-shirt.

She did the same, stuffing her shirt and shorts in her backpack. Before heading to the water, she stole a kiss from Clare.

"Oh, wait." Tim stopped and pulled his wallet from the pocket of his swim trunks. "Can you put this someplace safe?" He tossed the wallet to Clare, who caught it one-handed. She stuffed it into Jess's open backpack, corn silk clinging to it.

They walked to the dock. Jess dove in, and he followed. She swam out. The sun had warmed the top few inches of water, but the water below remained cool. She floated on her back. Righting herself and treading water, she located Tim who had surfaced, shaking water from his hair.

"I can't believe you have to leave tonight. It feels like you just got here."

"I know. I wish we could stay longer, but when you're a self-employed, small business owner, if you don't work, you don't get paid." He sent a splash of water her way.

"At least you're going home to a job." She splashed him back.

"You don't have a job to go back to?"

"No." She didn't elaborate on how Jackson's family owned the restaurant where she'd worked, so that bridge was burned—or would be burned—soon. At least restaurant jobs were easy to obtain.

"I'd offer you a job, but out of rock/paper/scissors, I think your expertise lies with rocks, not scissors." He laughed at his joke as she rolled her eyes. "Your hair still looks good though, Subaru."

"Thanks. I like the cut you gave me." Between thinking about the bridge she needed to burn and hearing his nickname for her, she felt a twinge of guilt. It had been one thing when she and Clare were only flirting, or maybe even kissing, but she wished she'd broken up with Jackson before she and Clare had slept together.

He dunked under, then came up and flicked his wet hair at her. "So, are you excited to finish your thesis?"

"Absolutely. To be honest, the department refers to it as a written technical report, but for all intents and purposes, it's a thesis. On top of that, I still have to pass an oral comprehensive exam and defend my written report in a final presentation. But, yeah, I'm eager to finish." Unease replaced excitement. "As much as I'm excited to wrap that up, I dread going home." She stared unseeing into the water.

"Because of Clare?"

She nodded. Besides calling or texting, she found it difficult to imagine how she and Clare could make long-distance work. Neither one of them had time for long road trips. Meeting Clare at some midway motel or hotel for a few hours sounded seedy, even if it gave them a chance to see each other. Plus, it would still be a long round-trip drive for both. And what if someone else entered Clare's life between now and then? She shook off the depressing thoughts.

"What am I going to do when I need my hair trimmed?" In addition to Clare, she was going to miss Ian and Tim. It wasn't like she had time to drive to Portland to visit them either.

"We could always meet somewhere in between. I know the drive to Olympia well." He winked.

She studied him, his knobby shoulders protruding from the water and his hair askew. "We'll figure something out. I want to stay in touch." Why did it feel like everyone who mattered soon wouldn't be a part of her life?

CHAPTER TWENTY-NINE

The sunset stirred the horizon into magentas and violets, but the deep colors quickly absorbed into the darkness. The high-pitched song of crickets floated through the warm air. Clare stopped to flick on a bug zapper before joining Jess on the swing. She kicked off her shoes and propped her bare feet on the coffee table. She wanted to enjoy one last drink outdoors. They both knew what would happen once they went inside. They only had two nights left. She doubted they would get much sleep, and she didn't mind in the least. She squeezed her thighs together in anticipation.

A phone vibrated. Jess picked it up.

"Is everything okay?" Clare sipped her wine.

"It's Tim."

Tim and Ian had left a few hours earlier.

"They can't be home yet, can they?" Worry crept in.

"They stopped in The Dalles, and he realized he didn't have his wallet. He wants to know if I have it." Jess frowned.

Clare gasped, horrified. "I forgot to give it back to him! I put it in your backpack at the lake. Let me see if it's still in there." She jumped up and ran inside, chastising herself for forgetting to return it.

Jess was still texting when she returned.

"It's here! I feel so bad." Clare held it against her chest.

"Don't feel bad. I'm surprised he didn't realize it was missing before he left."

"How are you going to get it to him? Are they going to turn around? That's so much driving, and it's so late." Despite it being partially her fault, Clare didn't want to have to drive, even if it meant meeting them halfway. She wanted to spend the evening, and the night, with Jess. That made her feel even more guilty, but she wasn't sure when she'd see Jess again.

"We're figuring it out." Jess typed, then returned her cell phone to the table. "I'm going to meet him in Leavenworth on my way home. He said he'll buy me lunch. I offered to drive to Ellensburg or Yakima, but he insisted."

Home. The word rang in Clare's ears. She didn't want to think about Jess going home. Even the word home insinuated that Jess belonged somewhere else, to a life she'd never seen, somewhere without her. She'd never met any of Jess's friends, never seen her apartment, never slept a single night with her in the city she called home.

Everything felt up in the air, like a juggler's balls waiting to fall. While having a concrete plan would have lent some stability to the situation and given her some reassurance, Clare also knew it wasn't prudent. God, they'd only known each other for such a brief time. It might not hurt to take a little breather, give each other a bit of space, and see if they felt the same for each other in a few months. While she didn't anticipate what she felt for Jess changing now, in a few months, or ever, she wasn't sure Jess could say the same.

It wasn't her, with her thirty-plus-odd years of life under her belt returning to her hometown, her friends, and her favorite coffee shops and restaurants. It was Jess. It had only been a handful of years since Jess had been able to legally drink. Clare wasn't sure she could rely on someone so young with so much life ahead of her to have enough wisdom and foresight after three months to say, "This is what I want for the foreseeable future." Could *she* even reliably say that? While she hated to admit it, time would tell.

Clare looked at the moon and the stars. It was such a gorgeous night, the temperature perfect, the ambiance almost surreal. She listened to the musical sounds of frogs and crickets. Occasionally, a bat dashed across the sky.

Normally, she could sit out here for hours, but tonight they would cut it short. She knew they had to make the most of what they had because they didn't have much time left. The center of her chest hurt when she thought about it.

"I think it's supposed to be a full moon tonight." Jess pointed to where the edge of the moon clawed its way over the top of the cliff.

"Hmm." She sipped her wine and traced little patterns on Jess's leg as they watched the alabaster sphere slink its way into the night sky.

"I think that might be a planet." Jess pointed at something bright.

Clare gave her points for trying to keep her composure, but she saw Jess twitch when her fingers grazed her inner thigh. It didn't hurt to build the anticipation a bit before they retired inside. Clare leaned closer. "Where?"

"There. Near the horizon."

"I don't know." Clare sifted her fingers through Jess's hair from temple to ends, much like she'd done after Jess's haircut. "Tell me something about you, something I don't know." Her bare foot pushed against the table, rocking them.

Jess laughed self-consciously. "I don't know. I can't think of anything, especially when you're doing that."

Clare chuckled. "I'm going to get more wine. Would you like a refill?"

"Yes, please."

Clare was only a few feet away when her cell phone vibrated on the table. She turned back. Lyn's name showed on the screen. "I'll only be a minute."

Clare hung up and stood rooted to the spot. She didn't know whether to laugh, cry, or break every dish in her kitchen. It might have given Lyn some satisfaction to relay the news, but ultimately, Clare trusted her. Lyn would never make something like this up.

She poured a single glass of wine. Her hand shook. She took a few calming breaths before walking back outside. This was nothing like how she'd imagined the evening going. She tried to swallow the hard lump choking her.

Jess rocked back and forth on the swing with her eyes cast heavenward. She turned when she heard the back door close.

Clare handed her the glass of wine and sat on the edge of the swing, stopping it.

"Where's your glass?" Jess raised the glass to her lips but didn't drink. "Aren't you having more?"

Disappointment and rage threatened to erupt from her at any moment. Clare fought to control her emotions. "I've had enough." Blood raced through her veins. Her pulse pounded in her ears. She stared at the cliff behind the house, hoping it would come crashing down on her to prevent this conversation from happening.

"What's wrong?" Jess reached out and touched her arm.

She shook it off. "Don't touch me."

"What's going on?" Jess leaned forward and set her glass of wine on the coffee table.

"How dare you? I trusted you." She spit out the words that felt like gravel in her mouth and laughed a singular, hollow laugh. "A boyfriend."

"Oh, God." Jess looked horrified.

"I should have known better." If she had, she'd be alone, but at least she wouldn't be hurting like this.

"Let me explain."

"What is there to explain? Do you or do you not have a boyfriend?"

Jess began to cry, tears seeping from the corners of her eyes. "Yes, but please let me explain."

Anger rose inside her. Clare stood, throwing her arms wide. "Why did you kiss me that night?"

"You kissed me!"

"You didn't stop me!" Clare started pacing. "You've had months to tell me, but you kept it from me. Intentionally." She covered her mouth with her hand before dropping it to her side. "My God, we slept together!"

"He means nothing to me. He doesn't even care that I arrived safely. He's barely texted two words since I got here."

"That sounds like a personal problem." Clare could see her words stung.

"I needed to break up with him a long time ago, and…I haven't. It's complicated."

Clare stared at her. "Except it isn't, Jess."

Jess looked confused. "What happened to, 'It's difficult to force ourselves to do certain things, especially if the task is an unpleasant one'?"

Clare pointed her finger at Jess's chest. "Exactly, it's difficult, but you do it. You force yourself to do it."

"It's over between him and me. It was basically over before I got here. Before *us*. I've tried to call and break it off with him several times, but he hasn't taken my calls. You have to trust me. Please." She sobbed outright.

"I thought I did, but that was a mistake. Now I don't know what to think. I don't understand how you could start something while in another relationship. Did you ever stop to think about other people's feelings? Did you consider how he would feel? How *I* would feel, after everything I've been through?" Clare paused, watching Jess's shoulders shake with sobs. Deep down she knew what she was about to say wasn't true, but she said it anyway. "Or maybe what this is isn't that important to you."

Jess froze. "Yes, I made a mistake, but there's something here, something between us, and you know it. Tell me there's nothing here. Tell me you don't feel it. Tell me you don't want me." Her voice shook.

Clare was silent. Jess's sobs mingled with the frogs and the crickets. "Yes, I did, but not like this. I won't be with a cheater. I won't be someone's second choice." Tears breached their feeble barrier, her emotions betraying her. She walked inside and turned off the lights, including the porch light, making her message clear: Jess needed to leave.

From the dark kitchen window, she watched her walk across the yard still sobbing, and strangely, it made her heart ache. How could she want her to leave so badly and be so heartbroken to see her go? She gripped the edge of the kitchen sink and waited a few minutes more before turning on the light and resolutely washing their dirty dishes.

Her emotions passed from furious, to defeated, to disappointed, not only with Jess, but with the situation itself. Everything had been going so well. She wasn't sure if she was glad that Lyn had overheard her conversation with Tim and Ian or not. If ignorance were bliss, she'd be leading Jess inside right now, lifting her onto the bed, making her arch and bend beneath her until she added another delightful memory to the precious others they'd made together. Her arousal soared at the thought, and she attempted to push it aside as she vigorously scrubbed their dinner plates.

Jess's pleas had nearly destroyed her. Of course, there was something between them. She knew that the day Jess pulled up to the ranger station and fumbled her way through registration. Of course,

Clare wanted her. She wanted her so badly that it hurt, more than she'd ever wanted anyone, and not just sexually. She threw the rinsed silverware into the drying rack, and a fork bounced out and ricocheted off the floor. She picked it up and washed it again.

Why hadn't Jess told her? Had she been truthful when she said that she'd wanted to break up with him but hadn't yet? Did her relationship with her boyfriend *really* mean nothing to her? Thinking of the word boyfriend in association with Jess made her nauseated. She hadn't seen this coming.

She'd trusted Jess, and it turned out to be a mistake. Clare saw Jess's immaturity come into play, but she felt strongly about this particular issue, whether it was youthful folly or not. She wasn't going to be involved with someone in a relationship. She'd been on the receiving end of such actions, and she wouldn't participate in doing that to someone else, at least not knowingly.

Tears fell onto her dish towel as she dried her wineglass. The closeness, the touches, and the beautiful evening had given her such high hopes for tonight. On a primal, organic level, she knew that Jess felt it, too. One poor decision and one phone call had ruined more than just one night.

However, Clare's body hadn't received the message that the night had been cut short. There had been no, "Loud and clear, over," only radio silence. Even after she finished washing the dishes, longing swirled inside her. Her desire wouldn't dissipate, and yet, her heart was full of cracks, threatening to shatter into a million pieces. Clare hurled the pristinely polished wineglass at the kitchen wall. It burst into smithereens, scattering shards of crystal onto the linoleum floor.

CHAPTER THIRTY

Jess stared out the mesh top of her tent at the night sky. As they often did, the stars enigmatically drew her to them. She wanted to lose herself within them, but she couldn't ignore the emptiness inside. If she felt like this tonight, she worried about what morning would be like with everything compounded under the harsh light of day.

Clare had made it clear she had boundaries she wouldn't cross. In addition to the pain Jess knew she'd inflicted upon her, Clare had also been angry. She felt sick knowing how badly she'd hurt her. Had her mistake ruined everything? Was there any way to salvage what they had?

Unable to sleep, she began to pack her belongings. She knew Clare well enough to know that trying to go to her now, trying to talk to her, to explain everything again would only make the situation worse. Clare's walls had gone up like a drawbridge. There was a slim chance that time might bring them down again but forcing the situation right now would not. There was no reason to stay another day.

With her duffels stuffed full and her bike secured on top of her car, she loaded everything else except for her tent, air mattress, and a small bag of toiletries. Come morning, she'd stop for some snacks and leave.

She flopped on the mattress and hoped for a few hours of sleep. That's about all she got. Morning brought sunlight and shadows, but no more clarity. She tore down her tent, packed everything in her car, and stared at her empty campsite. It looked like she'd never been there. She got in her car and drove to the general store for snacks.

Jess stuffed her receipt in her pocket and grabbed the Snapple and bag of Smartfood Popcorn. On her way out the door, she nearly ran into Lyn.

Lyn glanced between Jess and her packed car. "Oh, it's you. Are you leaving?"

Jess stepped past her. "Why do you care?" If she believed Lyn had been selfless with her delivery of the news, she might feel less annoyed. In truth, she was far angrier at herself than at Lyn.

"I don't. I care about Clare's happiness."

Jess kept from rolling her eyes. Barely.

"Lynette Weber, close that door! You're letting the cool air out!" Maggie yelled from inside.

Lyn let go of the door.

"Is that what you call it?" Jess stared holes into her.

Lyn ignored the question. "You must have thought I was joking when I told you she was fragile. How dare you?"

She wished the ground could open and swallow her. Jess was ashamed, but to have to wear her shame in front of Lyn was too much.

"Let me tell you something. Despite what you believe, whatever is going on between Clare and me is none of your business. She may tell you some things, but I guarantee she does *not* tell you everything. She's fully aware that you can't be unbiased." Calmer, Jess took a step back. "I'm no angel, but neither are you."

Lyn just looked at her, her lips parted. Jess walked away.

The winds picked up as soon as she left the campground. She fought to steer the car within its lane and tried to avoid hitting the tumbleweeds blowing across the highway. She figured the gale rushing through the canyon would subside once she reached the top, but it wasn't until she reached Ephrata that the winds tapered off. There were things she'd miss about Dry Falls, but the wind wasn't one of them.

Jess chastised herself. She should have broken up with Jackson before she left Seattle. Had there ever been a time when she'd been so angry with herself? She prided herself on prioritizing important matters. Completing a double major while working full-time was no easy task, but she made it happen. She'd known where she wanted to go to graduate school and what she intended to do while there, and she made it happen. So, why was she so lackadaisical about her personal life? Was it because her relationship with him inspired nothing in her, and that blasé feeling had overtaken all parts of the relationship, even hampering her ability to end it?

With her dad gone and graduation around the corner, that little nagging fear that she'd be alone hadn't helped. Now, look at her. Her attempt at self-preservation hadn't been fair to Jackson either. He wasn't the right person for her, and she should have told him that. Worst of all, she'd hurt the one person who meant the most to her, and that thought crushed her. She never thought it would turn out like this. What a mess she'd made of her life.

Her delay and disregard concerning her failed relationship may have cost her dearly. Before last night, she hadn't realized the potential impact of her procrastination. Nevertheless, Clare's words had sent her into a tailspin. She'd become the most important person in Jess's life, and yet her procrastination had resulted in the terrible situation in which she found herself.

She knew that breaking up with Jackson might not change anything between her and Clare, but she had to at least find out. Clare had trusted her, and lying, even lying by omission, had destroyed that trust. Whether it could be repaired would have to be seen. Clare simply might decide not to take her back. Was her mistake unforgivable? She honestly didn't know.

While it might be too little, too late, she needed to tell Clare her relationship with him was over. It might not change anything, but it was time to grow up. What she'd done, the choice she'd made, was wrong. She needed to fix things.

Clare entered the ranger station. Lyn greeted her without looking up from the papers on her desk.

"I told you to do the self-reflection for your annual performance review last week. If you had, you wouldn't have had to come in today." She admonished her in a tone that Clare would accept from few people.

"You're right. I should have. This is the last thing I need right now." She hadn't even bothered changing. She wore the same sweats she'd slept in, but she'd put on a bra, a testament to the minuscule bit of her pride that remained. "I miss the good old days when my supervisor would just tell me if I was doing a terrible job, and I didn't have to bother with all this self-reflection crap."

Lyn looked up. "Jesus. You look like shit, and you're in quite the mood. I take it that things didn't go well last night." She pushed her paperwork aside and clicked the end of her pen.

Clare stared at the pen in her hand until Lyn laid it on the desk. Her nerves were frayed. She'd barely slept. "That would be an understatement." She just wanted to get into her truck and nurse her heartache in private. How stupid she'd been, thinking she was finally ready to put herself out there again. Hadn't she been through enough already? She allowed herself to be vulnerable, and it only left her poor heart bruised once more.

"For what it's worth, I'm sorry this happened to you." Lyn stared at the floor. "I know you probably think I'm happy about how it turned out, but I'm not. I hate to see you hurt. It was nice seeing you happy, even if it wasn't me making you happy. I've thought a lot about our talk. I want you to know I'm not sitting here…I don't know…experiencing schadenfreude, or whatever."

Clare listened, then nodded. "Thank you. That means a lot to me." She hadn't expected that.

"Do you think you'll forgive her?"

"She withheld vital information from me. We'd become so close. I trusted her. If she'd just said something in the beginning…"

"Would you have still given her a chance?"

Clare shrugged. "I don't know. I suppose we'll never know."

"I saw her this morning." Lyn scratched at a mosquito bite.

"You saw her? What did she say?" She hated that she sounded so interested, so weak, so pathetic.

"Nothing much. She was leaving."

"Oh." Clare's stomach went into freefall. Jess had left. The news stung worse than she would have ever guessed. She assumed Jess would try to see her, try to say good-bye. She didn't necessarily want to see her and certainly didn't want to talk to her right now but knowing Jess had tried would have meant something. *Why* she needed it to mean something confused her. "I'm such a fucking mess."

"Maybe leave that tidbit off your review." Lyn stood and pulled her into a hug. "I'm here, as your best friend. I promise."

Clare hugged her back and felt a smidge better for the support. "Where's that stupid form?"

"I pinned it to your bulletin board." Lyn pointed to the wall.

Clare pulled down the form without removing the pushpin, ripping the top.

CHAPTER THIRTY-ONE

Jess had cried on her way to Leavenworth, so she took a few minutes in her car to compose herself and apply a bit of makeup. Still, her eyes remained red. She spotted Tim sitting at a corner table in the Old World Café.

He put away his phone as she approached. "Thanks for meeting me. I hope it's not too much of an inconvenience." He hugged her.

"Not at all. Thanks for coming a day early." She dropped her backpack on an empty chair. "I would have met you somewhere closer."

He shook his head. "No, I'm the one who forgot his wallet. I didn't want you to drive out of your way."

She slid his wallet across the table. "Ian didn't mind covering the shop by himself today?"

"No, he can manage it. He said to say hello." The server interrupted them to take their drink order, and Tim waited for her to leave before he spoke. "I say this as your friend, but you look awful. Why did you leave a day early?"

"I screwed up. I think it's over." She stared at the table as the tears resumed. So much for mascara.

"What happened? Did you and Clare fight?"

"My boyfriend came up." Their drinks arrived and the server took their order. Jess used the time to pull herself together. She unfolded her napkin and dried her eyes.

Tim scowled. "I'm surprised you told her, especially this late in the summer."

"I didn't. Her friend Lyn overheard us talking at the concession stand."

His eyes widened. "I'm sorry. I'm the one who brought it up. I guess it didn't occur to me not to talk about it in public."

She felt even worse because he looked so apologetic. "You're not to blame. I'm the one who should have broken up with him before I left this spring. When I hadn't, I should have been truthful with Clare, even if she wanted nothing to do with me. I never thought I'd be this person."

"Well, it sounds like you have some explaining to do."

"She's not speaking to me at the moment."

He stared at her, then tilted his head. "Have you ever watched those period movies with stagecoaches and women in fancy dresses?"

Was he drinking? "Um. Not often, but sure?"

"Where the gentleman gets out first, takes off his coat, and lays it over a puddle of mud for the lady to walk across?"

"Yeah, I guess so." She had no idea where this was going.

"Well, that coat is your pride, and you're going to have to lay it out there and let it get walked on." His voice softened. "I know we haven't known each other long, but I think we can agree we've become friends. So, I say this to you as your friend. You screwed up and screwed up royally. You can't worry about your pride. Lay it out there. You need to be honest with her. Tell her why you did it and apologize. Make it right."

Jess played with her straw. "That's easier said than done. I know I screwed up. Trust me when I say I wish I could have a redo." She sighed. "I need to figure out what to say and how to say it. I suppose I also need to figure out why I held on to Jackson so long. *I* need to have answers before I can explain it to Clare properly. I can't blow the one slim chance she might forgive me. You have no idea how much I've hurt her. She was beyond upset."

"She deserves to know everything. No one knows what your relationship with that douchebag boyfriend of yours was like except you. It sounds like it was a dead-end, and you knew it. You weren't off doing…" He motioned with his hand through the air. "…whatever with Clare when you had a boyfriend back home you loved or who was in love with you, from what I've gathered. However, that still doesn't excuse it."

Jess wiped her tears. At this point, the napkin had more mascara on it than her face. "I hurt her. I never meant to hurt her. If I had the chance to do it over, I'd do it differently."

"You wouldn't have kissed her?"

"Oh, I definitely would have kissed her. I also would have driven to Seattle a hell of a lot sooner to dump his ass." Jess sighed and squeezed her eyes shut, unable to face him. "It's worse than that. I slept with her."

"Well, that does make it worse. I assumed you had, but I wasn't sure."

"I slept with her *a lot*." She opened her eyes.

He winced. "Thanks, but TMI. I don't think how *many* times matter. You either did or didn't. It's a binary thing, like you can't be sort of pregnant."

Their food arrived, but she couldn't stop thinking about the argument. Clare had been so angry, showing a side of herself Jess had never seen before, but it was the hurt in Clare's eyes that left Jess decimated. She should have known the kind of effect this kind of betrayal would have, but she never expected Clare to find out.

That night on the island, Clare had shared things about her past and had shown her vulnerability, the chinks in her armor. She'd trusted her, and Jess had landed the blow right where it could do the most damage. God, what had she done?

They continued their meal with less sensitive subjects, namely whether Tim should grow a beard. He was in favor of the change, citing how the fall was a perfect time because it was hunting season, and hunters didn't shave until they bagged their deer. He argued it would be in fashion. Jess argued that they were gross, scratchy, food receptacles, and he should ask Melanie her opinion.

As they lingered near the door of the café to say their good-byes, he hugged her. "Thank you for bringing my wallet."

"Yeah, thanks for the talk. Speaking of your wallet, where is it?"

He patted his back pocket. "Got it."

"Thanks again for lunch."

"It's the least I can do. Get your life straightened out." He pointed at her as he walked away.

"Got it. Give Ian my love."

He'd given her good advice. She was going to have to sacrifice her pride and hope it was enough.

❖

Traffic slowed Jess's progress as she tried to get to Seattle's Queen Anne neighborhood where Jackson lived. She decided to close this chapter of her life as soon as she reached the city, even before she went to her apartment.

Seattle felt different, and she tried to put her finger on what it was. She settled on moist. She rolled down her window and inhaled. The petrichor from the recent rain wafted through the air as the sun warmed the ground and vegetation. It all felt so foreign. She'd grown accustomed to the arid heat.

She found a parking spot a few blocks away from Jackson's apartment. He lived on the second floor of a partitioned house. She had a key, but she knocked instead of letting herself in.

He opened the door, his hair wet and ruffled from a shower. He looked surprised to see her, like he might have been expecting someone else.

"Oh. It's you." He combed his hair with his fingers. "What are you doing here?"

She walked past him into the small dining area. His apartment wasn't messy like it usually was, which surprised her. "It smells good, like coffee."

"Do you want some?" He went to the kitchen.

"You don't drink coffee."

He shrugged. "I've learned to like it. Do you want some or not?"

"Yeah, thanks." She was beginning to feel fatigued from the lack of sleep.

He poured her a cup.

She blew across the top, took a sip, and recoiled. "What flavor is this?"

He fumbled around in two cupboards before he located the bag of grounds. "Coconut mocha."

"Difficult to remember, huh?"

She set the disgusting drink on the table. He didn't respond and stayed in the kitchen like he was afraid to get too close. It didn't escape her that there had been no affectionate greeting from him, neither physical nor verbal.

"I've been trying to contact you."

He fidgeted like a guilty five-year-old. "I haven't been using my phone much. I needed a break from technology."

"A break? I'm supposed to believe you're getting your technology MBA and need a break from technology? For three months?"

He shuffled from one foot to the other, his discomfort evident. He didn't answer her, silence being his apparent strategy to get through the conversation.

"I've been gone for months. Months! Do you know how many times I've heard from you?" She glared at him.

He stuck to his game plan and offered no excuse. Taking a deep breath, he sighed and leaned against the counter.

"We're done." Jess was tired of this game. "This has gone on far too long."

He said nothing.

"I need to use the bathroom. Get me a box or some bags I can put my stuff in, please." She headed down the hall.

The bathroom was messy, but not its normal state of squalor. She stepped over his wet towel and the boxers she knew he slept in, but the area around the sink was clean. As usual, an empty cardboard roll was all that remained on the toilet paper holder, and a half-used roll sat on the back of the tank. While she sat there, she changed the roll. She opened the door under the sink to throw away the old roll when something on the floor beneath the cabinet caught her eye. The overhang hid a pink hair tie. She picked it up. Blond hairs wound and knotted themselves around the elastic band's metal crimping. She set it on the counter.

When she pulled the garbage can from under the sink, she was amazed to find a plastic bag in it. She'd never known him to use one. Using the empty cardboard tube, she pushed aside crumpled tissues. She wasn't surprised when she saw the purple plastic wrapping from a tampon, different from the kind she used. Another push of tissues revealed a used condom and wrapper. With a grimace, she choked down her disgust. She scrubbed her hands and dried them on her shorts, not trusting the wrinkled towel hanging over the toilet. Before she exited the bathroom, she hung the pink elastic band on the faucet.

When she returned, not only had he found a banker's box for her to use, but he'd already begun to put her things in it, like the well-worn Sleater-Kinney T-shirt she liked to sleep in, the coffee mug her friend Molly had given her for graduation that said *Geologists know how to make the bedrock,* her UW sweatshirt, and her Kindle, which she assumed she'd lost.

She walked around the apartment looking for any remaining items that belonged to her. A pretty rock she'd found washed up on the shoreline near Ozette during one of their camping trips made it into the box. Her Vancouver Canucks cap hung on the back of his bedroom door along with her robe. Other than that, she'd left little evidence of their relationship in his apartment. That itself was telling. Still, hadn't the new girl noticed her things, or had she assumed they were his?

She set the box by the door and faced him. He still stood in the kitchen. She took his key off her keyring, set it on the table, and held out her hand. "I want my key."

He pulled out his keys, took her key off the ring, and extended it to her from a distance.

"I'll mail you your things." She slipped the key into her pocket.

"Okay."

She picked up the box and looked at him one last time. "We should have done this a long time ago."

He shifted uncomfortably, his eyes on the floor. "It's not all my fault."

"I never said it was." She stared at him, feeling nothing except annoyance. "You could have answered your damn phone, and we wouldn't have had to do this in person. Hell, you could have called to tell me you'd moved on, and it would have made us both happy. What a waste of my time." She shook her head and opened the door. "Tell whoever bought that coffee that it tastes like shit." As she shut the door behind her, she caught his stunned expression and smiled. She'd expected to be a little sad as she left, but she wasn't, at least not where he was concerned.

Driving, crying, and then keeping her emotions in check while dealing with him left her exhausted by the time she reached her apartment. It looked even more dim and uninviting than usual, and the air smelled stale. Jess sank into the couch, ate half her Big Mac, and finished the remaining fries she hadn't inhaled in the car. She couldn't recall the last thing she'd eaten.

She struggled to keep her eyes open. Unpacking could wait. Her laptop sat on the counter, and she'd locked up her bike. That was all that mattered, at least as physical objects were concerned. Her tears resumed, partially from exhaustion but mostly because her heart ached.

She glanced at her phone. Texting Clare was so tempting, but she knew it would do no good. This wasn't the kind of problem texting could fix. She might not have done anything right so far, but she needed to apologize the right way. Even if she did, she knew that there was a chance Clare might not take her back. She was young, but she wasn't naïve. Her stomach soured as she imagined begging for forgiveness, and Clare refusing to grant it. She pulled the blanket from the back of the couch and fell asleep within minutes.

CHAPTER THIRTY-TWO

Clare exited the ranger station and noticed her. It had been a week since Jess had laid eyes on her. Seven long, excruciating days.

"Can we talk? I won't keep you long." Jess stayed next to her car. She didn't approach Clare, as wary of scaring her off as she would a wounded bird.

"You shouldn't have wasted your time driving back here." Clare's eyes showed no emotion.

"Give me five minutes. Please?" Ten seconds into the conversation and she was already begging. Clare looked as beautiful as ever, but strain showed in her face, in her eyes that were a little too pink, a little too puffy.

Clare sighed. "Fine. Follow me." She got in her truck.

Jess followed her to the parking lot of the lake, and then to a nearby picnic table. It was telling that Clare hadn't invited her to her house across the road.

The park already seemed different, and only a week had passed. The trees had fewer leaves, the temperature milder, and the park nearly devoid of people. It felt eerie, too calm, and discordant with her heart that pinballed around in her chest.

Jess had rehearsed everything she needed to say during the hours it took her to drive to the park. Now that she sat in Clare's presence, her mouth felt dry, and her mind reeled. She wanted to take Clare in her arms and say she was sorry over and over, but she knew she couldn't. She'd lost that right. As she cleared her throat to speak, Clare spoke first.

"How did you know what time I got off work?"

Jess gulped. "I called the visitor center. They told me."

"Well, at least you didn't do this while I was working."

Jess wasn't sure how to interpret that. She couldn't remember ever being this nervous.

"I can't express to you how sorry I am. I realize that what I did was reprehensible. The first thing I did when I got to Seattle was break up with him."

Clare stared out at the lake, her elbows resting on her knees.

This wasn't going to be easy. Jess had to dig deeper.

"Let me start by saying this: I know I hurt you, and that was never my intention. You mean the world to me. You're the last person I'd ever want to hurt."

Clare sniffed but didn't respond, so she continued. If she only had five minutes, she better make them count.

"You are all I've thought about since I left. You, me, what I did. I was wrong. What I did was wrong. I realize that now. I should have done so many things differently. Instead of doing the right thing and breaking up with him before I arrived, or being honest with you when I hadn't, I stuck my head in the sand and hoped my problem would take care of itself."

She looked down at her shoes and thought about the feelings she'd been trying to deal with.

"You trusted me, confided in me, and it scared me. When you shared with me that Dominique cheated on you, I worried you'd never speak to me again if I told you. I was frightened, so I said nothing. I didn't want to lose you." Her throat felt hoarse.

Clare remained still and silent.

"I planned to break up with him as soon as I got home. He didn't mean anything to me, even before I came here for the summer, and I wrongly hoped the topic of him would never come up between us before I could end things. I wasn't honest with you. I am so sorry."

"Why *didn't* you break up with him?" Clare's voice sounded distant, hollow.

Jess had no good reason, no rational reason, only an excuse. "The same reason I started dating him, I suppose. I had no one after my dad died. My friends were all forming long-term relationships, and I didn't want to be alone. I wanted to be important to someone. In the back of my mind, if I didn't break up with him before I came here, at least I would be going home to something."

"So, he was your safety net, in case things didn't work out between us."

Jess shook her head vehemently. "No."

"That's what it sounds like." Clare toed the grass with her boot.

Jess looked at her. "No, definitely not, because I never expected to meet you. I never expected to feel this way. I didn't even know a person *could* feel this way. I never saw any kind of future with *him*. I just…" She sighed and rubbed at her sore eyes. "I was so afraid of being alone, of having no one at all left in the world who cared about me, that it seemed the lesser of two evils. I've thought a lot about the things I need to work on, the things that have scared me after losing my dad. And I'm going to. Work on them, I mean."

Clare blinked rapidly and looked away. Jess could see her chest rising and falling under her uniform.

"I don't want this to be what defines us," Jess whispered.

"What makes you think there's an *us*?" Clare didn't look at her as she said it.

The tip of Jess's nose tingled, and her eyes stung. That wasn't what she wanted to hear. Her tears lined up, ready to burst on stage, but somehow, she managed to keep them in the wings. "I know I hurt you. I swear it will never happen again if you give me another chance, even though I may not deserve it. I'm sorry."

Clare sighed and looked at her. "I believe you, but I hope you realize that saying you're sorry doesn't automatically fix this. This isn't a scratch, and an apology isn't a bandage."

The lump in her throat swelled. She couldn't speak. It wasn't supposed to be like this.

"I need some time. I need some time to think." Clare stood and walked to her truck.

Jess watched her walk away. She didn't look back once. When she drove away, she didn't drive toward her house.

Stunned, Jess sat there for a few minutes. It had all been for nothing. She'd practiced the conversation a hundred times in her head and imagined how it would go. While she knew it might not go as she hoped, this outcome felt worse than she'd imagined. Part of her had believed that Clare would forgive her and take her back.

With slumped shoulders and a sick stomach, she walked to her car. She'd have plenty of time to wonder where it had gone wrong. Was there nothing else she could do?

Chapter Thirty-three

Clare sent Lyn a text after Jess left. Lyn came by after her shift to check on her. She headed straight for the refrigerator and downed half a can of Diet Coke before flopping into her favorite chair. She hadn't even bothered to go home and change.

"You weren't expecting to see her. I'm sure it was shocking."

Clare stared at the wall from her place on the sofa. She hugged her knees to her chest.

Lyn tried again. "It'll get easier over time."

"Easier?" Clare furrowed her eyebrows.

Lyn blinked a few times as if the question confused her. "Being without her."

The contents of Clare's stomach surged upward. She swallowed hard, refusing to allow her body to betray her like that. She didn't want to think about being without her, *couldn't* think about being without her, and certainly didn't want to think about an existence where she was fine being without her. Being *with* Jess for three months had changed her. She couldn't recall how she used to exist before her.

On the other hand, what Jess had done broke her heart. It had been so unexpected, especially after what Clare had shared with her. She'd been looking toward their future together. She hadn't seen this coming.

"Or maybe, you could try to see her side of things." Lyn spoke cautiously and watched her intently.

Clare scowled at her. "What? Whose side are you on?"

"This isn't exactly comfortable given our recent conversation, but I'm trying to be a better friend. I'm on your side, and I want you to be happy. I've never made you that happy. I could never make you that happy. Maybe you shouldn't throw everything away quite yet. I'm not sure you realize how lucky you were to have what you had." Lyn sounded resigned.

"It wasn't mine to have." Clare looked at the floor. She knew it couldn't have been easy for Lyn to be so forthcoming. Was Lyn right? Had she been too harsh with her judgment? Cheating was cheating though. She didn't know if she could come around on that issue.

"Well, if you can't forgive her, you'll have to find ways to take your mind off her. Who knows what will happen with Brett? If you decide to report him and he gets sacked, you'll be first in line for the position. I suppose running the park will keep you busy." Lyn set the empty can on the coffee table.

"Maybe, but it's his word against mine. It might look like I fabricated the story to get the position. Plus, I don't even know if I want it." Her tone sounded one degree above catatonic, even to her ears.

"What? Haven't you spent most of the last decade working toward that goal?" Lyn sounded incredulous, the last word nearly squeaking out.

"Yes." Clare hugged her knees even tighter to her chest.

"That surprises me."

"You and me both."

"Maybe we should both look for jobs in different parks." Lyn arched her eyebrows.

Clare hadn't seen that coming. She had to give Lyn credit for showing such maturity. She nodded. "We both might need a fresh start."

Lyn jumped up. "It's nice outside. Let's have a drink." She pulled two ice-cold beers from the refrigerator and rummaged through a drawer for a bottle opener. She glanced at Clare's pajamas. "Do you want to change?"

"No." Clare rose from the couch despite her reluctance to do so.

Lyn handed her a beer before opening the back door. "Oh!" She stopped short, and Clare ran into her. "I almost stepped on that box. Why did you put it there?"

"What box?" She peered around her. "I didn't put anything out here."

Lyn picked it up, and Clare's eyes widened.

"Give it to me." She snatched the box away.

"What is it?" Lyn leaned in so she could see.

"It's her rock collection." Jess had shown it to her on one of the first nights they'd spent time together. She handed Lyn her beer.

"Rocks? Did she forget them? Why was it on your back steps?"

Clare ran her fingers over the wooden top. "She didn't forget it. She must have left it here today on purpose."

She unclasped the tiny latch and opened the lid. A folded piece of notebook paper sat on top. She picked it up. Beneath it, all the little holes held various rocks except one. Clare didn't know which rock was missing from the space. Jess must have taken one of the rocks with her. She remembered her saying that her dad had brought her many of the rocks from his travels. Perhaps one held extra-special meaning.

She opened the note and read Jess's short message in her neat handwriting.

Clare,

I never intended to hurt you. I don't want this to be good-bye.

I leave my most treasured possession with the person I treasure the most. Please take care of it.

I'm so sorry.

Yours,

Jess

Beneath the writing, Jess had attached Clare's house key to the paper with a Band-Aid. Lyn held her as she cried.

Clare left her therapist's office after her appointment and drove home. Over a month had passed since Jess left. It had been more than a month since she discovered she'd been betrayed a second time.

She'd been making plans for their future, wondering how they could have a life together. She'd looked forward to discovering what they had. It was like being a chapter or two into an intriguing book, and she'd been eager to see what the rest of the pages held.

In the weeks since, Clare had brought her therapist up to speed. She'd worked so hard in therapy and come so far, only to find herself back at square one: angry, devastated, embarrassed, betrayed, and ultimately heartbroken. Again, she started down the path to restore her trust in others. This time, it might be an exercise in futility.

In prior sessions, Dr. Markovich and Clare had discussed how the situation had been handled. She asked Clare whether Jess had owned what she'd done, whether she appeared remorseful, and if she acknowledged and discussed her feelings. Clare couldn't help but answer yes, but that didn't make it any less painful or excuse what Jess did.

One thing that resonated with her from today's session was that she'd be okay. In a move somewhat out of character, Clare believed it. Even after everything that happened with Dominique, her death and her infidelity, Clare had been okay. It might have taken her years to get to that point, but she met Jess and realized she had a life to live. With or without Jess, she knew she'd be okay, even if she was alone, even if she didn't feel anything close to okay now.

She knew she had to follow her heart whether she forgave Jess or moved on. There was no guidebook, no table of contents she could peruse to find that page that would tell her which decision to make. Fear would not be her guide. She knew she shouldn't run away simply because she was afraid of Jess hurting her again. Jess had stayed with someone she didn't love due to her fear of being alone. Look where that got her.

As she passed the ranger station, she saw Brett's truck. She'd been considering whether to report his behavior to the park system, both his relationship with a subordinate and the incident in the storage shed. But what proof did she have? What would they think was her motive? Lyn was right. Clare was likely the next person to head the park. Not only was she unsure she wanted the position, but she didn't want it to look like she'd gotten it via slander either.

Right then, she decided she wouldn't report him. It would involve numerous interviews and the fear of retaliation. The thought made her stomach churn. She didn't need that drama in her life. He would have to live knowing what he'd done and live knowing *she knew* what he'd done. That was enough for her. It felt good to have a sense of closure, even if it was only in her mind.

Her thoughts turned to Lyn. Their heart-to-heart had sparked something in her. Clare should have talked with her years ago. Hearing Clare say they would never have a relationship opened her eyes. Their friendship had blossomed again, Lyn even going so far as to advocate on Jess's behalf at times. It felt good to have her friend back.

Well, technically back, although probably not for long. Lyn was currently away. She had an in-person interview for a dispatcher position in the San Juan Islands. Clare had been surprised at how excited Lyn seemed about the job. Lyn called her a few hours ago as soon as the interview concluded. She thought it had gone well, and they seemed interested in her.

In contrast, the tempo of Clare's life slowed to a crawl, a normal effect of the cooler season and the closure of the campground. Fall brought with it fewer visitors and too much time to think, and the inactivity of the park seemed amplified this year. The park laid off seasonal rangers, leaving her, Brett, and two part-time rangers to manage the park. Luckily, he didn't seem to want to spend any more time with her than she wanted to spend with him, and that suited her fine. The layoff also meant that only one ranger worked per shift, so she had few interactions with him. But could she weather the long, slow off-season?

The electronic crackle of the radio she used to find comforting when she was at home or in her truck now did the opposite, so she rarely turned it on outside of work hours. Brett had brought on a temp-to-hire named Alicia that Lyn and Helen had been training to work nights. So far, she impressed Clare with her professionalism and her radio interactions. Helen told Clare that she was a fast learner and made smart decisions under pressure, both assets when it came to being a dispatcher. She hated to admit it, but he'd made an excellent choice. If the park up north offered Lyn the job and she chose to accept it, at least they wouldn't be short-handed. Thinking about the long-term absence of Lyn's voice on the radio, a familiar constant over the past decade, was still difficult to imagine.

Despite the more reasonable temperatures, even the climate made her irritable. She yearned for signs of life, greenery, something that felt alive, not the barren landscape that surrounded her. Soon the snow would blanket the park, a vast whiteness covering all. The park that had once been her everything now felt sterile and devoid of life. Her shifts passed in elongated states of inertia, her ability to focus on the tasks at hand waned, and she ripped off her uniform in relief after every shift only to experience the same depressing feelings at night.

Helen tried to console her, telling her it was stress or a case of seasonal affective disorder, but Clare knew better. She and Hank invited her for dinner at least once a week, telling funny stories over wonderful meals to try and cheer her up. Clare barely tasted the food and forced her laughter. When she returned home to her quiet house, she felt as out of place there as the garish painting she hated hanging above the sofa.

Days droned on into weeks. She lost weight despite exerting far less energy than she did during the summer months. Her service belt rode uncomfortably on her sharp hip bones.

She knew she couldn't live like this, not in this dreary and lifeless state, so she came to a decision. She *wouldn't* live like this any longer. On a gray, overcast day, as fall tumbled helplessly into winter, she sat at her dining room table with a pen and paper, and teary-eyed, she began to write.

CHAPTER THIRTY-FOUR

Weeks ago, Jess had made the final tweaks to her thesis and turned in her draft. Like a swimmer reaching the surface and gasping for air, it brought immediate relief from the stress she'd endured over the past months, but the relief had been temporary. After her graduate advisor and a few other faculty members recommended edits, she'd complete her oral exam and present her thesis. The state of her personal life was in shambles, and she missed Clare with every cell in her body, but she tried to power through.

"What are you doing tonight? Do you want to join us for drinks?"

Her coworker Dylan took off his dirty black apron and jammed it into his back pocket. She continued to buff silverware, eager to finish her side work and clock out for the night. The popular gastropub at which she found a job waiting tables didn't pay well by the hour, but the beer selection was enormous, the ambiance lively, the food renowned, and her tips reflected that.

"I can't, sorry. I need to study." She dropped shiny fork after shiny fork from her bar towel into the cutlery bin with a clang. She still needed to roll silverware after she finished buffing. It was boring and monotonous and gave her far too much time to think about Clare.

"You always say that." He leaned on the counter, his sandy hair flopping over his eyes.

"I say it because it's true."

An undergrad at the University of Washington, he was a junior or senior majoring in architecture or design. She couldn't remember and didn't care. He might have been flirting with her, but it didn't matter.

"Well, text me if you change your mind. We're heading to the Rabbit Hole, but I'm not sure how long we'll be there."

She wouldn't be texting him.

"Here, let me tip you out." She pulled out her black server book and counted out some bills. He was one of the better bussers. "Thanks for helping me turn my tables tonight."

He waved his hand. "You can give it to me later or tell one of the managers to put it in the safe. I know you haven't done your bank yet."

"It's okay. I keep a running tally in my head." She folded the money and handed it to him. "Have fun with everyone."

After he left, she returned to her task and thoughts of Clare. She stared out the windows at the street in front of the restaurant. Spots of rain dotted the glass, the storm either starting or having passed while she was busy. She was tired of the rain, tired of buffing silverware, tired of being without Clare, and tired of trying to think of ways she might have done something differently so that Clare would've forgiven her. They hadn't spoken since her apology.

She hadn't spoken with Jackson since their breakup, and that was fine with her. She felt a certain degree of relief. It took getting out of the relationship before she could see that it was better to be alone than to be with the wrong person.

Jess hated to admit it, but missing Clare on top of her stressful academic situation was starting to have adverse effects on her. Some nights she crawled back to her apartment barely keeping her eyes open, feet and back aching from a long shift or eyes bleary and brain pounding from too many hours in the library. The physical and mental toll was nothing compared to the emotional fatigue she endured from her heart being in pieces. Life seemed intent on taking away those who meant the most to her. No, she couldn't blame life this time. This was her doing.

She needed to be resilient. While her academic efforts technically amounted to a piece of paper, they also meant she'd soon be pursuing her dream. She had no intention of going out with a whimper. She'd worked too hard for too long. Her father would be proud, even if he weren't there to see it. She was going to ace this.

With her deadlines looming, she concentrated on passing her oral exam and defending her thesis. It was no small feat. Any members of the public who wished to attend would be present during her upcoming formal presentation in front of her advisor, other faculty members, and graduate assistants. She'd succeed or fail with an audience.

She peeked over the banquette. Her manager had retreated to his office. Before she could change her mind, she sent Clare a quick text.

Thinking of you

She waited, watching the dots. They started and stopped. When they didn't resume, she texted again.

My presentation is Thursday.

She held her breath. The dots appeared. Ten seconds. Twenty seconds.

Good luck. You'll do great.

Clare had replied. Maybe she didn't hate her. She held on to that. However, Clare didn't seem too willing to chat. Jess waited a full ten minutes before sending her final text.

I miss you.

It went unanswered.

Clare's mind wandered as she drove. She'd heard from Jess, a few texts last week that caught her off guard. She was surprised with how pleased she'd been to receive them. However, after reading them at least fifty times, she'd felt worse than before, like a junkie coming off a particularly good high. She turned up the heater.

Despite the cold temperature, no clouds obscured the sky. The ground was dry and devoid of snow, even though the area usually had a few inches this time of year. They'd had little precipitation throughout the fall and winter.

Something dark caught her eye in the rearview mirror. She turned to glance over the boxes behind her to make sure.

Smoke.

"Shit!" She pulled onto the shoulder, got out, and confirmed her fear. The black smoke came from the park, the northern section. Cars whizzed by, the force tearing at her hair and clothing, freezing gusts blasting her bare face and hands. From the growth of the column of smoke in the brief time she'd spent parked on the roadside, she could tell the wind pushed the fire along. What had been a thin tendril of smoke in her rearview mirror now billowed thick and black, the utmost reaches beginning to dissipate along higher air currents.

"Fuck!" Of all times, why was there a fire now? While common in the summer months, they rarely dealt with fires during the off-season. Then again, they usually had more precipitation than they'd received this year.

She'd seen it so many times in person that she could imagine what it looked like. Red-orange flames licked along the parched ground, swallowing up the canyon's dry shrub-steppe vegetation as the wind pushed the fire onward, scorched earth standing out charcoal black against the otherwise rusty-brown landscape. With such little moisture left in the plants, the fire would consume the brush rapidly, leaving nothing but the blackened ground.

She wanted to kick her tire but didn't. Lives could be at stake. She should go back. The ranger on duty would need help gaining control of the fire until the fire department arrived, but she didn't even have her Pulaski with her. She was torn. Obligation and desire waged a fierce battle within. Was the universe testing her?

She heard the piercing scream of the county's fire engines in the distance. In her mind, she envisioned their large yellow bodies barreling down the highway as fast as they could go. The knowledge that they were on their way should have made her feel better, but it didn't. She should be there. She knew what could happen during one of these fires. She'd lived through it, and still lived with its aftermath.

A fire burned, destroying the park's landscape and putting lives at risk. On the other hand, this hadn't been part of her plan.

The wind shifted.

With startling clarity, she knew what she had to do. She got into her car.

Chapter Thirty-five

Clapping filled the small auditorium, and some of Jess's favorite faculty members even stood to give her an ovation as she disconnected her laptop. Her presentation had gone splendidly, better than she could have hoped. She expected two faculty members and a graduate assistant to be present from the university, but she was both terrified and delighted to see many other familiar academic faces in attendance.

A bit nervous at first, she soon found a rhythm, temporarily transported to the park and all its geological wonders, and the presentation flowed from her with passion. The question-and-answer session ended up being fruitful, allowing her an opportunity to share additional information and giving her things to consider for future research. The presentation extended past its allotted time, but no one stood to leave or seemed to mind. She wished her father could have been there to witness her accomplishing this step in her career. He would have been so proud.

She wished Clare could have seen it as well. She'd played such a significant role in her summer of research and had been so interested and supportive. It devastated her that Clare hadn't been there to share this with her. Still, Jess had a feeling that she would have been proud, too.

As she put her notecards into her bag, she saw someone lingering in the seated section. Her advisor, Dr. Abad, gave her a soft smile. She leaned on an aisle seat, waiting to walk her out. Jess slung her bag over her shoulder and met her halfway up the carpeted stairs.

Aside from advising her, she also happened to be one of Jess's favorite teachers. Students and faculty alike highly regarded the esteemed professor. Her undergraduate *Geology of the Northwest* class had been the class that first drew Jess's attention to Dry Falls. The class she taught on stratigraphy had, hands-down, been Jess's favorite class. She'd been the faculty member to sign off on her independent study credit, and the letter she wrote had helped ease open the doors of the state park system to allow her to camp at Sun Lakes all summer. She supported all the students she advised, and maybe it was because she knew both of Jess's parents had died, but she'd been Jess's cheerleader beyond what duty required.

Dr. Abad grinned and touched her arm. "Marvelous. I knew you would stun them with your presentation as soon as I saw your first draft. I'm so proud of you."

"Thank you."

"I mean it. What you have done is extraordinary. I think you've logged more hours in the field than some of my colleagues have done in their entire careers."

Jess grinned as she continued.

"On a related note, there's something else I wanted to talk to you about."

When they reached the closed double doors leading out of the auditorium, Jess turned and pushed the door open with her backside. They stopped in the hallway, facing each other.

"Yes?"

Dr. Abad smiled. "A friend of mine contacted me a few days ago. We were undergrads together. He works for a consulting firm that does geological and hydrological research for companies looking to build, do restoration, or who are required to do environmental cleanup. They need someone intelligent and industrious who can hit the ground running and won't need a ton of oversight. Due to the recent demand, they've expanded, and they don't have time to hold someone's hand. You came to mind."

"That's so kind of you to think of me." Her eyes grew wide at the prospect.

"I know it's not your ideal job, but you have the skill set, and you've demonstrated your effort and talent this summer. Plus, you've shown you don't require extensive supervision. This opportunity would allow you to have a job upon graduation, something few of your classmates can say, plus it will give you a wide range of experience. I took the liberty of forwarding him your first draft. He was impressed." Her advisor smiled at her, her pride in Jess evident.

"I don't know what to say. Thank you. I'm definitely interested."

"Perfect. Send me your résumé, and I'll introduce you through email." Dr. Abad touched her arm again. "I'll let you go now. It looks like your friend is waiting for you. Congratulations again on your presentation."

My friend?

Jess turned and saw Clare leaning against a wall in the lobby, making the stately building's sole purpose appear to be holding her up. Exhilaration hit her, dizziness, too, like she was in a dream, and her world would twist and spin until she woke up, alone.

Clare looked stunning. A smile crept across her face, growing wider as Jess came closer. Jess moved on autopilot, like iron to a magnet. Her vision swam, and her skin felt warm. With her academic requirements over, the ache of missing Clare hit her all at once, threatening to land her on the cold, tiled floor. Her guilt and sorrow collided with the sheer joy of seeing Clare in person. Somehow, she managed to put one foot in front of the other.

She'd never seen Clare look like this. A different setting only increased the mysterious air about her. Jess would have to reach out and touch her before she believed her to be real. Clare's walnut-colored ankle boots gave her a couple of additional inches of height. She wore a burnt-orange, belted jacket that hung open and hit her mid-thigh. A silky, cream-colored blouse gave a glimpse of the dip between her breasts, and form-fitting jeans showed off her long legs. She looked like she'd stepped out of a magazine. Cooler weather clothes suited her.

"You're here." Jess's brain spun too fast to produce more complex thoughts. Her suit jacket felt like it weighed twenty pounds and held in her body heat like a thick blanket of insulation. Her blouse stuck to her back.

Clare eyed her. "Yes." She gracefully pushed herself away from the wall and embraced her.

Jess's cheek pressed against the soft collar of her coat. She closed her eyes and breathed deeply, Clare's perfume surrounding her. How had she forgotten how good holding her felt?

She must have used up all her words during her presentation because her brain felt empty, choking and spluttering like a car sucking on its last drop of gasoline. "You came."

"Of course, I came." Clare seemed amused by her elementary sentences. She released her.

Jess stepped back and cleared her throat. "I didn't know you were coming."

"I wouldn't have missed it for the world." The low timbre of her voice and the sudden sparkle in her eyes alleviated a tiny bit of the grief Jess had lived with the last few months.

"You didn't come in? I didn't see you inside."

"No, I didn't want to be a distraction. I peeked through the doors and watched from there. I wasn't sure I was supposed to be in there anyway." Her face broke into a huge smile. "It was a wonderful presentation. I thought you were *amazing*. I can't believe how many great questions you received. I'm so proud of you. Plus, you look fantastic." She held her hands and stepped back to admire her. "You take my breath away."

Jess felt her face warm, both from Clare's words and her gaze that flowed over her like warm maple syrup over a stack of golden pancakes.

"Is it possible to go somewhere and talk?"

Jess considered the request. They had so much to talk about. She didn't want to take her back to her dreary apartment, but she also didn't want to be somewhere where they couldn't talk privately.

"There's a bakery I like about ten minutes from here. We can get some coffee."

"That sounds good. I'm parked not too far from here."

Outside, Clare took her hand like it was natural, like this is what they did every day. They walked across the campus, their fingers intertwined.

What if she ran into someone she knew? How would she introduce her? As her friend? Her girlfriend? Jess wasn't sure they were either at this point. A girlfriend would have kissed her after not seeing her for so many weeks. A girlfriend wouldn't have cheated. All sorts of feelings came rushing back, coloring her initial elation. Luckily, they didn't encounter anyone she knew.

Eventually, Clare stopped beside a black Audi A4 and unlocked it with a beep.

"Is this a rental?" Jess assessed the car.

"No, it's mine." She climbed into the driver's side.

Like the clothing, it suited her. Jess got in. The car was luxurious, a massive departure from Clare's previous vehicle. It still had the new car smell. "Where's your truck?"

"That's part of what I want to talk to you about." She glanced at her. "I traded it in. It wasn't me anymore."

As they drove the short distance to the bakery, neither said much. There was too much to discuss during a short car ride.

Once seated with their orders, Jess spoke first. "I was offered a job."

"What? That's wonderful! What kind of job?"

"I don't have too many details. My advisor told me about it in the hallway. It's not my ideal job, but it's a great entry-level position that will give me experience in different areas."

"Here in Seattle?" Clare squirmed a bit in her chair.

Jess nodded and sipped her coffee. "I don't know what's going on in your life, other than you sold your truck. How's your job? I miss the park." It wasn't the park she missed. She wasn't sure how to talk to Clare. Where did they stand? Did Clare's presence mean she forgave her? Or was she there simply to support her?

"It was time for a change. It was time to do many things." Clare reached across the table and covered Jess's hand with hers. "That's what I want to talk to you about." She studied their hands. "I quit my job at the park."

"What? Why?" Jess almost yelped in surprise.

"I was unhappy. I will always love the park, but it's filled with so many memories, so many unhappy memories. I used to think I had a special connection to the park. For a long time, I needed to be there, like I was a part of it, and it was a part of me. Then, I realized that wasn't true. There are too many bad memories, too many ghosts." She paused, an added level of seriousness to her voice when she continued. "I know there are things between us, things we need to talk about, but this decision had nothing to do with us. It was about me, what I needed. I needed to move on from Sun Lakes. I decided to look forward, not back. So, I resigned."

Shocked, Jess turned her hand over and held Clare's. "I'm sorry you've been unhappy, but I can't believe you quit your job."

"Why?"

"Lyn told me you'd never leave the park."

At the mention of Lyn, Clare raised her eyebrows. "Well, Lyn has been wrong about me before. She and I talked. She finally understood that she and I will never date. She's been working in the San Juan Islands. I think she's happy, or at least *happier*." She smiled.

"You're still friends?"

"We are. She's come a long way." Clare stared into her cup a moment. "Speaking of the park, there was a fire this morning."

"What?" Jess's mouth hung open in disbelief. "In winter? Was anyone hurt?"

"I don't know. I saw it as I was leaving to come here." Clare looked at her and held her gaze.

"What do you mean? You didn't go back?" Her voice was hoarse. Clare shook her head.

"You always respond to fires." Then she understood, and her entire demeanor softened. She felt lightheaded. "You still came to see me. You saw the fire and still came." Jess squeezed her hand.

"Yes, I did."

Clare smiled at her, so tender and sweet that Jess almost cried. An understanding existed between them that hadn't been there before.

"I was beginning to think I'd never see you again." Jess cast her eyes downward. Admitting her fear was easier that way. "When I didn't hear from you, I assumed the worst. I thought all chances of you forgiving me had passed."

Clare caressed her hand with her thumb. "I needed some time. It was a lot to process, especially after what I'd been through. I thought about you every day, probably every hour. I went over what happened and why it happened. I have a better understanding of why you made the decisions you made, even if they weren't decisions I'd make. I understand now why you did what you did."

"You do?" Jess hadn't expected this. She felt exposed, more exposed than if she'd been standing on the table without any clothing.

"You lost both your parents. You were young. You must have been afraid, afraid of being alone, having to deal with your feelings by yourself, no one there to take care of you, no one looking out for you. No wonder you settled and began dating him. I tried to put myself in your shoes, but I admit that I don't know exactly how that feels. I can imagine, but I'm lucky to have both my parents. I've never experienced that, and I can't imagine how scary and lonely it must have been to think you were all alone in the world. You made a mistake; we all make them. But I do know this. You can't live your life with fear dictating your decisions."

Jess tried to swallow, but her throat was too dry. Clare had explained her life to her better than she ever could have. It didn't excuse what she did, but the fact Clare took the time to try to understand her meant something. She'd never had this. Being truly intimate felt wonderful and frightening. It meant showing Clare all sides of herself, flawed and all. She had to allow herself to be vulnerable, even if it terrified her.

"You don't hate me?" Jess's hands shook.

Clare slowly blinked and shook her head. "I don't hate you."

"I'm so sorry for what I did. I never wanted to hurt you. I still don't want to hurt you. Ever."

"I know." She tucked her hair behind her ear.

"Will you forgive me?" Jess whispered.

Clare looked out the window for a couple of seconds and then smiled at her. "I already have."

She felt immeasurable relief. If the sun broke through the clouds and a choir started singing, it wouldn't have surprised her. Her tears were imminent. She was unsure how she'd lasted this long. When they came, relief poured through her to see that she wasn't the only one in such a state. They wept through soft smiles then wiped away their tears with cheap, scratchy napkins. Finally, Clare spoke.

"After you left, I was upset for a long time. I was miserable and nothing felt right. I missed you, even after what had happened. I couldn't summon any of the passion I used to have for my job. The normal duties I had to do for work annoyed me. Knowing I either had to accept working with Brett, knowing he isn't trustworthy, or decide to report him weighed on me. Everywhere I looked reminded me of bad memories. I'd been there for so long, too long. I never thought there'd be a time when I didn't want to be there, but I realized that's how I felt. I needed to make a change in my life. It was time to start a new chapter."

"It's still hard for me to believe you quit your job." Hearing such surprising news left Jess a bit shell-shocked.

Clare looked at her and smiled. "Someone I know once convinced me that even though it might be terrifying, the best way is to jump in."

She couldn't help but let a small smile crack her demeanor as she recalled how frightened Clare had been standing beside her atop the cliffs at Deep Lake. "I suppose that's true. Sometimes you have to leap."

"I agree. An ocean wave will knock you off your bearings if you stand still. You have to dive into it." Clare winked at her.

"So, you quit? With no plan?" Jess shook her head, her fingertips over her mouth.

"Well, not exactly. One day, when I felt like I was at rock bottom, I sat at my dining room table and wrote myself a list."

"A list of what?"

"Of things I needed to do. I knew I needed a change, to think of what was best for myself, my well-being, and my sanity. I had this pervasive feeling of unhappiness, and it involved more than what happened between us, although that was part of it. So, I made a list of action items. Like I said before, it may sound selfish, but these were things I needed to do for myself. So, in the weeks that followed, I checked the items off my list one by one."

"What kind of things?" Jess was intrigued. Her drink sat abandoned as she listened.

Clare told her how she traded in her truck that no longer felt like her and turned in her resignation, to Brett's surprise and Helen's sorrow. She explained how she called a moving company, boxed up all her possessions, and donated Dominique's bike. She told Jess how she decided to leave the garish painting of Dry Falls that Dominique had painted hanging on the wall in the empty house for the next ranger to keep or discard. She described how she said good-bye to the park by visiting the cave one last time. She explained how the fragile, handmade basket felt heavier when she pulled it from its hiding spot, and how she discovered the pyrite sun Jess had left.

At the mention, Jess shyly smiled.

Clare continued. "I knew I could use my savings as a buffer while I looked for a new job, but I got lucky and landed a temporary position as a head ranger after only going on three interviews."

"What? Where?" Jess withdrew her hand as fear stormed her heart.

"Dash Point State Park. It's near—"

"Tacoma," she finished, stunned.

"I was going to say Federal Way, but yes, just south of here. It's only temporary." Clare ran her hand through her hair. "The head ranger is going on family leave, but they may have a regular ranger position opening up after she returns. Or perhaps she'll decide she doesn't want to return after she has the baby. Anyway, it'll give me experience running a park and having that on my résumé could land me something down the line."

"Congratulations. That's wonderful…your own park." Jess stared in disbelief. She hoped there was more.

"You once said you could never ask me to leave the park or my job, and you didn't. *I* chose to leave. I did it for me." She hesitated, then continued. "I've rented a house in Gig Harbor."

Jess absorbed the information with wide eyes. She'd never expected such huge news. It gave her hope, but she was afraid to assume too much. They'd be living in the same place, or at least not far from each other. Did Clare's forgiveness mean she took her back? She didn't have long to wonder because Clare continued.

"Most importantly, I realized that I can't imagine being anywhere you aren't, and I want to show you how serious I am. So, I'll be living and working here, and if you decide to take that job and stay in the area, maybe we could be *us* again. I miss us. I'd like to be with you, to live with you, to have a life with you." Her eyes shone with sincerity. "I love you." She finished, breathless, eyes glistening.

Jess had never seen her look so fragile as she waited for a response. Tears ran down Jess's face, but they were happy tears, and she didn't care who saw. She almost felt guilty, experiencing so much happiness in one day. Some people probably didn't have this much in their lifetime. She smiled, for her response was easy. "Yes. Yes, to all of it because I love you, too."

Clare laughed, still so gorgeous despite her watery eyes. She pushed back her chair and came around the small table. She stood above her, tilted her face up, and kissed her.

Jess felt wetness and tasted salt. She was unsure whose tears they were. She'd missed her, the feel of her, the taste of her, all of her. Clare pulled back slowly and gave her a knowing smile and one last quick kiss before sitting.

Jess looked around. The few people in the place seemed to be paying them no attention. When she looked back at Clare, she was smiling.

"I've given you a lot to process, and maybe it's too soon. I'll understand if you want to wait, but I hope you'll move in with me. When the time is right, together we can look for a place we'd like to live."

She thought she might die from the sweetness in Clare's voice. Never had she imagined her day would turn out like this when she'd gotten up this morning. Clare sat before her, offering her a life she thought she'd never have. Clare was hers if that's what she wanted.

She grinned. "I'd like that, living with you. I don't know if I want to take this job, but whatever happens, together we can find a place where we can both do what we love. I don't care where that is as long as it's with you."

Clare smiled, looking both relieved and euphoric.

Jess went on. "Life has dealt us both some terrible hands, and we've survived because we're strong women, but I think we've both come to realize that we *can*, but don't *have* to endure it by ourselves. It's so much easier with someone you love to lean on. I want you by my side. Always."

Clare's face crumpled. Tears clung to her lashes. She drew in a raspy breath and reached for her.

Jess looked at their entwined hands, hands that she knew well, hands that she'd studied, hands that she loved. "I want to be with you. I want to make these decisions with you. I want to be open and honest with you. Perhaps you'll get that permanent job or maybe you'll find a great offer somewhere else, but I want to go on these adventures with you. We'll figure it out together."

Tears trickled down Clare's cheek, and she brushed them away with a flick of her hand and a happy laugh.

"Show me." Jess grinned.

"Sorry?"

She stood, picked up Clare's coat, and held it open. "Show me this house of yours." She hesitated. "This house of ours."

CHAPTER THIRTY-SIX

When they reached the sidewalk, Jess turned and slid her arms inside Clare's orange jacket and tipped her head to receive a greeting appropriate for two lovers who had been apart too long. Clare poured everything she had into that kiss, all the emotions that had built up over the past few months. Her knees went weak when Jess sucked on her bottom lip.

Some minutes later—before they broke a few of Seattle's penal codes—Clare drew back. She hadn't noticed the drizzle until that moment.

Jess, her vibrant eyes ringed by mist-covered lashes, grasped her coat's lapels. "I love you." She kissed her. It was short, sweet, gentle.

Clare looked at her with adoration. "I'll never tire of hearing that."

Jess stood on her tiptoes and kissed her again. Minutes later, when the drizzle turned to droplets, they ran hand in hand to the car.

The house was an older Craftsman, but it was in a nice neighborhood, had been well-cared for, and had a beautiful view. The backyard featured a small garden and two mature shade trees.

"It already feels like you. Your house in the park never really felt like you, but that's not your fault." Jess smiled.

"If anything, it had become familiar, but no, it wasn't me."

Stacked boxes lined the walls of the living and dining areas and the master bedroom. It still felt chaotic and unorganized because she hadn't had any time to unpack. The smell of fresh paint still lingered, but she couldn't disagree with Jess's assessment. She liked it.

Jess began to wander toward the living room, but Clare gently grabbed her wrist.

"Your jacket is damp. Here, I can dry it by the fire." Jess turned, and she helped her shrug off her blazer. "Would you be more comfortable with your hair down?" She lightly tugged on Jess's tight ponytail. To her delight, Jess pulled the band and shook her hair free. Clare smelled the sweet scent of her hair products. It made her realize how many trivial things she'd missed about Jess.

Clare draped the blazer over a chair and lit the gas fireplace. The orange glow of the flames warmed the pale walls. She turned back to Jess who had been watching her bend over with no shame. When they looked at each other, the air felt heavier, laden with everything all the months of missing each other had encompassed. Based on Jess's undisguised appraisal of her, the next question surprised her.

"Do I get to see the kitchen?"

Clare chuckled and nodded. Reluctantly, she continued the tour, taking Jess by her hand. Jess headed straight for the gas stove while Clare leaned against the small island. She liked watching Jess explore the modern kitchen, running her hands over the appliances and counters much like she had the walls in the cave or the galley in the boat. It was hard to believe that Jess was here, standing before her, opening cupboards in their kitchen, and commenting on the best location for them to keep their wine glasses.

Jess opened the pantry, saying something about a spice rack, but all Clare could think about was how the front of her white shirt looked damp. The faint edges of her bra showed through the sheer fabric. She wondered what color it was.

"What's out there?" Jess cupped her hands, pressed them to the glass, and peered out the darkened window next to the pantry.

"It's our deck." Clare opened the adjacent door. They took a step out onto the deck but stayed beneath the eaves to avoid the rain that fell from the sky. She felt a hand on her lower back as Jess stepped close. It warmed her through her shirt. She draped an arm over Jess's shoulders. She reached back and pulled Jess's arm around her.

"I missed you," she whispered.

Jess looked at her and blinked slowly. "I've missed you, too."

She repositioned, sliding her hand under the hem of Clare's shirt, and then tucking it into the waistband of her pants near her hip. Jess tilted her head and kissed her, her other hand coming to rest on Clare's cheek. Jess's tongue in her mouth did wonderful things, things that had her mind heading all sorts of places.

That's all it took. Clare felt her arousal course through her. The ends of Jess's hair tickled her arm, her skin overly sensitive. Breathing hard, she nuzzled her nose into Jess's hair and breathed the sweet, familiar smell of her. She left a kiss on her temple. She knew what she wanted, but she didn't want to move too quickly either. This was nice, seeing their house for the first time together.

They gazed out across the water. The rain affected the visibility, but the scene remained striking. The droplets made the lights across Puget Sound twinkle.

"I can see us having a couple of lounge chairs out here. It's the perfect place to read or unwind with a glass of wine." Jess glanced up at her and smiled.

"Wine..." She brushed her lips over Jess's. "Sounds like a tremendous idea." She pressed their lips together but kept it light. Even so, another surge of desire settled low in her body. They separated but still held hands. "It's cold. Let's go inside."

Inside, she could already feel the effect of the fire, the air warm and dry. She rummaged through a box labeled *Kitchen Utensils* for a corkscrew. She couldn't find it. Why hadn't she purchased a screw-top? Jess wandered toward the living room.

"Are you worried about your car being on campus so late?" She pushed tongs and a silicone spatula aside. Maybe the corkscrew was in another box. She realized Jess hadn't answered and looked up.

Jess leaned against the back of the sofa and slowly undid each button of her shirt from top to bottom. Her eyes were dark, her gaze unwavering. It was peach. Her bra was peach-colored. Thunder boomed.

Clare forgot about the wine.

She *needed*. She needed to feel the fullness of Jess's breasts beneath the satin material. She needed to feel the weight of Jess's breasts in her hands, to touch their firm flesh and reactive nipples. She needed to drag her tongue over them, caress them, and make sure Jess felt as needy as she did. She needed to rid both of them of their clothing. She needed to find relief from the throbbing between her legs.

It took her three strides. They crashed together, all hungry mouths and active hands. She wouldn't be surprised to come away with a few scratches from Jess's attempts to tear off her clothing. They only paused long enough for Clare to emphatically draw the blinds, not wanting to introduce themselves to the neighbors in such a fashion.

Outside, the light rain that had teased them earlier hammered down on the greater Seattle area, but their home radiated warmth. Clare had asked the movers to unpack and assemble only a couple of things the day prior, including her bed and bedding. Yet, when Jess offered herself button-by-button, it was a blanket thrown on the floor in front of the fire where they landed.

Clare kissed her slowly, relishing the taste of her, the softness of her mouth, the way her body fit against hers. The fire warmed their skin. She positioned herself between Jess's legs and kissed down her neck to her chest. Jess threaded a hand into her hair. She brushed her face against each breast, the soft flesh against her cheek such a contrast to the stiff nipples. When her lips brushed over a nipple, she drew it into her mouth. She swirled her tongue around it and sucked gently, then more firmly. Jess pushed up against her and held her head tightly to her. She rolled her other nipple between her fingers.

"I forgot just how damn beautiful you are." She felt more than heard Jess's hum.

Having Jess unclothed beneath her felt more electric than the currents darting between the clouds above. It was all so familiar, the unique shape and feel of her, the undulating dips, the way Jess grasped and held her. Even the scent of her arousal. Yet it all felt new, alive, and exciting.

All the hiking Jess had done throughout the summer had made her strong and lean, all sharp edges and muscular appendages. Clare, however, might appreciate this version of Jess better. She was fit by any standard, but without hiking every day, some areas had softened, and as Clare explored her body, she found she liked spending time touching, kissing, and tasting those newfound curves. Jess's tan had faded. Clare only found the faint lines because she knew they were there.

She shifted lower, raking her teeth over ribs, gently biting the taut skin over her hip bone. She licked back up, over her stomach, her sternum, stopping occasionally to blow on the wet trail and watch the goosebumps break out over Jess's skin.

"You're killing me." Jess's voice, low and sultry, sounded like she'd macerated it in bourbon.

"I might want to prolong things a bit more if that's how it makes you sound because…that voice…" She moaned and rested her forehead against Jess's collarbone.

Jess chuckled, pulled her up, and captured her mouth. This time, it was Clare who swept her tongue into Jess's mouth. She pressed her body against Jess, rocking her hips into her in time with the kiss.

Jess met her, tilting her hips for better contact, pressing up, wrapping her legs around Clare's back, and digging her heels in for leverage. Clare managed to get an arm beneath her.

Jess wrapped her arms around her neck and dipped her chin, breaking their kiss. She gazed at Clare, eyelids heavy, lips parted. She tucked a strand of Clare's hair behind her ear and uttered a single word. "Please."

It nearly undid her. She lifted slightly and reached between them.

At contact, Jess's eyes squeezed shut. "Clare."

Clare entered her with two fingers, finally touching her in the way that she'd wanted to for months. Jess was liquid heat, smooth as silk, trembling around her fingers.

"Yes, like that." Jess responded by rocking harder against her hand.

She was so beautiful, her dark hair messy and fanned out, her skin glistening with perspiration in the orange glow of the fire. Clare could hardly take it. She dragged open-mouthed kisses along her neck, feeling the thudding pulse beneath her lips. She licked across her collarbone and tasted the salt on her skin. She kissed along her jaw, licked into her mouth, and then sucked on her plump lower lip. When Jess's breathing became ragged and her nails dug into Clare's shoulders, she rubbed her thumb in messy circles. It didn't take long before Jess slammed her feet to the floor and pushed up, pulsing around Clare's fingers, and arching with a cry. Clare eased up with her thumb but continued to slowly stroke her until she collapsed, damp and spent.

Clare pushed wayward hairs from Jess's forehead and cheeks and laid the gentlest of kisses on her lips.

She opened her eyes. "You're going to be the death of me."

Clare tilted her head to the side. "Wait a minute. You said I was killing you when I *didn't* give you an orgasm. Then I give you one, and I'm going to be the death of you?" She grinned and brushed their noses together.

Jess swallowed and shook her head. "Something like that, yes. Seriously, just…wow. I'm going to need a minute, and maybe some wine for real this time."

Clare laughed and propped herself up on her elbow beside her. She drew undulating trails up and down her torso. "Don't blame your wineless status on me. You know what you did."

Jess laughed softly. "It worked though, didn't it?"

After they'd demolished a pizza and a bottle of wine, they celebrated their reunion in the hallway up against a wall between stacked boxes and then two more times in the bed that would be theirs.

Much later, after extinguishing the fire and pulling rumpled sheets over them, they held each other in the darkness. Jess traced Clare's ribs with her finger as she spoke.

"When I first saw you today, I couldn't get over how amazing you looked. At first, I thought you looked so good because your hair was longer, or because you were wearing different clothes, or had a different car."

"No?" Where was this going?

"No." She propped herself up on one elbow. "When I look at you, your eyes seem to sparkle, your laugh sounds fuller, and you seem freer than ever. I think the decisions you've made for yourself have made you happy."

"I am happy. I'm incredibly happy right now." Tears, evidence of that happiness, threatened to appear.

Jess traced her cheekbones, kissed her eyelids, and snuggled close.

Clare listened to the light tapping of rain on the roof, soft and hypnotic. Her life had been so different a year ago or even last spring. How long would she have survived that bitter, empty existence? Jess had shown her there was more to life than sorrow and pain. She'd opened a door for her, but the decision to walk through the door had to be hers. She didn't regret that decision. The life ahead of her—of them—appeared full of possibilities.

"I love you," she whispered. She wasn't sure if Jess had already drifted off to sleep.

"I love you, too." Jess pulled her closer.

EPILOGUE

Jess sported a new haircut courtesy of Ian. She checked her rearview mirror and finger-combed a few strands back into place before exiting her car. She liked it. It made her look a little older and more sophisticated. He'd insisted that an exciting new job demanded a fresh cut, and she agreed, although she was just as happy to be looking her best for everyone who would be arriving in the next twenty-four hours.

"Clare?" She pushed the front door closed with her hip and carried the bags into the house. The warm smell of cinnamon and the fresh scent of evergreen greeted her.

"I'm in here." Clare's voice came from the kitchen.

"They didn't have any strings of LED lights, so I had to get the other kind. The selection was wiped out." She set the bags in the living room. "You know, if someone hadn't had to have vaulted ceilings and such a tall tree, we wouldn't have needed more lights."

Her playful chiding brought Clare in from the kitchen. She slid her arms around Jess's waist and kissed her on the neck.

"I want it to look nice. It's our first Christmas in our new home with everyone."

Jess leaned into her touch and closed her eyes. Clare smelled like vanilla. "Did you hear from your parents?"

"Mm-hmm. Mom said their flight is on time." Clare turned her around and ran her fingers through her hair from temple to ends. "You look beautiful."

"Thank you." She gave her a quick kiss. Clare's lips tasted like vanilla, too. "Ian said he and Camille would be over with Timmy after they close the shop. They said to text them if you want them to bring anything besides wine."

Clare laughed. "Lyn and Alice are bringing wine, too. So are Molly and her boyfriend. We're going to have enough wine for an army."

"And I bet we end up drinking it all." Jess grinned.

"It depends on whether Melanie is drinking. You know my theory." Clare wiggled her eyebrows.

Jess sighed. She'd heard Clare's theory before. "I'm not sure if she and Tim are having a baby, but if they are, they'll let us know. You don't need to play Nancy Drew." She secretly loved how excited Clare got being an aunt.

"I wouldn't mind another nephew or niece to spoil rotten." She tilted her head, her expression brightening. "Maybe they're saving the surprise announcement for my Christmas gift."

"After the noisy farm truck that you bought Timmy, Ian and Camille might ban all Christmas gifts."

"He loves it." Clare defended her gift choice valiantly.

She threw her arms over Clare's shoulders and brushed some hair off her forehead so she could see her eyes. "Have I told you today how much I love you?"

Clare looked at the ceiling and pretended to think. "Let's see, you got your hair cut, went to the store, made fun of my toddler toy choice—"

"I love you." She chuckled.

Clare's smile faded. She looked unusually serious as she brushed her thumb over Jess's cheek. "After all this time?"

Jess leaned back, looked at her for a moment, then slowly smiled. "After all this time."

"I love you, too." Clare cupped her face and kissed her with obvious tenderness. They separated, and Clare stroked her cheek one final time. "I need to go check on the appetizers. Oh! We got a Christmas card from Helen and Hank. You'll have to text them and tell them about your promotion." She glanced over her shoulder as she entered the kitchen.

"Where's the card? Does it have a cow on it again this year?"

"I put it on the dining room table."

Jess took off her coat and tossed it over the banister. She entered the dining room but didn't see a card. The table only held one item. She gasped upon seeing the familiar wooden box. Looking up, she saw Clare leaning against the doorway, smiling at her.

"My rock collection!"

"Did you miss it?" Her eyes sparkled, and pink spots bloomed on her cheeks.

Jess picked up the well-worn wooden box that held her precious rocks. She hadn't seen her beloved collection in over two years. "I wasn't sure you kept it." She ran her fingers over the top where her dad had burned her initials many years before.

"Of course, I did. You told me to keep it." She pushed off the doorway with her hip and walked toward her.

"Yes, but after everything, I wasn't sure you did." They might have had a rocky start, but they'd moved past it by trusting each other. Their relationship had never been stronger.

"Hmm." Clare stood behind her. She kissed her below her ear and slid her arms around her waist.

Emotions rushed back to her. Jess remembered the last few times she'd seen the wooden box. She'd chosen the perfect rock to deposit in the cave, a pyrite sun for Sun Lakes. After her unsuccessful apology, unwilling to leave things the way they were, she'd left the box on Clare's back steps with a note. Those times were far behind them now. She'd been parentless, afraid of being alone, living life and making decisions based on fear. Two years later, she lived with the love of her life, and all those important to her would be here tomorrow to celebrate the holidays with them. Her heart was full. She couldn't ask for anything more.

Clare stood beside her as she opened the lid. Jess expected to find the empty section that had once held the small golden disk, but to her surprise, the little compartment wasn't empty.

Clare knelt on one knee. She'd added a sparkling rock of her own.

About the Author

Alaina Erdell lives in Ohio with her partner and their crazy, adorable cats. She has a degree in psychology from Gonzaga University. Prior to writing, she spent time working as a chef. She enjoys painting, cooking for friends and family, experimenting with molecular gastronomy, reading, kayaking, snorkeling, traveling, and spoiling her beloved nephews.

Email: alaina@alainaerdell.com
Website: alainaerdell.com

Books Available from Bold Strokes Books

A Haven for the Wanderer by Jenny Frame. When Griffin Harris comes to Rosebrook village, the love she finds with Bronte de Lacey creates a safe haven and she finally finds her place in the world. But will she run again when their love is tested? (978-1-63679-291-0)

A Spark in the Air by Dena Blake. Internet executive Crystal Tucker is sure Wi-Fi could really help small-town residents, even if it means putting an internet café out of business, but her instant attraction to the owner's daughter, Janie Elliott, makes moving ahead with her plans complicated. (978-1-63679-293-4)

Between Takes by CJ Birch. Simone Lavoie is convinced her new job as an intimacy coordinator will give her a fresh perspective. Instead, problems on set and her growing attraction to actress Evelyn Harper only add to her worries. (978-1-63679-309-2)

Camp Lost and Found by Georgia Beers. Nobody knows better than Cassidy and Frankie that life doesn't always give you what you want. But sometimes, if you're lucky, life gives you exactly what you need. (978-1-63679-263-7)

Felix Navidad by 'Nathan Burgoine. After the wedding of a good friend, instead of Felix's Hawaii Christmas treat to himself, ice rain strands him in Ontario with fellow wedding-guest—and handsome ex of said friend—Kevin in a small cabin for the holiday Felix definitely didn't plan on. (978-1-63679-411-2)

Fire, Water, and Rock by Alaina Erdell. As Jess and Clare reveal more about themselves, and their hot summer fling tips over into true love, they must confront their pasts before they can contemplate a future together. (978-1-63679-274-3)

Lines of Love by Brey Willows. When even the Muse of Love doesn't believe in forever, we're all in trouble. (978-1-63555-458-8)

Manny Porter and The Yuletide Murder by D.C. Robeline. Manny only has the holiday season to discover who killed prominent research scientist Phillip Nikolaidis before the judicial system condemns an innocent man to lethal injection. (978-1-63679-313-9)

Only This Summer by Radclyffe. A fling with Lily promises to be exactly what Chase is looking for—short-term, hot as a forest fire, and one Chase can extinguish whenever she wants. After all, it's only one summer. (978-1-63679-390-0)

Picture-Perfect Christmas by Charlotte Greene. Two former rivals compete to capture the essence of their small mountain town at Christmas, all the while fighting old and new feelings. (978-1-63679-311-5)

Playing Love's Refrain by Lesley Davis. Drew Dawes had shied away from the world of music until Wren Banderas gave her a reason to play their love's refrain. (978-1-63679-286-6)

Profile by Jackie D. The scales of justice are weighted against FBI agents Cassidy Wolf and Alex Derby. Loyalty and love may be the only advantage they have. (978-1-63679-282-8)

Almost Perfect by Tagan Shepard. A shared love of queer TV brings Olivia and Riley together, but can they keep their real-life love as picture perfect as their on-screen counterparts? (978-1-63679-322-1)

Corpus Calvin by David Swatling. Cloverkist Inn may be haunted, but a ghost materializes from Jason Dekker's past and Calvin's canine instinct kicks in to protect a young boy from mortal danger. (978-1-62639-428-5)

Craving Cassie by Skye Rowan. Siobhan Carney and Cassie Townsend share an instant attraction, but are they brave enough to give up everything they have ever known to be together? (978-1-63679-062-6)

Drifting by Lyn Hemphill. When Tess jumps into the ocean after Jet, she thinks she's saving her life. Of course, she can't possibly know Jet is actually a mermaid desperate to fix her mistake before she causes her clan's demise. (978-1-63679-242-2)

Enigma by Suzie Clarke. Polly has taken an oath to protect and serve her country, but when the spy she's tasked with hunting becomes the love of her life, will she be the one to betray her country? (978-1-63555-999-6)

Finding Fault by Annie McDonald. Can environmental activist Dr. Evie O'Halloran and government investigator Merritt Shepherd set aside their conflicting ideas about saving the planet and risk their hearts enough to save their love? (978-1-63679-257-6)

Hot Keys by R.E. Ward. In 1920s New York City, Betty May Dewitt and her best friend, Jack Norval, are determined to make their Tin Pan Alley dreams come true and discover they will have to fight—not only for their hearts and dreams, but for their lives. (978-1-63679-259-0)

Securing Ava by Anne Shade. Private investigator Paige Richards takes a case to locate and bring back runaway heiress Ava Prescott. But ignoring her attraction may prove impossible when their hearts and lives are at stake. (978-1-63679-297-2)

The Amaranthine Law by Gun Brooke. Tristan Kelly is being hunted for who she is and her incomprehensible past, and despite her overwhelming feelings for Olivia Bryce, she has to reject her to keep her safe. (978-1-63679-235-4)

The Forever Factor by Melissa Brayden. When Bethany and Reid confront their past, they give new meaning to letting go, forgiveness, and a future worth fighting for. (978-1-63679-357-3)

The Frenemy Zone by Yolanda Wallace. Ollie Smith-Nakamura thinks relocating from San Francisco to her dad's rural hometown is the worst idea in the world, but after she meets her new classmate Ariel Hall, she might have a change of heart. (978-1-63679-249-1)

A Cutting Deceit by Cathy Dunnell. Undercover cop Athena takes a job at Valeria's hair salon to gather evidence to prove her husband's connections to organized crime. What starts as a tentative friendship quickly turns into a dangerous affair. (978-1-63679-208-8)

As Seen on TV! by CF Frizzell. Despite their objections, TV hosts Ronnie Sharp, a laid-back chef; and paranormal investigator Peyton Stanford, have to work together. The public is watching. But joining forces is risky, contemptuous, unnerving, provocative—and ridiculously perfect. (978-1-63679-272-9)

Blood Memory by Sandra Barret. Can vampire Jade Murphy protect her friend from a human stalker and keep her dates with the gorgeous Beth Jenssen without revealing her secrets? (978-1-63679-307-8)

Foolproof by Leigh Hays. For Martine Roberts and Elliot Tillman, friends with benefits isn't a foolproof way to hide from the truth at the heart of an affair. (978-1-63679-184-5)

Glass and Stone by Renee Roman. Jordan must accept that she can't control everything that happens in life, and that includes her wayward heart. (978-1-63679-162-3)

Hard Pressed by Aurora Rey. When rivals Mira Lavigne and Dylan Miller are tapped to co-chair Finger Lakes Cider Week, competition gives way to compromise. But will their sexual chemistry lead to love? (978-1-63679-210-1)

The Laws of Magic by M. Ullrich. Nothing is ever what it seems, especially not in the small town of Bender, Massachusetts, where a witch lives to save lives and avoid love. (978-1-63679-222-4)

The Lonely Hearts Rescue by Morgan Lee Miller, Nell Stark, Missouri Vaun. In this novella collection, a hurricane hits the Gulf Coast, and the animals at the Lonely Hearts Rescue Shelter need love, and so do the humans who adopt them. (978-1-63679-231-6)

The Mage and the Monster by Barbara Ann Wright. Two powerful mages, one committed to magic and one controlled by it, strive to free each other and be together while the countries they serve descend into war. (978-1-63679-190-6)

Truly Wanted by J.J. Hale. Sam must decide if she's willing to risk losing her found family to find her happily ever after. (978-1-63679-333-7)

A Good Chance by Ali Vali. Harry, Desi, and Desi's sister Rachel are so close to getting everything they've ever wanted, but Desi's ex-husband is coming back to get his revenge and rip apart their chance at happiness. (978-1-63679-023-7)

A Perfect Fifth by Jaycie Morrison. Streetwise pianist Zara Keller and Lady Jillian Stansfield couldn't be more different; yet their connection brings a new awareness of who they are and what they truly want in their lives—including each other. (978-1-63679-132-6)

Catching Feelings by Ana Hartnett Reichardt. Andrea Foster expected to catch a lot of pitches from the Alder Lion's star pitcher, Maya, but she didn't expect to catch feelings. (978-1-63679-227-9)

Defiant Hearts by Lee Lynch. In these stories, you'll find your lovers, friends, and lesbians you wish you knew—maybe even yourself. (978-1-63679-237-8)

Love and Duty by Catherine Young. All Princess Roseli wants is to marry her three lovers, but with war looming, she must instead marry Princess Lucia to establish a military alliance between their planets. (978-1-63679-256-9)

Murder at Union Station by David S. Pederson. Private Detective Mason Adler struggles to determine who killed a woman found in a trunk without getting himself killed in the process. (978-1-63679-269-9)

Serendipity by Kris Bryant. Serendipity brings jingle writer Annie Foster and celebrity pop star Bristol Baines together, and their undeniable attraction keeps them close, but will their different paths drive them apart? (978-1-63679-224-8)

The Haunted Heart by Jane Kolven. A ghost, a ring, and a quest to find a missing psychic—it's a spell for love. (978-1-63679-245-3)

The Rules of Forever by Nan Campbell. After reconnecting at their high school reunion, Cara and Lauren agree to embark on a textbook definition friends-with-benefits relationship, but trying to keep it uncomplicated is harder than it seems. (978-1-63679-248-4)

Vision of Virtue by Brey Willows. When virtue and desire come together, be prepared for sparks in this next installment of the Memory's Muses series. (978-1-63679-118-0)

Cherry on Top by Georgia Beers. A chance meeting leaves Cherry and Ellis longing for a different life, but when Ellis's search for truth crashes into Cherry's insta-filter world, do they have any hope at all of a happily ever after? (978-1-63679-158-6)

Love and Other Rare Birds by Angie Williams. Ornithologist Dr. Jamie Martin and park ranger Rowan Fleming are searching the Alaskan wilderness for a bird thought to be extinct and they're about to discover opposites really do attract. (978-1-63679-108-1)

Parallel Paradise by Mayapee Chowdhury. When their love affair is put to the test by the homophobia of their family, community, and culture, Bindi and Rimli will need to fight for a chance at love. (978-1-63679-204-0)

Perfectly Matched by Toni Logan. A beautiful Cupid named Hannah, a runaway arrow, and just seventy-two hours to fix a mishap that could be the best mistake she has ever made. (978-1-63679-120-3)

Royal Exposé by Jenny Frame. When they're grouped together for a class assignment, Poppy's enthusiasm for life and love may just save Casey's soul, but will she ever forgive Casey for using her to expose royal secrets? (978-1-63679-165-4)

Slow Burn by Missouri Vaun. A wounded wildland firefighter from California and a struggling artist find solace and love in a small southern town. (978-1-63679-098-5)

The Artist by Sheri Lewis Wohl. Detective Casey Wilson and reclusive artist Tula Crane are drawn together in a web of passion, intrigue, and art that might just hold the key to stopping a killer. (978-1-63679-150-0)

The Inconvenient Heiress by Jane Walsh. An unlikely heiress and a spinster evade the Marriage Mart only to discover true love together. (978-1-63679-173-9)